PRAISE FOR
D. RYAN GISH
AND
ENTHRALLED

"*Enthralled* is a story that lingers long after you've closed the book. It resonates vividly on a wide spectrum of levels that spans mature love, deep depression, and everything in-between, during rather uncertain times. Don't share your copy because you will long to read it again." –Christine Edwards, journalist and blogger

"A horror story that haunts. Gish shows the darker side of humanity through characters you can't stop thinking about. A must read." – Jaimie Engle, award-winning author and writing coach

INSPIRE. EMPOWER. EDUCATE

D. Ryan Gish

JME Books

Text copyright © 2016 D. Ryan Gish
Cover design © 2016 Philip Benjamin of Benjamin Studios
Edited by A Writer For Life
The text for this book is set in Fairfield
All rights reserved, including the right of reproduction
in whole or in part in any form.

Published in the United States by
JME Books, an Imprint of A Writer For Life, LLC,
Melbourne, FL 32935.

Visit us on the Web: awriterforlife.com

For bulk order discounts email awriterforlifecoach@gmail.com.

Summary: A man must keep his family safe when the undead begin to walk; only his
children may be the key, if he's willing to let them go.

ISBN: 978-0-9971709-3-1
ISNB: 978-0-9971709-4-8

Available in paperback, ebook, and audiobook formats.

10 9 8 7 6 5 4 3 2

JME Books are meant to empower, inspire, and educate readers.

For my brothers.

Special thanks to my friend Jaimie Engle for believing in me and this book.

Wake Up, O Sleeper

1

"Zombies," I said, waiting for the automatic doors to sweep open. "Every single one of them."

Beyond the glass, a myriad of shoppers stalked the aisles in search of items that would only briefly sustain them. I'd watched them all day from behind the deli counter, and I stopped in the entryway, grimacing as I realized I would soon be joining them.

A man shoved past with a case of beer, and my jaw clenched. "Excuu-use us," my daughter said, putting one hand to her hip. The man had enough sense not to look back. If he did, he likely would have turned to stone under my six-year-old's glare. "Some people."

"You don't talk to adults like that, Zoe," I said, then faked a cough so she wouldn't see me smile.

Before us, an elderly woman struggled to separate a shopping cart from the rest in the stack, and my smile faltered. She freed the buggy and continued on her way. I gazed back into the parking lot, wondering how much we really needed milk.

My stomach rumbled its irritation at the amount of my wife's fried rice I had consumed for dinner; an uncomfortable reminder that Sydney was home cleaning the dishes. There wasn't a chance in hell I could come home empty-handed.

"Let's make this quick," I said. "Try and keep up, Faris."

My son's hand slipped into mine. He was three, and I could hear his miniature boots clopping fast against the polished concrete as I put my head down and power-walked past the cash register. Someone called my name, but I shot down the nearest aisle, pretending not to notice. We took a sharp right at the end of the row, slowing when the bank of refrigerators came into view.

"Can we get cookies?" Zoe said, stopping at a display of Oreo's stacked in the center of the aisle.

"Absolutely not," I said over my shoulder, and dragged Faris the last few yards to our destination. A blast of cold air hit me as I opened the refrigerator, pulled out a gallon of fat-free milk, and let the door swing closed again.

"You know why they put the milk at the back of the store?" I said when Zoe had caught up.

"So you have more time to tell this boring story?" She pressed her nose against the glass and let her breath mist up the frosted surface.

"You love my stories," I said while she drew a "Z" over half of the fog, then took Faris's finger and traced an "F" beside it.

A man and woman watched from farther down the row. No amusement there. Faris squeezed my hand and we started back the way we came. Something about their expressions made me look again, but the couple had moved away in the opposite direction.

Zoe ran ahead, this time halting beside a bank of chips.

"They put the milk at the back of the store so parents have to drag their kids past all the junk food to get to it," I said and prodded her with a light kick to the rear.

"Hey, Shane," a loud voice came from my right. I cringed, my hope of making it to the check-out lane before being accosted now dashed. I turned to see the pimply part-time bakery worker hopping and waving in my direction, and I slugged toward the counter to see what he wanted. A line of people snaked through the tables of prepackaged pastries, reaching the sandwich station in the next section of the store.

"What, Tim?" I said, bypassing the queue, ignoring the impatient faces.

"Shane, I'm so glad you're here," Tim said. He stole an awkward glance over his shoulder. Then he bent his head and said in a much lower tone, "Something's up with Justin."

I took a deep breath. "Tim, I've been off for over two hours. I can't deal with this right now."

"Dude, I know you got your kids and all, but something's seriously wrong with him."

"Listen, Timmy," I said, trying to reign in my annoyance. "I am off the clock, and even if I wasn't, it is not my job to figure out what's wrong with the boss. I turned that job down, remember?"

"I really wish you hadn't," he muttered and shot another look toward the storage room door.

My arm jerked suddenly, and I felt Faris's grip on my hand tighten. The old woman with the buggy stared down at my son. Her mouth curled into what might have been a smile if not for the way her cracked lips lifted over her yellow front teeth. Faris seemed unable to tear himself from her gaze; his body trembled with every breath.

A cold chill brushed down the nape of my neck, and I took a few steps back, pulling Faris with me, but my daughter didn't follow.

"What're you lookin' at, lady?" Zoe said. When the woman ignored her, Zoe passed her hand directly in front of the elderly lady's face. "Hello-o."

The woman snapped out of her trance. She shook her head and turned her attention to Timmy.

"I'll have a dozen of those sour cream donuts you make so well," she said in a rather pleasant voice. *Much more pleasant than that look she gave my son.*

"That's another thing, Shane," Timmy said, holding a finger up to the woman. "I can't find any of the damn donuts. Justin's moping around somewhere in the back and Samantha's nowhere to be found. I've got a line the length of the Nile and people are starting to act really weird."

I lingered on the elderly lady a moment longer before returning my attention to Timmy. She seemed completely normal now, like her brain had turned off the senile switch and flipped on the sanity.

"Look, I can't..." My voice faded to nothing when the door to the storage area creaked open and Justin, the evening shift manager, slipped through. His glasses sat askew across the bridge of his nose and half of his shirttail dangled over his waistband, but not enough to conceal his open fly. Yet it wasn't his disheveled appearance that took my words away, or the powdered sugar smeared all over his mouth and chin. It was the look in his eyes. So much like the old lady's and they were aimed straight at Faris.

I backed away from the counter, this time ensuring I had both of my children within my grasp. "Sorry, Timmy," I said. "We gotta go."

"Uhhh," Timmy said, only now noticing our boss standing in the doorway like a Royal Guard after an all-night bender.

"Don't…forget your milk."

I quickly stepped to the counter and grabbed the gallon of milk. As I backed away, I felt Faris yank on my arm. But this time it was much harder. I spun to see the hunched old woman tugging at my son, her gnarled fingers wrapped around his forearm. Faris's mouth gaped open, his eyes pleading, screaming the words his tongue refused to form.

Zoe cried for her to let her brother go. The line of people watched with blank stares and did nothing. Timmy gasped. Justin sneered. My son closed his eyes, and the old lady held fast.

I had no other choice.

The milk hit the floor. And so did the old hag.

2

The bounce of the tires as the truck pulled up the front drive jolted my senses. I blinked, suddenly aware that our exit and short commute home from the grocery store was absent from the banks of my memory…and if I didn't hit the brakes my garage door would soon have a Dodge Ram-sized hole in it. Zoe gave a startled yelp as the truck came to an abrupt halt with mere inches to spare.

"You guys alright?" I said, twisting to get a view of my children in the back seat.

My daughter was sobbing by the time I'd gotten out and opened her door. At some point between the chip aisle and our driveway, the pink and purple ties my wife put in Zoe's hair had failed utterly; the stray locks fell over her face like a curtain of straw, soaking up the snot and tears. I helped her down from her booster and she darted for the front door, wailing for her mother. *Syd will have to deal with that mess.*

I reached back in for Faris. He grinned like he'd just gotten off a rollercoaster. *So much like his mother.* He raised his hand for a high five, and it was only then, when the red marks on his forearm were in front of my face, that the incident at the grocery store came barreling back.

My hands quivered as I fumbled to release the buckles of his car seat. "Does it hurt?" I said, hauling him into one arm.

He shook his head, but he was no longer smiling.

The sun had been above the horizon when we'd left the store, but darkness had crept in while I was spaced out behind the wheel. *I didn't even turn the headlights on.* The temperature had also dropped. October in Florida was far from freezing, but the breeze that blew over us as we walked to the house caused Faris to shiver and nuzzle closer to me.

Syd's gonna kill me for not putting their jackets on.

I pushed the front door open with my foot and trudged into the kitchen, our dog Bowie, a mutt as black as shadow, barking at my heels. Zoe was in her bedroom whining to her mother about my crazy driving. I sat my son on the counter to inspect his welts.

"How did that happen?"

I jumped and spun around to see Sydney scowling at our son's arm.

"I…," I managed before being swept aside.

"These look like fingerprints."

"They are."

"Who did this?" she said through her teeth.

"It was a little old woman."

"An old woman? Why?"

"I don't know why, honey. Everyone was just…shopping…" *And watching, and it wasn't just the old lady.* "Then people started acting strange."

Syd scooped Faris off the counter, and hugged him. "Are you okay, big boy?"

He nodded, but covered his ears with his hands.

"You have an earache?" Sydney said. "I told you to make them wear their jackets, Shane."

"Because a jacket would cover his ears?"

She glared at me and began rifling through the cabinet above the stove. She came back with a red bottle of liquid. "Here, take some Tylenol," she told Faris as she set him down and poured him a small dose. The way he drained the cup reminded me of Sydney taking a shot of tequila.

When he had run off to find his sister, Syd lowered her voice and said, "What do you mean, people were acting strange?"

"It's hard to explain," I said. "People were just staring. My manager and that old lady…"

"You should be manager."

I heaved a sigh. "We've talked about this, honey. I'm not cut out for decision-making."

"So everyone in the store was staring at you?" Syd said, waving away my lame rebuttal.

"Not everyone, just a few," I said. *And they weren't staring at me...* "The old lady was the only one that came close to us. She grabbed Faris's arm and tried to pull him away from me. Luckily, he was holding my hand. I knocked the lady on her ass, and—"

"You knocked her down?"

"Uh, yeah..."

My wife smirked for the first time since we walked in.

"You find that funny?" I said. For some reason I had envisioned the opposite reaction.

"Yeah, kinda. Have you ever been in a fight with a man?"

I started to defend myself, but she wasn't finished. "I mean, last year it was the girl that pulled your hair, and before that it was girl on the bike—"

"You would tackle someone that tried to rip your hair out, too. And the girl on the bike was an adult who threw a Gatorade bottle at me..."

"She didn't throw it at you, Shane, she tossed it in the grass next to you. Then you threw it back and made her crash into a light pole."

"Whatever." My face was heating up. "Did you not see the marks on Faris's arm? What would you have done?"

"Oh, I would've done more than just push the old bat," she said, but her smile faded when she looked into my eyes. She wrapped her arms around my waist, and laid her head against my chest. "Your heart is pounding."

"I can't stop thinking about the way they were looking at us."

"Guess I'll have to do something about that after Zoe and Faris go to bed." She pushed away from me and opened the refrigerator. "In the meantime..."

A can of beer arced across the kitchen, catching me by surprise. I fumbled it once, cracked it open, and took a long gulp.

"Umm, where's the milk?" Sydney rummaged through the refrigerator. Finally, she stood up and crossed her arms. "Really, Shane?"

I took another gulp of beer.

"Well, you get to deal with breakfast tomorrow." She kissed my cheek and went off to get the kids in their pajamas.

I tried to clear my head by watching the way her hips swayed in her tight jean shorts, but it was useless. All I could see was the old woman lying on the floor.

And the demented grin on her face.

3

I lingered in the hallway that night after putting Faris to bed. My wife was still reading to Zoe—*Green Eggs and Ham* for the seventh time that week—and the pictures lining the walls drew me in. Zoe and Faris at various ages; Sydney and I at our wedding; Bowie as a puppy; my brother, Johnny, Dean, and I on one of our hunting trips. The one of three kids at the beach...

A hand caressed my back and I jerked. "Will you quit doing that?" I said.

"Is that how the old lady was staring at you at the grocery store?"

"How long was I out this time?" My eyes remained fixed on the old and faded image of the three boys, so out of place amongst the newer, professionally done portraits.

"You and your brother looked so much alike," she said, weaving her arm in mine. "And Sean is..."

I pulled away from her and made for the living room. The memory didn't hurt like it used to, but talking about him still made me want to puke.

"You can take it down whenever you want, Shane."

"Would you?" I said as I plopped into my recliner and rubbed my eyes. Maybe it did still hurt like it used to.

Syd squeezed in next to me; the pale, smooth skin of her arms cold against mine, her thick red hair splashing over my face. It smelled of the cucumber shampoo she used, but it itched my nose. "Have you ever seen Faris scream?" I said when she had tucked her mane behind her.

She shook her head.

"I saw it today. He was terrified. He closed his eyes as tight as he could and opened his mouth, but nothing came out. It was the worst thing I've ever seen. I remember thinking how I wished that had been the moment he decided to talk. I wished that scream was the first sound I'd ever heard come out of his mouth. Seeing it but not hearing it was…disturbing."

We sat in silence for a long time. I closed my eyes, but peace did not come, that damn picture adding to the turmoil in my mind.

"Your bother called while I was in with Zoe," Sydney said. "He left a message for you to call him back."

I wedged my phone from my pocket and pressed the center button. The screen stayed black. "It's dead. I'll call him in the morning."

"*Candy Crush* does drain your battery," she said, laughing. "You can call him from my phone. He said it was important."

"Important doesn't mean the same thing to my brother as it does to most people. Calling to tell me the newest issue of *Saga* just came out is important to him." *When is that coming out, anyway?* "I'll call him in the morning. Early enough to ruin his Saturday sleeping in."

"That's mean."

I laughed and got up to plug my phone in. "I know. I can't wait."

When I returned from the bedroom, Sydney was on her cell with her best friend, Haley. The sound of giggles and gossip made my stomach turn so I went out to the front porch to smoke the first cigarette I'd had since before taking the kids to the store.

All that for a gallon of milk I didn't even bring home. I sat in the nearest wrought iron chair and watched one of my neighbors wander by. A little dark to be taking a stroll, but to each their own. I flicked open my Zippo and lit a cig as I settled into the semi-uncomfortable seat. Syd and Haley would be yakking for at least a half hour, and I considered calling Dean up to see if he wanted to play *Call of Duty* before remembering my phone was on the charger by my bed. Dean was a childhood friend that lived a few houses down from us. I considered it a genuine stroke of luck that his wife, Haley, became best friends with mine.

I smashed the spent cigarette in the ashtray, and meandered back into the house. Soft snores echoed down the hall from Zoe's room. Faris had fallen asleep in the middle of the story I read to him. Thank goodness for easy nights.

The TV was still off in the living room. As I reached for the remote, Sydney cleared her throat. She leaned against the doorframe of our bedroom, slender and beautiful in my favorite lingerie. Black fishnet stockings led the way to a pale green garter belt and matching lace chemise. Her fiery hair tumbled over her shoulders in wide spirals, her green eyes beckoned, the corners of her lips curved into a mischievous grin.

She backed into the bedroom, and I rushed after her like an eager teenager. We fell asleep in each other's arms that night, unaware that the next time we shared a bed it would be hundreds of miles away, with a loaded gun under the pillow.

4

I woke in a panic; the gaping mouth of a boy as he sank into the abyss clung to my mind, as it had countless nights before. Lost in the dark, I sat up panting, searching the sheets for a boy who wasn't there.

A short snort came from the mound next to me, and its steady rise and fall snapped me back to reality. I put my hands through my hair, thankful I hadn't startled Syd.

Something cold touched my forearm. My hand lashed out and the slap of my palm on the back of my wrist was both loud and painful. I rubbed the spot, thinking it had just been in my head, a remnant of the nightmare. The blue numbers of my alarm clock were more blinding than illuminating as I scanned the room. I saw nothing. I fixed the sheets and flipped my pillow. *If something were here, Bowie would've woken me up.*

A slight shuffle near the side of my bed.

I craned my neck, squinting into the black. *I didn't imagine that.* The intensity of the clock's glow softened as my eyes adjusted: the outline of the treadmill in the corner, the row of porcelain dolls lining my wife's dresser…and a small figure standing a few feet away. *Just out of reach.*

"Faris?" I whispered.

A slight movement of the head, a step closer.

I relaxed. "What's wrong, buddy? You scared the crap out of me."

Faris moved to the edge of the bed, and blue light washed over him. He stood wrapped in his favorite blanket, holding his ears in both hands. His brow and cheeks were scrunched, his small teeth gnashed

16

together. I slid to the edge of the bed and drew him to me. Over his shoulder I read the clock's numbers for the first time. It said 1:24, and I cringed, knowing I wouldn't be returning to sleep any time soon.

"Is it your ears again?"

He nodded in the crook of my neck.

"Let's get you some more medicine."

I started to lift him, but he resisted. He stepped back a little and his hands moved from his ears, formed a few words, but then stopped.

I signed back this time, the motions poor and choppy. *What else is wrong, are you scared?*

Now his face became drawn and his hands flew about in gestures I couldn't come close to following. I placed a hand on his, interrupting their flashing movement, and said, "Slow down, I can't read it that fast."

He looked down and shook his head, then climbed into bed to lie beside his mother. I pulled the comforter over us and snuggled in next to him. His skin was cold and clammy, but as the minutes passed, the tension in his forehead and jaw eased, and his breathing evened out.

I stayed awake a long time after my son had drifted off. The events of the day rotated in my head like pebbles in a dryer, clanging in and out with no semblance of order. The little old lady's mad stare, my boss's blank stare, dreams of drowning children. All this mingled with the scare Faris had given me earlier. The clock read 2:11. *Friggin' ridiculous.* I lifted the comforter gently and got out of bed. *I need a cigarette.*

I found the gym shorts I'd left on the floor that evening and pulled them on. Faris slept soundly, so I picked him up to take him back to his room. I was glad to see his temperature had risen to normal, but that would change if I left him there. His heat combined with my wife's would make it impossible for me to fall asleep.

Bowie padded at my heels, through the living room and past the kitchen. Zoe was still snoring as we neared the end of the hall, and I peeked in to see her sprawled sideways, her legs and blanket hanging over the rail. *I'll straighten that out once Faris is down.*

I smiled as I closed her door, leaving a small crack, but stopped short when I saw Bowie sitting on his haunches several feet up the hall; his head cocked, and a low growl vibrated toward me, more felt than heard. The hair on my arms and back of my neck stood on end. Faris suddenly felt heavy in my arms…and cold again. Through the doorway of his bedroom I only then noticed the glow globe he used as a night light had been turned off. The sphere should have been spinning steadily, shining orange light through hundreds of tiny holes. Instead, darkness swallowed the room. Even the narrow window to the left was a black void as the thick *Transformers* curtains repressed whatever moonlight may have attempted to make its way inside.

I stepped in, my eyes scouring every shadow, every corner a person could hide in, but saw no one. "Stupid dog." I inhaled and let the air, along with a portion of my unease, escape slowly back into the room. I took another step when something captured my eye directly in front of me. I leaned forward, peering at the wall over Faris's bed. Something was written there in large letters. Another step and I could make out a vague four-letter word. As I drew nearer several more words *(or were they all the same?)* blurred into view around the first, scribbled in red and covering half the wall.

"A-R-G..."

Faris went rigid in my arms. He gasped, and his legs thrust out so hard I nearly dropped him. My son's eyes flew open and caught my own; his eyes, blue and bloodshot, looked at me...*looked through me*. His left hand gripped my chest, the nails biting into bare flesh, the other shot out to rest firmly over the side of my face. A jolt of cold screamed through my cheek, spread over my skin, and shot down my spine. My knees buckled, and I swayed, the weight in my arms disappeared. Then the world went black.

5

There was only darkness. Thick and pulsing, it swarmed about me like millions of insects acting as one. It embraced me and pierced me; it was comfort and despair, promise and malice. It was all those things in unison, but none of them. It beckoned, desired, coveted; whispered until I could stand it no longer. My scream drowned in the emptiness.

Then it receded. A blacker shape formed before me, a shadow in the darkest place I could imagine. It swelled, and as it did, orange lights appeared within—thousands of flames burning in the belly of a beast. A few flickered and went out. More were extinguished, and then more, faster until only few remained.

The shadow lifted and I was atop a high tower. Above me a blanket of grey threatened to block the sun. In one direction, a wide pillar of smoke billowed into the gloom.

The tower was set in the center of what could have been a farm, but the borders seemed to fade out like an unfinished painting. A horde of glowing orbs materialized below, similar to the flames I'd seen earlier, but as I peered into the haze I saw they were eyes. They darted about in chaotic patterns: some of them unhurried, some of them swift, all creeping ever closer.

The voice of a young boy rose from the mist beyond, chanting, chanting, he sang, *Behold thy son, my King, a Saint of the Boughs...*

The words weakened and I was falling. The washed white wall of the tower blurred by and then I was soaring over the frozen earth toward a dim forest. Trees and eyes rushed past and a trail appeared.

The Bitter Path lay before me...

I swerved along the way until the trees weren't flashing by quite as quickly. An intersection laid ahead and the trail I was on ended. The paved street stretched to oblivion in either direction, but I was led to something looming near the path from which I came. It stood head high in staunch contrast against the black scrim of trees sprawling behind and above.

'Till death do I serve Thee...

I drew closer until the blank sign consumed my entire field of vision. An invisible hand began etching into the light wood; deep and black, the letters smoldered, releasing tendrils of heated smoke into the starless sky, and when the last one had been inscribed they burst into flames so red and thick that the engraved word could not be interpreted.

I was forced nearer, helpless as the blazing word singed my lashes, my nose, my face. It scorched my eyes and seared my mind. Then at last the heat subsided. The flames retreated to the thick grooves, and the word shone clear for an instant before the unseen finger redrew each letter out of existence, beginning with the last, working slowly in reverse.

When the pale wood was blank once again, it converted to brilliant white, then shining silver, and I was suddenly staring back at myself. Seething pain sliced into my forehead. I attempted to pull back, struggled to escape, but I could not. Great gashes carved themselves into my skin, the reflection in the sign enhancing the agony as I watched one letter after the other slash across my brow.

Guard my Heart in Truth, the child sang and the pain left me.

I touched the incisions, traced them with a finger. My lips parted to speak, to utter the word I had been branded with, when a hand appeared from the nothingness, crushing my throat. My vision blurred, consuming fire ignited in the gaping wounds above my eyes, and terror seized me. My mind, my heart, my soul cried out while the merciless fingers tightened. Insane laughter tore through the night as I crumbled, cruel and ubiquitous, and then the swarming darkness swept over me once more.

6

The light flooded in. Blinded, I gasped, but air refused to come. I clawed at the place those twisted fingers had been, cold as ice, squeezing tighter and tighter.

The pressure built behind my eyes and I felt them bulge in their sockets. I was suffocating, well past the point of panic when the clamp around my throat and chest released.

I sucked in a great garbled breath. Several more followed amongst a fit of coughing so severe it made my head throb.

Distorted shapes circled about the brightness. The blood in my face drained to the rest of my body. I blinked away tears and sniffed up the mucus pouring from my nose.

After a time my eyes focused enough to see my son kneeling over me, his hands tiny shadows fluttering against the light shining from the bedroom ceiling. I couldn't understand the rapid gestures now any more than I'd been able to earlier that night.

"Faris…" I started. My raw throat burned and my hands clutched my neck though nothing was choking me now. *Had there ever been?*

"What happened?" I rasped. I pushed myself to a sitting position and rubbed the side of my forehead where a large knot had formed. "What'd I hit my head on?"

He shook his head. *I woke up and you were on the floor,* he said with his hands.

I hugged him and then tried to stand. I wobbled to my feet on the second try, and when I looked up the breath I had worked so hard to catch escaped me in a single gust. The walls shifted in. My head whirled, my legs buckled, and my knees hit the carpet, sending a jolt up my thighs.

Faris had turned the light on while I was *(dreaming?)* unconscious. The obscure writing above his bed, barely visible in the darkness, now leapt off the wall like a neon sign.

In red crayon, a single word had been scribbled over and over on every wall, ending abruptly a few feet from the floor. The writing above the bed stretched higher as if…

…as if a child had stood on it and wrote as high as he could reach.

I turned to my son. "Did you…?"

But Faris shook his head, his shock matching my own. His hands repeated, *I didn't, I didn't,* and I believed him.

At least I believed he wasn't aware that he'd done it. At three, he couldn't even sign the alphabet, let alone spell out an entire word. Yet there was no doubt the sprawling letters had been done by his hand; the capital "A's" were like the roofs of the houses he liked to draw, long and crooked; the "R's" appeared…

The sign.

Like waking from a fleeting dream, I'd forgotten everything before the powerful fingers had wrapped about my neck.

Now the images flooded back, a tidal wave of jumbled horrific images surging through me. I remembered it all: the imposing darkness, the tower, the eyes, the child's singing voice…the ominous sign.

I felt the blood red letters slicing into my head. I saw it covering my son's walls with my open eyes; a burning blade carved it across my lids when I clenched them shut. The name of the mythological vessel Jason sailed in search of his golden fleece: ARGO.

7

What the hell was happening? What did the name of an imaginary ship have to do with me? Why was it written all over Faris's room?

And that child's voice…

I beheld my own child, asleep next to my wife, as I hovered beside the bed and wished I could shut my eyes without seeing orange eyes and red letters. *How could he doze off after what just happened?*

Bowie hopped up next to Faris and snuggled close, my son's black guardian against the darkness. He lifted his ears when I grabbed my cell phone from the nightstand and watched me leave the room.

A minute later I was on the front porch letting my tension sift away with each drag from the cigarette.

The mosquitoes swarmed when I turned the outside light on, so I flipped it back off before sloughing into the chair. The moon was out, though, and it kept enough of the night at bay.

I pressed the top button of my phone and lit another smoke while I waited for it to load. A series of beeps told me I had voicemail, but I was stunned to see I had seven. Plus a text from my brother.

ASSHOLE! CALL ME ASAP!

The text had come in at 2:04, just before I'd taken Faris back to his room. It was now 2:30. I'd passed out, had a vision, discovered my son was a fantastic graffiti artist, and made it outside for a cig in less than twenty minutes.

I listened to the messages, but after the third one of Judah yelling at me to turn my phone on and call him I deleted the rest. I flipped to my missed calls. My thumb hesitated over my brother's number. Did I even want to know?

Nothing he says can make your night any worse.

I shrugged and tapped the number.

"Shane," my brother's voice bellowed. His police radio squawked in the background, and I had to pull the phone away from my ear to keep from going deaf. "What the crap, dude, I've been calling you all night."

"My phone died, and I forgot to turn it back on after I plugged it in. What's going on?"

"It's been a bitch of a night, big brother. A ton of domestic violence calls. Assaults out the wahzoo. A lot of it's going on near our neighborhood, so I've been trying to see if everyone's okay."

"Well I appreciate it, Judah, but we're surrounded by white trash and rednecks. Domestic violence isn't really out of the ordinary."

"It's how many there's been tonight, moron. SWAT got called out to Walmart two hours ago. When they got there, two guys were holed up in Sporting Goods taking shots at anyone they saw."

"Did they take'em out?"

"Eventually, after the guys shot two deputies. I swear things are so ass backward." He paused a moment to answer a call on his radio, then said, "I saw Johnny earlier."

"Thought he was off tonight."

"He was, but that's what I'm saying, man. When off-duty firefighters and paramedics are getting called out, you know things are crazy. He even brought Jordan over to stay with Devon. You know how the twins get when they have to be home alone. Why do you think I switched to day shift?" A siren blared and died away on his end. "You seen anything strange?"

You don't know the half of it.

"Uh…" Movement caught my attention, and I could barely make out something edging up my street. Not a person, though… "Um, I think there's a cow walking down the road. That count for strange?"

"A cow? From the sorry excuse for a farm around the corner from you?"

"Probably." Another shape emerged from the woods a few yards behind the animal. The figure was taller, and on two legs. "Now there's a person following it." I watched the shape as it ambled after the cow less than three houses away.

"Does he see you?"

"I don't know," I said, looking down to light my third cigarette. "It's just the old man chasing his cow, I'm sure." But that theory fell apart as soon as my lighter's flame disappeared and I raised my head. The cow had passed by, but the man… "What the…"

"What?" Judah said. "What happened?"

"The guy's not following the cow anymore."

"Does he see you? Get back in the house and lock the doors." My brother was shouting now, telling me to call the police. The man had stopped his pursuit of the cow in the middle of the street and turned to stare at me.

"He definitely sees me."

"Get inside, Shane," my brother said. "I'm seri—"

"Gotta go, Judah." The figure took a slow step onto the grass. I hung up the phone. My brother's irate voice cut out, and I suddenly felt very alone.

8

Inside, Bowie barked wildly. His scratching at the front door, like nails grating against Styrofoam, sent chills down my spine. The ground lit up around me as the porch light went on, stretching my shadow across the yard, which ended a head's length away from the approaching stranger. *Sydney's awake.*

The door opened a crack and my wife stuck her head out. "What's going on?"

"Nothing, babe," I said, not turning around. "Go back inside."

"Yeah right," she said. "Your dog's gonna wake the whole neighborhood."

"Just stay by the door. We may have a situation here."

The area of East Bay where I lived was little more than a swamp and all properties had to be built up several feet before houses could be constructed, leaving a drainage ditch along the front of every lot.

The figure stumbled slowly up this incline and attracted my wife's attention for the first time.

"What the..." she muttered.

"That's what I said."

I took a few steps off the porch. My fists clenched into tight balls and a warm tension eddied in my stomach. "You need to get out of here, man," I called out. He halted for a moment, tilted his head, and increased his pace up the hill. I glanced back at Syd to see wide eyes and an open mouth. The tension in my stomach turned to rock. I met him halfway up the yard. "You're trying my patience."

He bared his teeth and snarled. I stepped back. The man had appeared normal until the sound left his mouth, just a weird guy, maybe drunk, chasing a cow. But now I was about to freak out. He felt...*wrong*, more animal than human.

He kept coming, a few yards away, his piercing gaze far from friendly. His eyes flicked over my shoulder to where my wife stood, and I snapped. My fist connected with the man's nose. Blood gushed from his nostrils in thick spurts and he dropped, landed flat on his back, and rolled halfway down the hill.

I turned to tell Sydney to call the cops, but she pointed and shouted,

"*Watch out.*"

I came around in time to see his hands reaching for my face. I batted them away and swung again. My knuckles swiped past his cheek, but before I could pull back his teeth locked onto my wrist.

His jaws clamped down, his teeth tearing through my flesh like hot knives, shooting fire up my arm and across my shoulders. I hit him over and over with my free hand until something gave. He released my wrist, but my blows had barely dazed him.

Fresh blood flowed from the newly opened wounds about his cheekbone and lips. He reared back, his head twitching, his eyes as blank as my boss's had been, and his lips curled into a grin that sent my pulse racing. *The old woman...it's the same sick grin.*

That cold chill streaked down my neck, this one much stronger than the one at the supermarket.

Rivers of blood streamed from his nose and mouth; from his eyes and ears it poured as if being purged from his body. He cocked his head back and released a deafening high-pitched screech.

Gooseflesh rippled over my arms, and I stepped away. The sound reverberated through the still air, clouding my thoughts as the burning in my wrist reached a new peak. I heard Sydney cry out, but I didn't have time to turn.

The man charged. I planted my bare feet in the dirt and stood my ground, the stone in my stomach boiling and twisting.

We collided, and I hit the ground and rolled, gasping. The man...the *creature*...clawed at the ground beside me, struggling to regain his feet. I no longer stood between him and the porch, and he scrambled into the gap, his focus now on my wife.

Desperate, I reached out with my injured arm and latched onto the man's ankle just as he lunged for the porch.

Pain ripped through me as his weight stretched the punctures, but I held on. Sydney screamed, and the man's face hit the concrete path a few feet from the porch. Growling and thrashing, his nails scraped at the walkway.

Syd had backed up against the door with nowhere to go. I tightened my grip, swallowed the agony pulsing up my arm, and heaved.

There was a tearing sound, and the body slid backward.

I dove onto his back and pounded my bleeding knuckles into him until a pair of arms engulfed me, and I was yanked away.

9

"Shane." The nasally voice was distant, from somewhere outside the haze of red that filtered my vision.

It came again, this time closer, louder. *"Shane."* My head started to clear, my struggle to reach the crumpled mass before me ebbed, and I relaxed into the strong arms that restrained me.

"I think you killed him, Shane." I knew the voice, had heard it nearly all my life. Like a man with a constant head cold, Dean spoke through his nose, trying his best to break through my rage.

My lungs wheezed with every belabored gasp. I reached over my head and grabbed a handful of stiff, short hair to ground myself. "Watch the do," Dean said and released his grip on my shoulders.

He had a sharp nose, thin lips, and small shifty eyes that were rarely serious. Patting down a ruffled patch of spiky blonde hair, he eased away to give me some space.

Dean's wife, Haley, followed my wife as she paced back and forth across the lawn, her cell phone by her ear.

Syd grunted, threw the phone on the ground, and said something to Haley I couldn't hear.

"What're you doing out here, Dean? It's the middle of the night." I stood up and anchored my hands on my knees to catch my breath.

Sydney darted to my side to keep me upright. Blood trailed down my leg from the wound on my wrist. The deep holes had torn into two ragged strips that ended halfway up my forearm.

I straightened my back and put some pressure on the wound with my right hand.

"Your brother called me and told me to get my ass outside," he said, taking off his shirt to wrap around my arm. "You might need stitches." Dean prodded at the semicircle of gashes, and I winced. "Did he bite you? Human bites can get pretty infected."

"Yeah, I'm pretty sure I'm gonna turn into a zombie."

"Well, I'll be the first to shoot you if you do." Dean stepped close to the body, nudged it with his toe. "Judah will find this interesting. What happened anyway?"

"Long story," I said, "and you can tell Judah I don't need my little brother watching over me."

Dean squatted and used his sandal to nudge the man on the ground, harder this time. "Tell him yourself. We both know why he does it."

Sydney caught the last part of our conversation and stopped pacing.

The muscles in her jaw tightened and loosened. "I can't get a hold of the cops," she said. "It keeps saying all lines are busy. How is that even possible? What are we gonna do?"

"Well, we kinda need to speak to the police," I said. "Keep trying, please."

She clenched her teeth again and went to find her phone.

"Hey, there's a cop," Dean said. Headlights rounded the corner, tires screeching as the squad car slammed to a stop in front of the house. "He got here fast."

"You knew he was coming?" I put my hands behind my head and let my chin drop to my chest.

A dull ache was creeping up the back of my head. Sydney sat on the edge of the porch and pulled me down next to her so she could rewrap Dean's shirt over my wounds.

Judah threw open the door and swaggered up the lawn, ticked about something.

A string of curses preceded him. The slam of two more doors brought my head up, and I was surprised to see Devon and Jordan running to catch up.

"Shit the bed, big brother," Judah said. He had shaved his head bald and started to grow a disgusting mustache that made him look like a cross between the Monopoly Guy and a Spanish Conquistador.

He flipped the guy over with his boot and knelt down to feel for a pulse. "Did you have to kill the guy?"

"Pretty sure I did." I pointed to the twins, huddled so closely it seemed they'd fuse back into one person. They wore matching pajamas; their dark, curly hair pulled back from their tiny girlish faces in tight ponytails. "We having a party?"

"Tweedle Dee and Tweedle Dum over there rang my phone off the hook for the past forty minutes because they were scared. I just spent the last four hours dealing with marital spats, drunken bar fights, and two idiot psychos with a death wish. Oh, and my brother just killed someone. I don't really feel like partying right now, Shane."

Dean raised his hand. "Um, which one's Tweedle Dum?"

"Dammit, Dean." My brother approached his friend, made a fist, but let it fall to his side. He shook his head and tried to hide his smile. "Can you take anything seriously?"

"What're we gonna do about this, Judah?" my wife asked.

My brother breathed in deeply. "Honey, you and Jordan check this guy's vitals. I'm pretty sure he's dead, but a couple nurses' opinions wouldn't hurt." The twins hesitated. "Son of a whore. You see dead people every day at work. What're you afraid of?"

Devon glowered at her husband and took a small step toward the body. She screamed when my front door burst open.

Sydney and I jumped off the porch and whirled around to see our son hunched in the doorway, his eyes squeezed closed, hands pressed against his ears so hard his face had turned red. Bowie darted past as Syd and I rushed to Faris.

I tried to pull his arms down as his mother embraced him, but jerked back when I saw the blood seeping between his fingers. It ran down his cheeks and neck, dripping to the concrete, soaking into Sydney's nightshirt.

"Holy…" The others had gathered around and I lifted my son's face level with my own. "Faris…open your eyes, son," I said, my voice trembling. He cringed and squeezed them tighter. "Open your eyes, Faris."

Slowly his lids parted, and Sydney gasped. His irises swam in dark red pools; the corneas so bloodshot only the faintest hint of white remained.

"What happened, sweetheart?" Sydney asked, her voice breathless and trembling.

Faris shuddered, the lines on his face strained, but he lifted his hands to answer. Slowly, methodically, he signed. *It's coming.*

He tilted his head to his shoulder to cover an ear, but his hands continued. *Need to go to…* His hands stilled, then he balled them up and started pounding the sides of his head.

I grabbed at his arms and finally got him to quit hitting himself. When he inclined his head, I saw fear gazing back, real and unbridled. "Go where, Faris?" I said. "I'm right here, buddy. I won't let anything hurt you. What's coming?"

He gritted his teeth, but his forehead wrinkled the way it did when he couldn't think of how to sign something. A second went by and he lifted a closed fist, knuckles out, thumb flush and pointed skyward. Then he crossed his first two fingers. He opened his hand again, but gave into the pain, clasping the sides of his head.

"I don't understand you, son," I said. "What're you trying to say?"

"I think he's spelling, Shane."

"He's three, Jordan. He doesn't know the alpha—"

I shivered when I realized she was right. Those *were* letters. And I knew exactly what he was trying to spell.

I leaned closer to whisper the word he couldn't say, but he flung his head back, shut his eyes, and screamed as he had at the grocery store.

Except this scream, silent and terrifying, was far louder. I reached for my son, but before I could touch him, a chorus of shrieks filled the night. From over the trees, the sound surrounded me, resonated through my head. My blood froze as I remembered the screech that had come from the man now lying dead in the grass. The volume increased as more and more voices joined, the cacophony growing to a pitch so deafening I had to cover my own ears.

The others were doing the same, and I realized Faris had been holding his ears long before the screaming ever started. He'd been holding them for most of the day.

Then my thoughts shattered. My bones vibrated. The shrill noise entered every pore in my body.

My teeth rattled, the intensity rising until my eardrums were on the verge of bursting. Then as suddenly as it began, it was gone.

Its final echoes faded into the darkness, and when the low growls issuing from my dog as he stood sentinel at the edge of the lawn was the only sound remaining, my son collapsed.

10

I burst into the house, my son cradled in my arms. Sydney followed with some of the others; a jumble of crying and mumbling and shuffling ensued, but I barely heard any of it. His bed was a ruffled mess, and I laid him down for the second time that night—the third if

I counted dropping him as I passed out. His chest rose and fell in quick, heavy bursts. The blood had begun to dry sticky on his ears, neck, and hands, but had ceased its flow.

I turned, calling for a wet towel, and bumped heads with my wife.

"Sorry," I said. "I'll get it." But Jordan, Devon, and Haley blocked my exit from Faris's room, their mouths hung wide.

"Wh-why is…who wrote that?" Devon stuttered. Her eyes were glued to the wall across from her. Jordan rested her head against the doorframe.

"Faris did," I said. "Can you move so I can get something to clean him up with?" They moved aside, but Jordan grabbed my arm as I made for the opening.

"That's what he was trying to spell outside, before the screaming started."

I sighed. "I don't really have time to explain this." I took another step, but Jordan's nails dug into my bicep.

"Where did he hear it?" she said and squeezed. "I work with sick kids and a lot of them are deaf. You know I can read sign language because I talk to Faris all the time. And you know I saw what he said about needing to go somewhere. He answered you by signing the first two letters of the word written on every wall of his room. Now tell us where he heard it."

I put my hands behind my head. The ache was creeping up my neck again, and I could feel my pulse thumping in my injured forearm. "I'm just a little busy right now," I groaned. "Can we talk about this later, please?"

She released her grip, and I took yet another step toward the hallway when Devon said something that froze my feet to the carpet. "We know what it means."

I turned back, my quest for a wet towel completely forgotten. "What did you say?"

"He's awake," Sydney shouted before I could press my sister-in-law any further. "Can someone get me a freaking towel?"

"I'm going," I said, then to the twins in a lower voice, "To be continued." I stalked through the door, grabbed a towel from the linen closet, wet it in the bathroom sink, and handed it to my wife. The girls crowded around the bed, changing Faris out of his soiled jammies, finally being of use.

"How you doing, boy?" I said as Syd wiped the gunk from his face. He gave a weak nod and shifted his attention to the girls as they scrubbed his hands with the other end of the towel.

His eyes were still red, but the blood had receded some, replaced by a lighter pink. Haley brushed his unruly auburn hair from his forehead so the towel could do its work.

"How about a bath, sweetie?" Sydney asked, and his head bobbed again.

"I'm going to talk to my brother about the dead guy in our yard," I said when they had gotten him in the tub. No one answered.

I stopped by the master bathroom and piled every antibiotic I could find onto the counter. The drying blood stuck to Dean's shirt and tears formed as I peeled the makeshift bandage away from the ravaged flesh underneath.

I stuck my arm under the faucet, pumped soap into the wound and rubbed at it as hard as I could without screaming.

The peroxide came next. I gripped the side of the sink while it bubbled over, my knuckles turning white in the few places they hadn't been split open.

I rinsed out the cuts and applied alcohol. I did scream then, but crammed my mouth into my shoulder to mute the sound. I rinsed again, applied pressure until the bleeding stopped, and wrapped my arm back up with gauze.

When I got outside, Judah and Dean were loading the dead man into the back seat of the squad car. I lit a cigarette and walked over.

"You're just gonna take him?"

Dean's grin was out of place to say the least. He gave the body a final shove and slammed the door.

A foot slipped out, and it bounced back open. "Son of a…" he said as he flopped the foot back inside and swung the door closed, still grinning.

"What could you possibly be smiling about?" I said.

"I love this shit," he said. "Dead people, the screaming flash mob a block away. Little kids freaking out. It's like we're in a horror movie."

I took a drag and blew out a long white string of smoke. "You ever stop to think, Dean…"

"What?" he said.

"Ugh, never mind. What are you gonna do with him, Judah?"

"I'll think of something," he said. He pressed the button on his radio and spoke something in police jargon. Only static answered. "I can't get a hold of anyone. Dispatch isn't answering, my sergeant isn't picking up his phone or radio, no one on my squad is talking..." He put his hands on his hips and hung his head. "Can the girls stay here until I get off?"

"If you take that guy off my hands, I'll babysit anyone you want," I said.

"How's my nephew?"

I stomped the butt of my cig out on the grass. "He's awake, and his ears stopped bleeding. Syd's got him in the bath."

"I've never seen him like that," said Judah. "It scared the hell out of me."

"A lot of things are scaring me right now," I said.

My brother gave me a hug and started to his car.

"Hey, do you know what Argo is?" I called after him.

"Why?" He stopped and stood with his back to me.

"Faris wrote it all over the walls of his room tonight."

Dean gave me an inquiring look and my brother turned around, his eyebrows pinched and low.

"Freaky, I know," I said. "He also said we needed to go there, in between holding his ears in pain while blood poured out of them and fainting after all the screaming started. He was pretty adamant about it."

"Does he do that often?" Dean said.

"Yeah, you should see his pillows when he wakes up in the morning. Idiot." I lit another cigarette and observed my brother who was staring off into the night. "Well? Do you know what it means?"

He backed to his car, his eyes still spacey, and reached behind him to lift the door handle. The door creaked open and he sat down, absently digging in his pocket for his keys.

He slouched sideways and stuck them into the ignition. Finally, he straightened and faced me, hands gripping the wheel. When the moonlight hit him he seemed more a ghost than a man.

"Yeah, brother," he said, "I know what it means...and I also know where it is."

11

His taillights shrunk down the street, winked at the stop sign, and then disappeared around the corner. I stood and watched, unable to turn away, though my brother and the man I'd killed were long gone.

The man I'd killed...

I searched for a sense of guilt over what I had done...shame, pride...anything at all, but the only thing that plagued my mind was worry. Worry for my brother, and the dead man in his back seat.

I shivered and crossed my arms over my chest. When did it get so cold outside?

"He'll be okay," Dean said from behind me.

"He usually is." *But not always.* I schlepped up the driveway, the thought of that shrieking madman in the backseat of Judah's squad car weighing heavily on me, when I glimpsed a set of headlights sweeping around the same corner. The car rushed down my road and pulled up my drive.

"What're you doing here?" I couldn't help but ask as my parents stepped out and rushed toward me. My mom's hair lay flattened on one side, but the thin ironed curls she worked hard to achieve each day still held on the other; my dad's was a brown and gray mess. Both had changed out of whatever they'd been sleeping in, though, which meant they wouldn't be getting back into their car and driving home any time soon.

My mother embraced me like she hadn't seen me in ages, yanking my neck down to her level. Sharp ripples of pain snaked around my sides from the center of my spine.

My whole body ached; I hadn't noticed until now. I cringed as she released her grip, and I straightened, the fingers of pain reaching into my abdomen and thighs. Not to mention my throbbing arm.

My mom hadn't answered my question. She gave a sidelong glance at my father who studied me over baggy eyes and tight lips. "Judah woke us up with his unending phone calls," he said, voice gruff, more annoyed than angry. "Said we should all be together right now, wouldn't tell us why, but when that racket started your mother insisted we just come over."

"Racket?" I said. "You mean the screaming?"

He nodded and yawned. "Rednecks and their parties."

Dean and I exchanged glances.

"I saw that," my dad said, shifting his eyes from Dean to me, and then to my bandaged forearm. "You wanna tell us what's going on?"

I sighed and lit a cigarette so they'd have to stay outside while I filled them in. I wasn't eager to move into the house. My mom would crap a brick when she saw Faris.

"Guess I should start with the grocery store…"

12

My mom did indeed crap a brick when she saw Faris. Actually, she crapped several of them as she dashed into the house after I got to the part in the story when her grandson had passed out on the porch.

Frankly, I was impressed she made it past the old lady grabbing him.

"So what're you thinking of doing," my dad said from the hall outside Faris's room. "Hauling Syd and the kids halfway across the country to some farm you've never been to because your boy writes on the walls and you have a weird dream after fainting?"

"When you put it like that, it makes me sound like a pansy," I said. "That's not what you're insinuating is it, pops?"

He shrugged and laughed. "You know I'd never call you pansy. Your brother, yeah, but not you."

"Whatever, old man. But I am seriously thinking about doing exactly what you just suggested. How could I not have known the twins' mom got remarried?"

"Not like you pay any attention when they talk, Shane," Dean said.

"And you knew the guy she married was named Argo?"

He shook his head. "I don't pay attention either."

"What'd Judah say about it?" my dad asked.

"Why does it matter what he said?" I threw my hands up and stomped down the hall toward the living room.

"Because he took a dead man off your lawn and drove off with him," he said, following. "Which is illegal, I'm sure."

"And we both know *why* he did that."

"Yes we do, and he'll continue to do things like that until he finds a way to cancel that debt he thinks he owes you."

"He doesn't owe me anything. We're brothers." I stopped. My hands were trembling. I sat on the couch, elbows on my knees, and inhaled. "He doesn't owe me anything."

My dad sat next to me and put his hand on my head. "You and I know that, but he doesn't. You two are thick as thieves, and you did what you did because he's your brother. He just wants to show you he would do the same for you." He ruffled my hair and stood back up. "And you didn't stop him from taking the dead guy, did you?"

"Ughhhh." I slapped my temples with the pads of my hands. "I can't think about this right now—"

My phone rang, and I pulled it out with a grunt, knowing full well who it was. "It's like he knows when we're talking about him," I said to my dad, then pushed the answer button and said, "Hey Judah, what now?"

"I'll tell you what now, you stupid son of a..." I pulled the phone away as a string of expletives barked into the living room. My dad raised his eyebrows, and I smiled for the first time in the last hour.

"I can't understand you when you don't use your big boy voice," I said when he'd stopped cursing. "Something upset you?" My dad laughed and walked down the hall.

"Like the corpse in my backseat that sat up and tried to eat me?" Judah's pitch became high and panicked. "If the glass shield wasn't between us he would have ripped my head off."

"He what? But that's impossible, Jordan said he was dead."

"Yeah, well he came back to life." His words edged with fear.

The cold chill sank into my stomach, mixing with that warm ball of tension. "So…he's alive?"

"Uh, not anymore. I shot him in the head. Three times."

"Are you alright?" It was the only thing I could think to say. My mind was reeling again. That guy had been dead. Even the twins had confirmed it.

"Nice to know you care. I'm fine, but we have bigger problems."

"Bigger than someone rising from the dead?"

"Probably not, but it affects you more at this point. Things have gotten worse in town…exponentially. They're calling in the National Guard, sealing off the city. I don't think we want to be here when that happens."

"Martial Law?"

"And everything that goes with it."

35

"I wonder where we could go," I said. A leading question, but one that needed to be answered. And not by me.

For the first time Judah was silent. His heavy mouth breathing told me he was still there, rasping in and out for what seemed an eternity. Finally, he said something, but it was so soft I couldn't make it out.

"What?" I said. "I can't hear you."

"I said...I think you should take everyone to the Argo."

I had anticipated his response—had counted on it—but when he actually said it, when the words actually left his mouth, it was like a wrecking ball had slammed into my chest.

My pulse began to thud, sweat seeped onto my palms. *Am I really going to do this? Pick up and go to a place that...*

That what? That gave me chills every time I thought of its name? It did; it made my whole body quake, but at the same time...at the same time it felt safe. A refuge against a coming storm. And a storm was coming. Of that much I was sure.

I hung up the phone and found myself in the bedroom closet. I couldn't remember consciously making the decision to go in there. Stacks of junk occupied every inch of the high shelf that lined the closet's perimeter—old board games, once-completed puzzles, boxes of Lego's, more boxes of comic books, the safe in the corner...

The safe, barely the size of a microwave, was the one easily accessible thing in my closet.

My fingers brushed along the top, came back with the key, and turned the lock. I reached in and brought out the only two material objects that I truly cared about.

My great grandfather's guns. A pair of immaculate revolvers, they had been fashioned by some gunsmith whose name died with the man for whom they were made.

The steel gleamed even in the dimness of the closet. I ran my thumbs over the letters intricately etched into the dark walnut hilts. *F.M.* My great grandfather's initials and my son's namesake.

I laid the weapons on top of the safe and again reached in, pulling out a brown leather gun belt that had been passed down along with the revolvers. It was lined neatly with .45 caliber bullets, the two holsters engraved with the same detailed scrollwork as the initials on the guns' wooden grips.

I fastened the belt and ensured each revolver was loaded, spinning the cylinders before slipping them into their holsters. My hands had been trembling in regular intervals since the encounter with the man in the yard, but for the first time I felt them still. I drew the guns, smooth and quick, a frequently practiced act, and took aim at the opposite wall. My hands were steady, and I grinned.

The shuffling of footsteps approached, and I turned my head toward the bedroom door. My wife stood in the entryway, and the night's hardships showed clear on her tired face.

"Faris?" I said, securing the guns in their holsters.

"Asleep," she said through a yawn. "We're really going, aren't we?"

I nodded and walked to her, held her by the arms. "But first there's something I have to do."

13

"Stay in the car," I said to Jordan as we pulled into her driveway. I killed the engine and quietly dropped out of the truck. *One twin down, one to go.*

I was beginning to regret the promise I'd made to Judah over the phone, but options were becoming scarcer by the minute.

The highways would be blocked off in less than an hour, and we couldn't leave until Devon and Jordan packed a few things.

And then there were the dogs. We owned four altogether: I had Bowie, Jordan and Johnny had Shelby and Samson, and Devon and my brother had a massive lab named Jax that would take up more space than the other three combined.

It had taken twenty minutes to get Devon to her house and back. I'd given her all the time I could, but she still griped my ear off about making her leave without "taking anything".

As if three bags and a dog the size of a bear wasn't enough. She'd be leaving two of those bags at my house, but she wasn't aware of that yet. It took less time to let her pack what she wanted than it would to argue about trunk space.

That had been an easy trip. This one wasn't shaping up quite so nicely.

I heard the dogs barking as soon as we pulled onto their street, and I cut the headlights before turning up the drive.

Unlike Jax, Jordan's dogs rarely barked unless they heard

something in the yard, my first clue that something was wrong.

I handed Jordan my shotgun. "You know how to use—"

"Just point and shoot, right?" she said. She pulled back the action and rocked it forward again.

I smirked, and then crept up the drive, pressing against the garage door. Under other circumstances I would have simply driven away, but I wouldn't have left without my dog and I didn't expect Jordan to leave without hers.

The house was small. The outer walls formed a rectangle that surrounded two bedrooms and baths, a kitchen, and a snug little living area.

Something heavy had been thrown through the front picture window, and from my position I could hear at least two people shuffling around inside.

They weren't being quiet about it either. *What if Jordan had still been here?* The thought gave me chills. It also strengthened my desire to get this over with.

The dogs took priority here and thankfully they had been left in the back yard. I edged along the garage door and around the east corner of the house, kneeling where the privacy fence halted my progression.

Sweat poured out of me despite how cool the breeze was. My heart pounded, my torn wrist hammering in sync. My bowels shifted, and I suddenly had the urge to shit.

I drew a revolver and my stomach settled somewhat. I'd already killed one man tonight, sort of, and here I crouched, gun in hand, prepared to kill some more. How did things get turned around so quickly?

I lifted the latch to the fence's gate and swung it outward about a foot. My teeth clenched as the hinges screeched loud enough to be heard in the next town.

"Shelby, Samson," I whispered, hoping I could get the dogs to come to me without having to actually enter the back yard.

I waited a few seconds, but the dogs continued barking at the rear of the house. I took a breath, and Jordan's scream stopped me cold.

I bolted to the corner of the house and froze. A dark figure pulled Jordan away from the truck. I stepped around the corner when the front door burst open and two men charged out. *Crap.* I backed into the shadow of the house.

A gunshot rang out and the figure dragging Jordan collapsed at her feet. She yelped, and huddled against the truck, sobbing.

The light from inside the house fell on the two men as they stepped away from the door, and I realized they both wore police uniforms. One also held a handful of jewelry; the other had Johnny's Xbox 360…and the gun.

"Whadda we have here?" the man with the gun said.

"Looks like we got ourselves a little hottie," said the other and spun the silver hoop in the center of his bottom lip with his tongue.

He shoved the jewelry in his pocket and crossed the short span of driveway until he stood directly in front of Jordan. "Why don't you come inside with us and we can have a little fun?"

Jordan gasped as the man reached for her. She slid along the truck, stepping sideways over the body of the crumpled figure so it was now lying between them.

"Aw, come on now, sugar," the man said, "we just wanna stick it in ya and then we'll be on our way."

"B…but you're cops," Jordan breathed.

"Nah, the cops are around the corner taking a long nap." The man with the lip ring reached again, but as his fingers closed around Jordan's bicep, the hand of the figure on the ground grabbed the man's ankle.

He yelped, stumbled, and fell.

The dark shape was on him in a flash, teeth gnashing at the startled man's hands as they struggled to fend off the attack.

His friend shouted, pointing his gun. Jordan scrambled for safety. I watched in shock as the figure chomped down on the man's right hand. He yanked and his hand came back with three less digits.

The creature spit out the fingers and lunged. The man's arms flailed, but he was powerless to stop the attack. Bloody teeth clamped over his neck.

Two shots finally sent the assailant tumbling, but it was too late. The man's throat had been ripped out; a spring of blood pumped onto the ground.

The figure twisted, unhindered by the two bullets in its ribs. Its head thrashed and it let out a piercing screech. The cry was cut short by a third gunshot. The side of the thing's head exploded and it finally lay motionless in the grass.

"Joe?" said the gunman. He realized he still held the Xbox and tossed it away, then knelt beside his dead accomplice. "Joe?" he said, over and over.

My senses trickled back, and I stepped from the shadows. Jordan hunched behind the truck's rear bumper, safe enough for now. The man had his back to me and I closed the distance, my great grandfather's revolver trained on the back of his head.

"Don't move," I said.

He moved.

With a startled grunt, the man whirled, his gun searching for the source of the voice. I shot him between the eyes.

Jordan came out of hiding, giving the bodies a wide berth as she made her way to me. I took in the three men lying dead in front of Jordan's house and squeezed my eyes shut, thinking just maybe they wouldn't be there when I opened them.

"Shane?" She put a hand on my shoulder. "You're shivering…"

They were still there. "Two…" I couldn't think straight. The blood…the screech…the gunshots…

"Two what, Shane?"

"I…I've killed two people…"

"You saved me, Shane," Jordan said. "From being raped and probably killed. You took your time with it, though."

I tried to go over what had just happened, and found that I couldn't. It was all a blur of screaming and movement. I hadn't saved Jordan…that thing on the ground had. *I just watched.* How long would I have stood there, hiding in the shadows, if nothing was there to distract them?

Those cold fingers made a fist in my stomach, forcing everything else up into my throat.

I staggered to the side of the house, pressed my head against the rough concrete.

The first guy had let me off the hook when he rose from the dead, and here I just replaced him with two more.

I took a deep breath, closed my eyes. And then I threw up.

Lucha Libre (Part 1)

1

We embarked a little after four o'clock Saturday morning. After the incident at Jordan's house, we tried repeatedly to reach my brother. When that failed we called Johnny, but he didn't answer either. We had to go without them. I didn't know what else to do.

Dean and I had to drag Devon into the vehicle, kicking and refusing to leave without her husband as Jax barked and growled at our heels; Jordan sauntered in on her own, her eyes distant, and climbed into the backseat without a word. Haley and the twins rode with Dean in Devon's Honda Pilot, Sidney and the kids were center with me in our Mercury Monterey, and my parents followed in drogue. They had been adamant about staying; sure the cops would bring the city under control by morning, but when I burst into the house and half-explained half-stuttered what had happened at Jordan's they finally gave in. Now if my dad could find it in him to drive faster than 75 mph, we'd make it to the Argo around three or four Sunday afternoon.

We made it out of Florida and into Georgia safely and in good time, though we did pass a convoy of Humvees traveling south on I-95 less than five miles from our exit. Even Devon had to admit it was a good thing we left when we did. The kids slept in back, snuggling their blankets. Sydney had told Zoe we were going on vacation, and she passed out with an excited smile on her lips. But Faris knew where we were headed. He seemed calm enough—he hadn't complained about his ears since the screaming had died down—but his stare said otherwise before disappearing beneath the weight of his eyelids.

The intended route took us up I-75 to Macon where we would

exit and take the back roads directly north toward Gatlinburg, Tennessee. Judging by the mayhem in our part of Florida, I thought it wise to stay as far from Atlanta as possible, and hopefully circumvent most other large cities.

We didn't, however, take the highwaymen into account.

2

Dead air screamed from nearly every station on the radio by the time we exited the highway and turned north along US-129. The irritating buzz of static hummed from the rest. No radio meant no news.

Dean spied the roadblock about halfway between Macon and Eatonton.

"You seeing this?" Dean's voice came through the Motorola walkie-talkie that my parents happened to have lying around for no reason in particular. They never went to the beach but they happened to have awesome lounge-chairs, never went camping but happened to have lanterns and tents, and never traveled but just happened to have pretty decent walkies. I suspected they went to the store sometimes thinking, *Hey, the kids might need this someday.* In any case, today was the day we needed the two-ways. Each car had one, and since cell phone reception was more out than in, it made communication much easier than pulling into the passing lane to flag down the lead car for every little thing—like the millions of pee stops we had to make for Zoe. The girl's bladder was the size of a grape.

"That's a negative, over," I said.

"I'm so blind I shouldn't even be driving," my dad piped in from behind us. I pushed the button and laughed.

"You don't have to laugh into the walkie, Shane," Dean said. *"Keep it to your own vehicle."*

I laughed through the two-way again.

We slowed and I could see what Dean was referring to. The roadblock lay about 500 feet ahead and consisted of four run-down cars parked bumper-to-bumper across the four-lane road. There were a few cars queued up at a dead stop, and about ten people walking around.

"I think you'd better lock and load," I said through the radio.

"Done," Dean came back.

"Grab the guns out of the glove compartment and give me one," I said to Sydney, suddenly relieved I had spent twenty minutes pulling all my guns from the closet shelf and scrounging for ammo before we left. "Keep the other. If things get dicey, shoot anyone that comes close to the car." I lifted my butt off the seat and settled into a more upright position. "And stretch the gun-belt over the center console in case we need to reload in a hurry."

Syd held out my revolver between her forefinger and thumb like it was a dirty diaper. The other she laid in her lap, barely giving it a glance.

"It won't go off unless you pull the trigger."

"I've never shot one before, okay?" she said. "It makes me nervous."

"Well, just hold it for me in case I need it."

Her face scrunched and she lifted the gun with both hands. "I got this. Just keep your eyes on the road."

That would have to do. She probably wouldn't hit anything if she *did* end up firing off a few rounds, but sometimes people got lucky.

"Pops, you good?"

"As good as we can be, I guess."

"Alright, we're getting close and I don't see any cops," I said. "If these people need help, we'll help, but be ready to floor it around on the shoulder. Dean, we'll follow your lead, so think on your toes."

"Roger that. Red Leader out."

What a dork.

We crept closer and my gut began to churn. The feeling intensified, and when we neared to within 100 feet, I nearly soiled myself. What lay before us reminded me of something out of *Mad Max*. The windows of the three cars in front of us were smashed in, their drivers either sprawling in the road or hunched over in their seats. The cars had been halted a few yards from the roadblock. Half a dozen men in *lucha libre* masks rooted through the trunks, while another four watched our approach.

All were smiling. There was no way I could know that, but I did.

"No stopping, Dean," I said and realized I wasn't even holding the radio. I picked it up and pushed the button. "No stopping, Dean. Floor it."

The Pilot jolted forward, fishtailing onto the shoulder. My foot depressed the accelerator, and our own vehicle lurched ahead. I could only hope my dad reacted as quickly to the situation.

For a moment, as Dean moved off to the right, I had a clear view of the road. Dean's sudden, erratic swerve caught the highwaymen by surprise, and they scrambled to cut him off. The man nearest the roadblocks barked loud, muffled orders. His partners immediately abandoned their pillaging efforts and sprinted into action. They were far more organized than they appeared at first. Our spur-of-the-moment escape plan depended on the element of surprise. Now that it was gone, we would have to hope we were either smarter, faster, or better with a gun than the men rushing at us from at least three different angles.

Or luckier.

3

We made decent progress in the seconds before the highwaymen closed in—Dean flew around the parked cars within a few yards of the roadblock, myself and my dad close behind. A few sparks of hope, and then the first shots were fired.

4

"Get the kids down," I screamed at the windshield. They were sitting ducks in their car seats, but my wife wasn't moving. *"Syd, the kids!"* That registered and she climbed over the seat, unbuckling Faris with one hand and Zoe with the other.

The van's tail-end threatened to slide out as I followed Dean's example and swerved onto the shoulder. The incessant sound of the road's safety grooves *clack-clack-clack*ing against my driver's side tires rammed home the fact that we were actually taking evasive action.

I spun the wheel and veered further back onto the road than I expected. A quick flash of yellow and a dull thump informed me that one of the *luchadores* hadn't envisioned the swift change in direction

44

either. My eyes went to the side mirror in time to see the man spinning like a top. I winced and sucked air through my teeth as I made the universal expression for, "Ewwww, that suuuucks," then widened my eyes in pure shock as my dad's car barreled through the guy, flipping him over the hood and sending him airborne before I had to turn my attention back to the road.

Sydney had barely settled the children to the floorboards when the window behind me blew out—the one Zoe had been sitting next to mere seconds before. Syd screamed and fell flat on top of Faris in the center aisle. She lowered out of view, attempting to cover every inch of our children's bodies with her own. If we got out of this alive, I was going to tell her how lucky I was to have her.

The overcorrection put me back on the road, which was bad because the asphalt was blocked not far ahead. Dean passed the stationary cars on the shoulder, but I didn't have time to make it back behind him without swerving too drastically and losing traction. The last thing I wanted to do was roll the van. If I slowed down I could probably make it, but the highwaymen were closing in. My dad remained right on my tail and there was no way he would be able to follow me at this speed.

Which left only one option. We were going through the roadblock.

"Brace yourselves back there." I had decelerated slightly in order to stop the vehicle from fishtailing, but now I stomped on the gas. The speedometer jumped past 60. I hoped it would be enough. And that my dad had caught onto the idea. Space rapidly grew short.

I heard three plinks on the outside of the driver's door as the van reached 65. We were riding the line now, heading for the gap between the roadblock's bumpers (which were the same color as the cars, generally identifying a plastic molded piece of crap, much to my relief) and on a collision course for two more highwaymen. Like deer, they seemed entranced by the vehicle speeding toward them. At the last minute, the one on the left nudged the other out of his daze and they dove their separate ways just before I crashed through the barricade. Several more plinks sprayed the exterior of the van and then my forehead was thrust into the steering wheel. The air bag deployed. Bolts of agonizing heat exploded from my nose, and my teeth clattered together. My foot slipped from the gas and I struggled to accelerate as I moved my arms like a little kid in a slap fight trying to get the airbag out of my line of sight. A slit of light at the upper portion of the windshield presented itself and I took full advantage.

And I saw…nothing.

5

There was only empty road ahead. I checked my rear-view and saw my dad's car scraping through the decent sized hole I had created. It was riding a little lopsided.

"Where's Dean?"

"What?"

"Nothing, Syd, stay dow—" The SUV almost sideswiped me as Dean made his way back onto the road. My stomach found its former place in my throat as I maneuvered to avoid side-swiping him. The airbag had begun to deflate, increasing my range of vision, but I felt warm liquid flowing freely over my mouth and down my neck.

"Great."

"What?"

"Nothing," I said. "Just stay down until we stop. I think we're clear of the *luchadores* but—" I checked my mirrors again, "—it's probably not a good idea to stop yet. Doesn't look like they're chasing us though."

"Lucha-whats?"

"*Luchadores.* They're Mexican wrestlers that are more like acrobats…" I stopped talking to try and plug my nose with a wad of my shirt, hissing as I pushed up too hard. Definitely broken.

"What do Mexicans have to do with anything?"

"They were wearing *lucha libre* masks… Ugh, can we have this conversation later, please? My nose is broken and blood is getting everywhere."

"How'd you break your n—"

"Shane you there?" Thank heaven, it was Dean. I felt around for the walkie-talkie and about gave up when I touched the tip of the antenna near the gap between my seat and the door. Dean repeated his query as I fumbled for a grip on the antenna while simultaneously attempting to spill as little blood as possible on the upholstery. The front-end of the van was undoubtedly a smashed mess, but that didn't mean the leather interior had to match.

"Shane here. Is everyone okay? Over."

There was a moment of silence over the air and then my dad piped in. *"We have a flat and some broken windows. The engine's rattling. Not sure how far we can get in this car. Dean, pull over as soon as you think it's safe. Over."*

"Red Leader acknowledges."

"Holy shit, you're gay," I said, blowing red snot in all directions.

"Mini vans are gay."

"Enough," my dad said, not sounding amused. There really wasn't much to be amused about. My father had killed a man (or maybe I had, and my dad just made sure). Either way, the tone had changed, and I didn't feel much like talking anymore.

6

We pulled over five minutes later. Sydney, Zoe, and Faris were safely strapped in their original seating positions. My daughter's hair was a blonde flag flapping in the breeze that entered through the shattered window. I was at a complete loss as to whose genes had won out in creating those straight, thin locks. Her mom's hair was brilliantly red and unmanageably wavy. Mine was falling out, but at a time when I still touted a full head of hair it was equally thick, curly and dark brown. Faris's had sprouted enough to determine it would be curly, and the color was all Sydney. Poor boy.

Once at a stop, everyone but the kids piled out of their respective vehicles. The clock on the dash read 11:05 a.m., and the cool Georgia air was a nice contrast to my heightened temperature.

Our eyes, drawn by a common force, drifted south in the direction we had come: still no cars heading our way. Another blessing.

But you haven't seen any coming from the opposite direction either. The voice of intuition. And it was strong.

"I think we need to get off this road," I said, almost to myself. "And quickly."

"But no one's coming," Devon said.

"I know. In either direction."

"You think there's another group down the road?" my dad said. His mussed up hair appeared to have gotten grayer since our last pit stop. He stood around five foot eight, 200 pounds (exactly how I would look given another twenty-five years and no exercise—minus the hair of course, that bastard still had his). He held my mother around the shoulder. I could see his hands trembling, but it may have been my mom's body that shook.

I sighed. "Yeah, I do. It's just a hunch, but it would explain why they didn't bother chasing us." My nose had stopped bleeding, but any passage of air was impossible and my voice was beginning to sound like Dean's. I caught a glimpse of the purple mass of broken blood vessels under my eyes in one of the car windows. It resembled an eggplant that had been smashed by a sledgehammer.

"Sydney finally get tired of your bull crap?" my dad jeered, gesturing toward my bruised face. "You always were my favorite, you know," he said to my wife.

"I keep him in line," said Syd, following it with the first real laugh I had heard all day. It was nice to hear, even if it was at my expense.

"Mom and dad, you're with Dean and the girls. We'll divide the luggage in your car between Devon's car and mine. Put Jax in with Bowie." I added, "Let's move," and clapped a few times when no one did.

The twins, Haley, and my mother headed to the Pilot while Dean, my dad, and I unloaded then reloaded the four or five bags and suitcases from the Saturn's trunk and threw them into my van.

Sydney came over to check on the kids. They both had to pee. So did the dogs. I let my wife deal with that particular crisis.

7

We accelerated back onto the cracked asphalt of US-129, one car shorter, hearts a little heavier. We devised a quick plan that probably wouldn't work while the kids and animals were watering the crabgrass that covered the gradual slope on either side of the road. The one map we possessed showed only a few small streets within the next two miles, only one of which curved north in the direction we needed to go. With any luck, we would reach that side street before we ran into the highwaymen that may or may not be waiting for us.

I was the lead car this time. Sydney was once again in the center aisle with the kids, sitting upright at the moment but positioned in a way that she could duck and cover them in a moment's notice. The luggage from the car we left behind took up every inch of the back bench that wasn't occupied by a dog.

The silence in the cab was beginning to get to me so I plugged in my iPhone and set it to shuffle. Acoustic guitar and banjo filled the van, something by *Mumford and Sons*, but my mind was too distracted to enjoy it.

Before the song ended, I turned onto the side road we'd agreed on. I killed the volume in anticipation of a call from either Dean or my dad. We'd gone over the plan already—which was to follow this road to the next gas station (or any sign of civilization for that matter), but I knew my friends and I knew my dad. One of them would call. I was betting on my dad.

"You see anything up there, Shane?" My dad just couldn't help himself.

"Nada," I called back. "Nothing but farmland on the right, trees on the left, and empty road ahead." *And no cars at all. Please don't let there be another roadblock up there.* My head started throbbing again and I was getting woozy, probably from the loss of blood. My forearm ached for the first time since leaving the house. We were rolling up a steep incline, making it impossible to see what lay beyond the hill's crest. We would most likely see one of three things when we reached the apex. The first, and the one I was setting my hopes on, would be a gas station or any type of store. The second would be nothing at all; just the usual scenery. This wouldn't be ideal, but it would be better than the final alternative. That, of course, would be another roadblock complete with bandits wearing brightly colored masks.

What actually presented itself as we passed over the hill a few minutes later was a depressing mixture of all three.

I slowed to a stop and put the van into park. Sydney immediately came in with the questions: "Why are we stopped?" "What do you see?" "Are there more *luchados*?" Dean joined in a moment later, reiterating the same questions, except pronouncing what Sydney had called *luchados* correctly.

"Everyone be quiet for a second, please," I said into the walkie-talkie for both the other car's benefit as well as Sydney's. To my surprise, I was answered by only silence. The Pilot's passengers couldn't see over the hill and had to be anxious to know what was down there, but I desperately needed to gather my thoughts. The roadblock in conjunction with my aching face sent my head swooning. If I didn't take a minute, I was going to pass out.

"I'm getting out for a sec. Just stay put, okay." I opened the door and stepped down before my wife could protest.

My feet hit the asphalt and I staggered. I leaned against the side of the van, breathing deeply in an attempt to slow my heart rate. A car door opened and I saw Dean and my father exit their vehicle. I let them come to me. They would need to view the scenery below if we were to figure out a course of action.

They made eye contact with me briefly before peering into the distance. Neither said a word. My dad laid a hand on Dean's shoulder, then took a few unconscious steps forward as though it would improve his vision. Dean just stood, staring.

It was about 11:45 in the morning, the mild cloud cover unable to hold back the fall sun. It didn't look like it was going to rain anytime soon, but it almost certainly would eventually. With any luck, we would be long gone before that happened. The air was getting warmer but far from unbearable, nowhere near as humid as Florida would have been. It actually felt nice, and made me wonder why we lived in a place that rarely saw below 80 degrees. I had actually forgotten about the events we experienced not thirty minutes ago, and all but forgot what waited for us down the hill. Nice weather could do that. At least I didn't feel like fainting.

"Whadda you make of that, Shane?" Dean asked, bringing me out of deep space where there were no such things as highwaymen, the temperature was always in the 70's, and there was never a need to flee one's home at odd hours of the night.

My dad and Dean pulled themselves away from the slope and were now standing before me, lending me their full attention. *Another decision I'm expected to make.* The swollen blue face of a little boy flashed through my mind, and I thought of Judah. He'd contribute, probably wouldn't shut up about what he thought we should do. And we'd probably argue, but at the moment I found myself wishing he were here anyway so I could just sit back and let him have his way.

As it were, the time I spent sitting in silence had allowed me to think some things through.

"I don't know exactly," I said, "but I have an idea of what happened down there."

8

The view, beautiful in its rural simplicity, was marred only by imagination. That is to say nothing actually appeared out of place from atop the hill. From this vantage, a rolling landscape of peach trees stretched to the east and northeast as far as the eye could see. To the west, clusters of tall poplars occupied the 200 or so yards of buffer between us and US-129. The peach groves picked up again on the other side of the highway. What I could smell of them through my inflamed nostrils was enough to clear anyone's head.

Imagination inserted its influence when I noticed the complete lack of human beings in or around the stand-alone gas station/farm store that stood a half mile down the equally deserted roadway. Questions like *Where is everybody?* and *What happened down there?* or *Is everyone dead?* provided a depressing soundtrack to the scene below. Such questions were hardly helpful.

"Whadda you make of that, Shane?" Dean had said as the voices were asking their own questions and the movie reel in my head flickered with visions of mask-wearing ass-holes and bloody massacres.

I was positive highwaymen like the ones that confronted us down the way had taken control of the entire area—highway, side roads, gas stations, the whole bit. The people that should be gassing up or driving their vehicles, or just buying Gatorade at the farm store, had been cleared out or tied up somewhere. Or killed, if the scene at the roadblock was any indication. Based on what we had seen a couple miles back, I was leaning toward the latter. And I now desperately wanted an orange Gatorade. The electrolytes would compliment my blood loss marvelously.

I told this to my dad and Dean (minus the part about the Gatorade), and then waited for any input or ideas—contributions of any kind, really. When there was no response, I began to get flustered, which was the last thing I wanted. I don't think clearly when I get anxious, I just get angry.

"Give me something, guys. The van needs gas, there could

be…probably *are* more bad guys down there, and I'm running on empty. "

Fresh smirks outlined their faces. Wondering what the joke was, I raised my eyebrows and a fresh jolt of pain made me wince. This cracked them up.

"I just can't take you seriously right now," said Dean. "You're face looks like a bruised ball sack."

"Ugh," I said, rolling my eyes, which also hurt. *How does moving my eyes make my nose hurt?* I thought, irritated more by that than by the visualization my friend had forced into my head. "So…any ideas?"

Dean said, "We can either take our chances and try to use those gas pumps, which almost definitely will mean someone going inside the store to start the pumps—"

"And get a Gatorade," I added.

"And get the moron a Gatorade…" Dean continued. "Or we can floor it past the station altogether and hope we find actual civilization again before we run out of gas."

"Now we're talking. Pops, you have anything to add?"

"Ideally, I think it would be best to bypass the gas station." He was haggard and for the first time in my life, the thought occurred to me that my dad was getting old.

"Obviously," he said, "this situation isn't ideal. We were on 129 for a while without any sign of gas. This isn't the Interstate. Gas stations don't come as frequently, especially in rural areas like this. It could be a long time before we find another, and you just said you need to fill up."

Dean and I nodded agreement.

We had to stop at that gas station.

9

"You enjoying all this?" I said as we rolled down the hill.

"We used to play this game when we were kids, remember? The end of the world?"

"Playing in the woods was fun. This isn't really the same."

He shrugged. "Only difference is we aren't playing anymore.

And I seem to remember you being pretty good at that game. Always the last one standing."

"You all were two years younger than me. Of course I was the last one standing."

"Point is," he said, waving me off, "if I had to choose who to be stuck with in this situation, it would be you, Judah, and Johnny." He peered out the window and added, "And Haley, obviously."

"Obviously."

"So what's the problem? You've been handling things pretty well, I think."

I tightened my grip on the steering wheel. "I've been fumbling around like a terrified fool, Dean. You call that handling it?"

"You don't look terrified to me," Dean said.

I thought of my children, of Sydney, the men I killed. I lit a cigarette and pulled on it long and hard. "Well, I am. I'm more scared than I've ever been in my life." I blew a stream of white smoke out the window, thinking of the apprehension on my wife's face when I told her what we meant to do; when we kissed our loved ones, not telling them what they already knew: that this may be the last time they see us alive. "But I'm even more angry."

Dean pressed his lips together and nodded.

"You guys alright?" my dad asked over the radio, breaking through the quiet. The others were told to stay in the Pilot and keep a lookout. If they saw something—anything—they were to let us know immediately. But that didn't include asking questions like "are you alright?"

"Yeah, we're fine," Dean answered. Then added exactly what I was thinking, "Keep the air clear unless you have something important to tell us. Over."

"Roger that, boys. Good luck."

"Thanks. Over and out." Dean clipped the radio to his belt. "We really gonna do this?"

I shrugged. "I don't see another option, do you?"

"No, I just wasn't sure you were ready to add more bodies to your list of people you've killed in the last 24 hours."

"Well, I hope we don't meet any more bad guys," I said, "but I'm so pissed right now I just want to shoot something."

He shook his head and laughed again, his metro-sexual hair and dress clashing with the shotgun laying across his thighs. "No, as long as you don't become a serial killer or anything." He paused as a thought lit up his face. "We could stop these guys from doing anything like this again. Where's all the cops anyway?"

"The city probably. Must be just as bad here as it is at home." An image of my house popped into my mind, but then I caught a faint whiff of something that struck me as completely ironic and let out a laugh.

"What're you laughing at?"

"I just pictured going into a shootout with you wearing your American Eagle polo and jeans, trying not to mess up your hair." I put my foot on the brake. "Are you seriously wearing cologne?"

"Ha, at least I *have* hair, douche, and mine will do just fine in a shootout." He lifted the front of his shirt to his face and sniffed, shaking his head. "I like to smell good, alright?"

I took my foot off the brake and continued crawling forward. "I wish Judah and Johnny were here," said Dean, now smelling his armpits.

"No doubt."

"But then again, Devon would never have let Judah stop."

"And since he does everything she tells him, he would have driven right through and then ran out of gas down the road."

Dean grunted, knowing I was right. The only reason Devon hadn't made a fuss about us stopping was because she knew we wouldn't have listened to her. "Freaking Judah."

"You ready?" I asked.

He lifted the shotgun, and slid back the action, much like Jordan had done in her driveway the night before, but much less sexy. "Ready."

I pushed the buttons on the driver door that lowered Dean's window. He shifted in his seat to achieve a decent firing position, literally riding shotgun. I think I understood how the Earp Brothers must have felt as they strolled down the dusty main street of Tombstone to the alley near the OK Corral where a gang of outlaws waited. I felt cool and confident though I had no reason to be. The Earps had earned their confidence with blood and steel. I was as inexperienced as any rookie cop his first day on the job. Unlike targets, people tended to move. And targets didn't fire back.

I pulled the left revolver from its holster, and the wooden hilt felt cool in my hand. I had strapped the cartridge belt around my waist before setting off, quickly realizing why gunslingers took their guns off when relaxing. The belt and holsters bunched at the base of my back and hips making it extremely uncomfortable to sit behind the wheel. Still I had fired the revolvers many more times than I had my Glock that Dean now had tucked in his waistband, and felt much more certain of my aim.

Bowie and Jax shuffled around in the space in back made vacant by the absence of my wife and kids. They were only with Dean and me because they wouldn't fit in the Honda Pilot once Sydney, Zoe, and Faris were added in. I had mixed feelings about bringing the dogs (like there was any choice). I knew Bowie would respond to my orders, but Jax was another issue. He was an obedient dog…for my brother. But he had a problem with acknowledging the authority of most other people. If it came down to it—and the opportunity presented itself—I would not hesitate to set the dogs loose on anyone that threatened us. At the very least, they would cause a certain amount of chaos. I just worried about getting Jax back into the vehicle in a hurry. If he took too long (or didn't listen at all) he would be left behind, simple as that. My brother loved his dog almost to the point of being inappropriate, but I doubted if he would blame me if it came to that.

We swung into the gas station parking lot, tires screeching slightly, and pulled up to the inside pump that sat closest to the farm store entrance. The idea was to provide a buffer between us and any assailants that may come from the direction of the road. The two rows of pumps would provide a certain—yet dangerous—amount of cover. I'd heard bullets rarely cause gasoline to explode, contrary to what you see in the movies, and hoped the theory held true today. If it didn't, I doubted it would make a difference if we were parked in front or behind a pump if it blew. Either way we'd be crispy critters.

The filling station was small but of common design. Four pumps in two rows of two, protected from the elements by a freestanding flat, metal awning that didn't quite connect to the farm store's gabled roof. The store itself was also small by today's standards, bathrooms inconveniently located around back, and not many places to hide inside.

We got out and moved quickly to the store's front door. The words *Doge's Stop 'N' Go* were written across the glass in hand-painted block letters. I drew the other revolver; Dean ran with his finger beside the shotgun's trigger in the way they instruct the military, barrel aimed low and to the side. We entered like clowns falling out of an overstuffed circus car, both of us screaming at the top of our lungs. I had read somewhere (in a work of fiction, no doubt) that yelling disturbed an enemy's train of thought, possibly buying a few precious seconds before realizing they should be firing their weapons. I wanted all the time we could muster.

Neither of us had spied anyone through the store windows, but they could have been waiting in ambush. Our approach was not exactly disguised, and we weren't taking any chances. To our relief, the aisles to the right and register area to the left were empty…at least of *living* people. I shrugged at Dean, feeling a bit idiotic after yelling my head off to an empty room. But my teeth clenched when I saw the first body laying between the two aisles closest to the door amid an array of Milk Duds and Air Heads. I wouldn't have thought the human body contained that much blood had I not seen it pooled around the dead man's body. It was drying, but had not yet taken the darker, coagulated gel-like form that blood takes when it's been sitting for a long period of time.

"There's another one over here." Dean was already over the counter and behind the register, clicking on the pumps. I didn't bother going to see for myself. Everything I had envisioned taking place at this gas station had actually happened.

"This didn't happen too long ago," I said as I turned to the door. "We need to make this quick."

"Why?" Dean said as he hopped over the counter. "Aren't you having fun?"

We hustled to our predetermined positions, me manning the gas pump, Dean covering me with the shotgun.

I pumped with my right hand, reserving my left for shooting. The van's tank was roughly two thirds of the way filled and I was beginning to think there wasn't going to be any. Then my dad was yelling through the walkie-talkie.

10

"You've got company, Shane. On the other side of the road, coming

fast." The communication from the walkie-talkie on Dean's hip shattered any hope of getting through this without bloodshed.

"How fast?" Dean asked, taking his hand momentarily off the shotgun's slide to press the TALK button on the radio.

"Full sprint. They know you're there."

Dean didn't answer. I hung up the pump (two thirds would have to do) as he clipped the radio to his belt and I noticed my right hand was shaking. Hell, my whole body was shaking. The adrenaline rushing into my bloodstream was like an electric shock to my system. This was getting ridiculous. I absentmindedly pulled the right revolver from its place on my hip. Dean's eyes were wide, eyebrows raised in an expression that said, "Holy shit, whaddawedo?" An expression that I was probably mimicking perfectly.

I peeked around the pump, inhaling deeply as I moved, taking longer to exhale. The initial adrenaline shock had passed and I realized with both guns in my hands that they were no longer shaking. From beside me, a puff of air blew past my neck and I was comforted to know Dean had followed my example.

"They're gonna try and surround you," my dad informed us. He couldn't keep the panic out of his voice, although he fought it bravely. *"I see eight altogether, split into two groups of three and one group of two."*

I nodded in the direction of the pump standing adjacent to the one we both crouched behind. Dean took my meaning and darted across the open space to his new cover. I made the decision to use the pumps to our advantage, rationalizing that it would be better to take the chance of a bullet igniting the gas than fighting out in the open. *Just keep telling us where they are, pops.*

From here, there was no plan to speak of. The walkie-talkie told us they had reached the pumps and the two groups of three were stalking around either side of us. The two in the middle were sidling between the pumps closest to the road. *Three each on the sides, one each in the center.*

"Guard my heart in truth, that my aim may follow," I breathed, the words of the child from my vision coming from me without thinking.

I caught Dean's attention and mouthed the numbers 3-2-1.

11

I tasted warm metal, smelled the swirl of sweat and gasoline. I heard the *clomp* of their footfalls, boots on cement, before they appeared around the pumps. Blurry and outlined in dark red, they skidded to a halt, three in a row, their surprised expressions concealed behind bright colored masks. My hand set a bead on the far left figure and my other locked onto the one beside, their obscured faces streaking between the revolvers' sights…and I squeezed the triggers.

My ears rang and I fired twice before the shotgun roared to life, distant but so very near. Crouched low, my feet crossed one another in smooth steps the way my brother had shown me years ago; my fingers squeezed and released, squeezed and released, alternating left and right. The initial shot hit the figure on the left in the throat and he tumbled like a felled tree, blood spraying into the overcast sky like crimson branches. The second and third found their marks as well. The man in the center staggered backward with a fist-sized hole through his chest, while the third was whipped clockwise from the slug in his shoulder.

The shotgun exploded again and again, and I continued pulling the triggers. A bullet went wide of the man I had winged, but the next ripped through the head of his partner to his left, sending blood, brain and bone onto the pavement several feet behind. The one I missed teetered on his heels, clutching his shoulder, and collapsed. I dove left, firing in the direction of a fourth figure near the pumps. The bullet lodged into the side of the pump, but it bought me some time.

So far I hadn't heard the sound of any guns but our own, though the men on my side of the station had all been armed.

With the left flank incapacitated, I dashed for safety behind the closest pump. Without thinking, I opened the rear passenger door and let loose the hounds. Bowie and Jax bounded out, sprinting around the van and between the pumps as I ran around the front of the vehicle to cover Dean.

Dean's first shot had disintegrated the man in the middle's upper torso and had winged both assailants to either side of him. The other two blasts I heard had removed the face of the guy on the right and sent the man on the left six feet backward to join the first with a chest full of lead. None were moving. Dean was about to break cover to advance on his fourth man when I reached his side.

The dogs barked wildly. I slumped against the pump, straining to hear anything over the clamor. And then it stopped. For a fraction of a second I heard absolutely nothing. I closed my eyes, waiting for the sound of gunfire that would mean the end of my dog.

Instead came two desperate, agonized screams. My eyes popped open as relief swept in.

"Let's go while they have'em occupied," I said. Dean's face was a bit pale, but he nodded and moved away along the van to the right.

He went around the pumps, I went through them, and actually laughed when we converged on the spot the dogs had found their victims. Bowie had clamped down on one of *luchadores'* arms, causing him to drop his gun, and was now attempting to rip it off completely. I had never been more proud of him.

But Jax is what had spurred my laughter. The enormous Labrador straddled the other man, his jaws engulfing the terrified man's neck just below his mask.

Dean and I trained our guns on the two highwaymen and I called the dogs off (I wasn't positive Jax would back off, and if he didn't, I wasn't coming between him and his prey). To my relief, both dogs heeled to my side.

"Take the masks off and lay where you are," I said as threateningly as possible, my snarl sending waves of pain through my nose and into my forehead. They listened well; perhaps because the two of us had just blown away six of their friends. Both were middle-aged, white, except the one Bowie had taken down sported a tear drop tattoo under his right eye. Both were terrified. Obviously, they hadn't expected resistance.

"I'll ask you this once, and if I don't get an answer I like or if I feel it's a little far from the truth, I'm going to shoot one of you." My voice sounded strange to my own ears, like someone else was speaking for me. But the words were coming from my own mouth, and I realized with an internal shudder that I meant every word. I also realized I meant to kill them both, whether they gave me answers I liked or not. "Are there more of you down the road?" I waited. They exchanged glances, but said nothing. I shot Tear Drop in the leg. "Last chance," I said calmly through his screams.

"No. No. It's just us. It's just us!" The one with Jax's teeth marks indenting his throat cried hoarsely. He had a thin beard that could have been decent if it hadn't been matted with blood from his neck.

I leveled my gun over him.

"What's going on, Shane," my dad's voice burst from the walkie talkie. We were on the road side of the pumps and in clear view of our family that waited less than a mile up the hill to the south. Neither of our eyes left our captives.

Dean took the initiative and answered, "We're getting answers. Keep the kids away from the windows."

There was a long pause before my dad spoke again, saying the one thing I hadn't expected. *"Do what you have to do, son."* Then the radio was silent.

I shuddered again, visibly this time. Dean saw it and asked, "What're you gonna do?"

I had known the answer to that question before my dad had come on the radio. To the man who answered my last question, I said, "How did you know we were here if you were watching the main road?"

I expected a lie, but instead got much more. "W-we had a roadblock on the main road, but set a spotter in th-the trees bet-tween the highway and this road." He paused to take a breath (Jax had done a number on his throat, but I suspect he had gotten off easy). "H-he was the spotter," the man continued, pointing to the guy I'd shot in the leg. "You were seen coming down the road. We all w-would have gotten to you by the time you turned the pump on if his cell had a signal, b-but he had to run back to tell us you were here."

Made sense. They were the other roadblock.

"Why'd you come after us?" I said, but I thought I knew the answer to that as well. *They wanted revenge for the guy we hit at the first roadblock.*

"You killed one of ours," the highwayman confirmed. That was all, but his eyes betrayed his thoughts. They wanted blood. Now more than ever. And those eyes sealed their fates.

Dean's face was grim, no longer pallid as it had been after the shooting had ended; the heat of anger lit up his features, and when he pulled the Glock from his waistband, it told me everything I needed to know.

"We killed more than one," I said, thumbing back the hammer of my revolver. I always wondered why people did that, thumbing the hammer of a double-action pistol seemed pointless when simply pulling the trigger would suffice, but now I knew. It was to see the flash of understanding in the eyes, the mouth, the *face* of the one whose life is about to end. And I did see that flash when I pulled the trigger, as the light from the man's eyes snapped out of existence. I wondered if Dean had seen the same as he executed his man, and I swallowed hard. For that was what this was, wasn't it? An execution.

12

We walked around the south pumps on our way back to the van. The ground surrounding the final two highwaymen was a gory mess, although we had thrown the masks back over their decimated faces. The decision to walk around the south pumps, dogs following obediently, to avoid having to skirt over those dead bodies was subconscious, the kind of thing that was so logical one didn't actually remember thinking about it; a decision that haunts me still.

Dean had called the other vehicle over the walkie-talkie, giving my dad the okay to join us, warning him to idle on the road and not to bring the Pilot too close to the pumps. They were about halfway down the hill and we were nearly halfway to the van, when I stopped abruptly.

"What is it?" Dean asked. His head shifted in either direction, searching for a threat I may have seen that he hadn't.

I said nothing. In fact, I *couldn't* say anything. I could only stare in astonishment, in shock at the blood and brain spatter scattered on the pavement to my right. The *luchador* associated with said gore laid in a lump a body's length away.

It wasn't the combination of blood, skull fragments, and grey matter that had shocked me, however. It was the image that I perceived in it. I never professed to be a prophet, but what I saw (or was made to see) etched itself in my mind's eye as a portent of things to come: a foreboding omen, looming on the horizon and terrifying in what it promised.

Dean, having seen my alarm, shook my shoulder with his free hand— he'd returned the Glock to his waistband, but still held the shotgun ready. "Shane," he said in a hushed, insistent tone. "What do you see?"

The shake brought me back to the present. I wagged my head to clear it and repeated the question Dean had asked, directing it to him, aiming his attention at the mass of mess beside us. "What do *you* see?" He shook his head and shrugged his shoulders slowly. "I see what was inside that guy's head. What'd you mean?"

"Look *into* it, Dean. What do you see *inside*?"

His brows lowered as he considered the mess a second time. "Huh."

"Huh, what?"

"It looks like," a short pause, "it looks like a tree made of bone or brain surrounded in red leaves," another pause, "a starburst of blood." He had seen the same picture in the crude Rorschach display, but had obviously not seen what was behind it. The promise of more blood on the horizon…and something deeper I could not interpret

The rest of our party had arrived in front of the gas station by that time. I nodded to Dean and said, "We should get out of here."

He agreed—although reluctantly; I could see his curiosity had been sparked—and told my dad we were pulling out, to follow us, and we would reassign seats down the road. All good ideas considering in order for people to switch vehicles they would have to view the newly decorated parking lot, and the more time they kept idle, the more time they had to take in the scenery.

Dean got in the driver's seat and started the engine as I fumbled to get the dogs back in the van. I noticed movement in my periphery and twirled, gun in hand, to see the guy I had winged attempting to get up. Dean had thought to gather up all the guns he saw lying around, but my heart leapt into my throat nonetheless. It had been a mistake to assume the man was dead without checking; a mistake that could have cost one of us our lives if he had another weapon.

The man made it into a sitting position by the time I climbed though the passenger door, and I gestured for Dean to check his mirrors.

"That won't do." He shifted into reverse and spun the tires. *Thump.* Dean shifted into drive and spun the tires the other way.

"Ew," I said through closed teeth. Behind us the man lay face down in the dirt, this time in a not-so-comfortable position. I took a final peek at the convenience store as it dwindled into the past and put a hand to my head.

"Crap," I said, "I forgot the Gatorade."

13

"This far enough?" Dean said. They were the first words either of us had spoken since leaving the gas station.

I nodded as row after row of peach trees floated by. A mild shudder came over me and I crossed my arms over my chest, clenching my sides as if to keep my ribs from seeping through the skin. *When did it get so cold?*

The SUV rumbled onto the shoulder and stopped with a jerk. Dean unhooked his safety belt, climbed over the center console, and collapsed into the back seat. I let him alone and tumbled out the door, adjusting the guns that hung from my hips like ten pound kettle bells. The afternoon sun had warmed the air considerably, but as I shuffled to the van, passing Haley, the twins, my mother and father without raising my head, I still felt cold. Bowie stayed by my side until we reached the van and then jumped through the open passenger door. I leaned in to see the dog's rear as he made his way to the back and then the faces of my children were all I could see. If Zoe and Faris comprehended what had transpired, they showed no sign. Faris flashed a crooked grin and waved; Zoe said, "Hi, Daddy," and went back to playing her Nintendo DS.

I would do anything for you.

I faked a smile and climbed into the seat as a new chill enveloped me like a wet blanket.

Sydney squeezed my knee, but said nothing as she followed the SUV back onto the highway. I tried to come up with responses to the questions she might ask, but failed. Other than cold, I felt very little. I wondered what Dean was thinking in the backseat of the vehicle in front of us, crunched beside his wife while my mother badgered him for information.

We were probably six or seven hours from our destination. My body shivered uncontrollably now, and again I wrapped my arms around my chest as tightly as I could. *Maybe if I squeeze hard enough I could disappear inside myself for a while.*

I closed my eyes.

When I woke we were pulling up the long tree-lined drive of the Argo compound. I had slept for nearly seven hours.

I had dreamt as well. I couldn't remember the substance, but I knew it wasn't the usual nightmare of drowning children because when I opened my eyes to the entrance of what was to become our new home, the crimson silhouette of a sprawling tree obstructed my vision. Then it faded and what I saw made me doubt whether or not I was still sleeping.

The Argo

1

The sign spanned the width of the road above the compound's front entrance. In my vision it had stood beside the drive, but this banner—the same light wood with the same word painted across its face in bold red capitals—was no less daunting as we passed beneath it at a slow crawl. The sky loomed dark, the stars faint and distant, casting little light through the canopy of trees lining the drive. The night seemed to seep between the gnarled branches and black leaves that reached for our vehicles as we passed.

We drove nearly a mile before the forest finally ended and we emerged from the gloomy path onto the main lot. My fear, along with the brooding dark, vanished as I beheld for the first time the place we would dwell for the next few years. The stone house stood two stories high. The roof, a burnt orange mountain range of shingled slopes and valleys, added a castlesque ambience appropriate to the house's grey walls and foundation. Crowned molding framed the massive windows that looked out over a landscape of maples, and oaks. But perhaps the most striking feature of this amazing house was the sense of humility that surrounded it. It spoke of wealth, but not arrogance. It whispered security and family rather than screaming decadence and snobbery.
Set farther back and to the left sat an old chapel with a high bell tower; it's similarity to the one in my dream stood the hair on the nape of my neck on end. Run-down to say the least, the church mirrored those seen sporadically along southern country roads: peeling whitewashed wood slatted horizontally with a steeple that protruded from atop the bell tower. Two arched casements of immaculate stained glass flanked the immense front doors. A ship sailed over an ocean of vitreous

serpents and mermaids on one side, while a tree grew in an open field under a spanning night sky on the other. Brilliant and stunning against the drab backdrop of the chapel, the colorful mosaic of glass stood out like a lighthouse in a foggy harbor, brightening the church along with the spirits of anyone fortunate enough to take in its magnificence.

We parked beneath the overhang extending from the garage on the house's eastern end and were met promptly by the twin's mother and stepfather.

"You made it," Mrs. Argo said in a low pitched, pleasant voice; a voice quite the opposite of my mother's, which could attain a high, scratchy tone at times. Mrs. Argo and my mom were of equal height and of comparable size; that being short and neither thin nor fat. Her hair resembled her daughters', dark, thick, and curly and reached her shoulder blades, unlike my mother's whose thin, light brown waves ended just above her shoulders. Altogether, Mrs. Argo was an attractive woman in her late forties, a promising peek into the future for Judah and Johnny if the twins followed in their mother's footsteps. I waited patiently as the Argos doted on Devon and Jordan, inquired into the whereabouts of their husbands. When it became my turn to shake with the house patron, he greeted me with a cheerful smirk, his eyes straying to my crooked and bruised nose more than once.

"The honeymoon's over, huh?" he said in such a matter-of-fact manner that it caught me a little off guard considering I had never met the man. His smile seemed authentic, however, and I couldn't contain a reserved laugh that reintroduced pain to my entire face. I suspected that was his intention since he cracked up when I raised my hand to my nose and gritted my teeth at the fire that ignited there. "Let me know when you're ready to set that. It'll hurt like a bitch, but it's better to do it sooner than later."

"Thanks a lot, Mr. Argo. I'll keep it in mind."

"It's Luke from here out, ya hear?" he said, flashing his teeth as he stepped off to give his step-daughters another embrace.

When we had been greeted, Mr. Argo—or Luke—took my father ahead of us while Mrs. Argo—Anna, please—lead us to the house to show us around.

The house's entryway flaunted a polished cherry stairwell that led to the eight bedrooms above. An open expanse reached the ceiling of the second story and the sparkling chandelier that hung there reflected sparkles of multicolored light throughout the room. The walls were painted a pleasant grey-blue complete with white molding along the tops and bottoms with chair-rails lining the centers. To the right and left, archways led to the living, family, dining, recreation, and sitting rooms that made up the ground floor. Beside the staircase ahead, stood the door to what I later found to be the kitchen, which connected to the dining room on the other side of the wall.

After we'd taken in the decor, Anna led us upstairs to our bedrooms. The twins took the rooms they stayed in when they came to visit, and they quickly went in to call their husbands. They still hadn't been able to get a hold of them since before noon and were worried. I didn't blame them; I was beginning to get worried myself. Syd and I were given two adjacent rooms at the end of the east hall, one for us and one for the kids. Zoe and Faris were dead to the world so we laid them in the matching beds the Argos were so kind to supply and left them to sleep. Then we checked out our new digs, which were more than adequate.

Our room had a king-sized bed centered on the far wall. Two dressers, matching vanity, bed-side tables, walk-in closet, what else could we possibly have asked for? How about a 40" plasma TV? Nope, we had that too. But when I turned it on to check the news, all that came out was static. From every station.

"That's not a good sign," Sydney said.

I clicked the TV off. "Maybe they just don't have cable."

She scanned the room. "Maybe, but not likely."

It was late and Syd had driven a long way without a break. The exhaustion showed plain on her face as she unpacked a change of clothes and crawled under the covers. She was always pale, her Irish blood gave her little choice in that, but tonight she appeared a ghost in the dimness of the bedroom. Her vibrant red hair seemed to have lost its luster and swirled in limp twists against the pillow. I considered the anxiety I had put her through on the journey here and decided she was as beautiful as I had ever seen her. Perhaps more.

"You coming to bed?" she asked, her long lashes already fluttering closed.

"I just took a seven hour nap." I also realized I hadn't had a cigarette in over eight hours.

She yawned and shrugged. I knew the urge to talk about all that happened was eating her up inside, but sleep had taken over. I kissed her forehead, and trekked down the hall to find my father. I knocked softly, but didn't receive an answer. *Probably sleeping.* I walked down a few doors to find Dean, but didn't hear any voices or movement inside so I decided he must have been sleeping as well. That left Jordan and Devon, but I didn't particularly feel like talking about their husbands at the moment so I bypassed their doors and made my way back downstairs to have a smoke with the dogs.

Then I'd have to find Luke. I touched my nose with the tip of my finger and the pain spread. This was not going to be fun.

2

It was 2:00 a.m., and I wandered outside once again, cigarette in hand. The Argo boasted a staggering 500 acres, consisting of cattle, swine, horses, crops (mostly corn, soy, and tobacco, but could easily accommodate a number of vegetables), a large natural lake and uncountable hills and wooded areas. It wasn't a large farm, but it would support the property's residents if worse came to worst.

A chicken-wire fence ran the perimeter of what the Argos called their back yard (I called it the back ten because it spread at least that many acres wide and half as many deep). The dogs, having been around one another enough to avoid most fights associated with dominance, currently lay together along the garage side of the house. They had enjoyed their initial frolic about the farm and had finally worn themselves out.

As I entered through the gate on the far side of the garage, Bowie mustered the energy to mosey over for some attention. I hunkered to scratch his head, but I think he could tell my heart wasn't in it because after a couple short strokes he huffed like a teenage girl whose daddy wouldn't let her leave the house until she changed into something less revealing and returned to his buddies by the garage's stone wall. My stomach was a constricted ball of ice; my face a persistent throb of agony that drummed from my bandaged nose after Luke's confident fingers had performed the excruciating task of straightening it out. At least it took my mind off the soreness in my forearm.

"You got one for me, number one?" I didn't have to turn to know it was my dad; he had two sons, and I was…well, number one.

It wasn't favoritism, though. He favored whichever one of us was around at the time or did something he liked.

I rose, and noticed that not only had he snuck up on me, he had also succeeded in opening and closing the fence gate without me hearing. I must have really been distracted because my dad was not that smooth. Actually, he was downright clumsy. I produced a pack of Marlboro Lights, and held it out to him.

My dad's face contorted as he took one.

"If you wanted Benson & Hedges," I said, "you should've brought some, you freaking snob."

"My children show me such respect," he said, taking a puff.

"Whiner." My pulse quickened. He wasn't here to make small talk or because he needed a cigarette.

"You've been spending a lot of time awake and alone tonight, boy," he said after taking a few drags. "Wanna tell me what's on your mind? Lord knows you've been through it today."

And there it was. I breathed in, and let it out in a long audible gust.

"Getting you to talk about your feelings," he said, "is like getting kids these days to actually talk to someone in person instead of texting or Facebooking."

"I have a feeling not too many people are on Facebook right now, pops."

He held his cell phone at arm's length, then raised it above his head. "Probably right, I still got zero bars." He returned the phone to his pocket and said, "Before you were born I used to shut down when I got stressed. Your mother would try to get me to talk about things, but it usually led to an argument and a night out at the bar. After we had you and your brother, I would go into your rooms after you'd fallen asleep and I'd spill my guts. It was easy talking to babies that couldn't talk back yet or judge me."

My dad flicked his cigarette butt onto the driveway. I tried not to see his face, but it was impossible. His brows curved in a kind arc over his honest blue eyes, his mouth arched upward in an endearing slant that mine could never achieve. His sincerity took over my inhibitions and I clung to his every word.

"You woke up one night when you were older," he said. "Right in the middle of me explaining why I lost my job at the church. You remember that?"

I did remember, but I was unable to speak. In the darkness I stood there, enthralled by my father, just wanting to hear his voice.

"I stopped mid-sentence, and you said, 'What's up, pops?', and then I just told you everything. When I was done, I remember thinking, 'my son's gonna think I'm a loser.' Remember what you did?"

"I…" But I couldn't finish. I remembered like it was yesterday, but the words wouldn't come.

My dad took a step closer and bent his head. "You said I was your dad no matter where I worked, no matter whose scapegoat I was. You said you were proud of me for taking a stand and that you loved me."

Tears threatened and I tried to turn away, but he pulled me back, both his hands gripping my shoulders.

"I wasn't scared to talk to you about things from that point on," he said.

"But I'm not like you, dad. I get stressed, I smoke cigarettes. That's about the extent of my emotional management."

"You're more like me than you know, Shane. Judah's got the scatterbrain, but you have the responsibility. For your family and those around you. That's not to say Judah's not strong, but *you're* the leader. You always have been, whether you like it or not. And I know it isn't easy. Responsibility, *leadership*, is about as hard as it comes."

My father released his grip and stepped back. My cigarette, forgotten, was a cylinder of ash hanging flaccid between my fingers.

"I feel angry, dad." I hadn't even realized I was speaking until the words were said. "I mean, I killed five men today, one unarmed and under my control. But I feel no regret…they *made* me kill them…"

I didn't know how to continue. So many images clogged my mind—red trees, orange eyes, dead men, that ever persistent drowning boy—I couldn't put a comprehensive thought together.

"You and Dean did what you had to in order to protect this family. You were brave, and you made decisions in the heat of the moment that I don't think I could have made myself." He reached for me again, but let his hand drop to his side instead. "I envy your steel sometimes, son. In many ways, you're more a man than I am."

I reflected on the people I had killed. The fake cop, the mask-wearing highwaymen. Was this the world in which we lived? That people could do that to one another?

"Do you think people are naturally evil, dad?"

He put his hands on his hips, pondering the question like a battered, overweight Peter Pan. "I think there is darkness in the hearts of every man," he said. "Selfishness, greed, lust...all these things feed the darkness, and we're all guilty of them at one time or another. But there is also goodness lurking beneath. I don't believe that people are naturally good or evil. We make choices that influence the lives we lead and the lives of those around us. And those choices are what determine which side of the fence we stand on." He paused, shifting his weight to the other foot. "It's our decisions that define us, Shane."

Decisions. Again the images flooded in. Older, familiar pictures. Childhood memories of a day at the beach with my best friend's family and my brother. Three boys playing together, splashing in the ocean, and the wave that came out of nowhere. I had made a decision that day, and it had played a significant role in the man I had become. "What if you make the wrong decision?" I said. "And the cost is...too much?"

"I think your brother would say you made the right choice," my father said. It was scary how well he knew me, knew what I was thinking without ever saying it.

I fumbled for another smoke. "His life meant another's death," I said. A lump was forming in my throat. I tried to swallow it down. "And now everyone's looking to me for direction. How do I make decisions that affect other people's lives after that?"

My dad shrugged. "I don't know, son. But you're not alone."

"What are you doing out here at two in the morning, anyway?"

He stared out into the rural darkness that was both terrifying in its absolute nothingness and satisfying in its lack of human alteration. There were no city lights here to hide the stars, no traffic to drown out the crickets, and for the first time I allowed myself to be somewhat content. *This too shall pass,* my dad prophesied in my head from his repertoire of sayings, though this one was frequently said in association with gas build up.

"You just bored me to tears telling me why I needed to talk about things," I said, "and you're gonna try and get away with not answering me?"

"I kinda had a dream tonight that freaked the hell out of me." My father's tone of voice broke my body out in gooseflesh. I didn't consider myself superstitious, but I *obviously* believed that some dreams held meaning, that some dreams were significant.

"A lot of that going around," I said, trying to put him a little more at ease.

"Yeah," he sighed, "and this one's a doozy."

3

"So this man is kneeling before two teenage boys," my father began in his new eerie voice, "twins I think. Dressed in cloaks of green and purple, these boys…these kings…grasp the shoulders and head of the kneeling man, one hand of each twin atop one shoulder, the other placed upon the back of the head. The kneeling man isn't dressed for royalty, but appears to be dressed in attire worn by a people of another world." He shook his finger. "Or maybe it's the other way around, it's the boys that are dressed weird—in the dream their clothes feel right, though. Anyway, this man wears ragged blue jeans. A long brown leather coat drapes around his feet, concealing a faded black cotton shirt. It also hides the pair of revolvers hanging on his hips from worn leather cartridge belts."

He glanced at my hips, but my guns were upstairs in my room. "A lot like yours, actually. The guns aren't visible to the boys, but they know they're there. The man's hair is a long, wavy auburn, like the color of tea, which falls about his lowered face, pretty much hiding it from view. Words are spoken by the twin kings, but I can't make out what they're saying. The kneeling man bends lower, touching his forehead to the ground, and then rises as the lips of the twins move once more. He is taller than the kings, but not by much; older, but not by many years. His back is to me, but I know the man remains silent. The kings' hands touch the man's shoulders once more and this time the twins are the ones who kneel. They don't touch their faces to the ground, this is out of respect rather than duty. Then they rise again and say a final lost word. The man nods and turns—"

He broke off suddenly, like he had just pieced something together. "What is it?" I said.

I didn't like the hardness I saw in my father's eyes when he turned them on me. "He looked like you, Shane."

He faced the night again, leaving me to ponder the things he'd said. So unlike anything I had expected, the telling of his dream left me speechless. I lit a cigarette for us both and we stood in silence, staring off into space.

Finally, after untold minutes had passed, I said, "So you dreamed of me. But what does it mean I should do?"

"I thought that at first, too, but now I'm not so sure."

"Not so sure of what?" I asked, incensed. "You said the man was me."

"No, I said the man *looked* like you, not that it *was* you." He took a sharp breath and let it out quickly. "I think the man with the guns was Faris."

"Faris?" My son was no more than three years old.

My father put his hand on my arm and peered down at me. "When you scrunch your eyebrows like that it's a tell-tale sign that you're either scared or angry," he said with a smile. "Maybe it's a glimpse of what's to come like you think your vision was. Or maybe not. But if we're taking these things seriously now, and since we just packed up and drove 500 miles cross country in the middle of the night I'm guessing we are, I think what it means is pretty obvious. We have to keep Faris alive."

"Well I don't intend on letting him die," I said.

"Yeah, you're a regular gunslinger now. I think I let you watch too many Westerns as a child."

I rolled my eyes. "I honestly have no idea how Dean and I are still ali—"

The words caught in my throat along with the smoke I was exhaling, making me retch wildly. Something had caught my eye, and I attempted to point it out while frantically trying to catch my breath. "*What the hell is that?*" I finally got out once the coughing fit had passed.

My dad followed the finger I had aimed to the sky, but after a few seconds he wrinkled his nose and shrugged. "I don't see anything."

"There. It's dark like the sky, but you can definitely make out a shape and its moving fast."

He squinted and stepped forward. For several more seconds he stood there like a doofus, but then a sudden gasp told me he had seen the object. "What the hell *is* that?"

That cold ball of ice was back, tightening my stomach like a vice. Whatever it was, it wasn't good. And it just happened to show up on the night we arrived at the Argo? Not a likely coincidence. "Maybe we should wake everyone up."

4

"Where did it come from?" Haley said. It was cool and breezy on the lawn behind the house, and it hadn't been easy dragging everyone out of bed to stare at the sky. Haley stood beside Sydney, her dark brown hair a tangled, slept-on mess that didn't quite reach her shoulders. She stood a head shorter than my wife, who ranged between 5'4" to 5'6" depending on the shoes she wore. Haley's eyes, sitting large above her small, slightly pushed up nose and pouty lips, matched her hair: confused and annoyed.

"I don't know, Hales," Dean said. "Let's wait and find out." He gave me a tight-lipped sneer, and twirled his finger around his ear.

"I saw that, dick," Haley half-yelled.

"I saw dat, dick," Zoe sang.

"Oh, great," Sydney said, throwing an irritated glare at Haley. "Don't say that word, Zoe."

Normally, Zoe would've had something to say back, but being awakened in the middle of the night and clearly still groggy, my daughter did not respond. Of course Faris woke when we were retrieving Zoe, and so he joined us as well (not that I would have left him alone in the house anyway, my father's dream still being fresh in my mind).

Dressed in her *Little Mermaid* pajamas, my girl reached up, signaling for me to lift her, and laid her head on my shoulder. Syd held Faris, who was now very alert in his matching *Lightning McQueen* jammies. "Can you see it, princess?" I whispered into her ear. Her little head shook in the negative against my neck, utterly disinterested.

The half-moon was north-west of us and clearly visible despite the nearly indistinguishable clouds hanging motionless above us. They were of the sort you didn't notice at night unless you tried to see the stars or it began raining. I glanced at my cell phone, but it told me nothing. The time wasn't even right.

"Any word from your husbands?" I asked the twins, who huddled together in the rear of the group against the increasing cold. The wind blew from the west; not enough to chill our bones, but cool enough to need something more than the light jackets we brought from Florida. At least Zoe and Farris looked warm enough in their fleece pajamas and slippers.

Devon, always the quieter one, didn't even acknowledge that I'd spoken.

"My phone doesn't even have any bars," Jordan barked, like it was my fault. *How many times has she been asked that question?* My mother alone had probably asked a dozen times.

"I still don't see it," my mom said, frustration clear in her voice.

"Try crossing your eyes," my dad said, visibly content that he could see it and she couldn't.

My mom slapped his shoulder. "This isn't one of those 3D art things, stupid man."

"Well, I can't see those frigging things, and you can't see this. Sorry if I'm glad we're even for once."

She continued squinting and finally stomped her foot into the ground in a mild tantrum. Not used to failure, my mom crossed her arms in an audible huff, producing more than a few chuckles from those around her.

"It's like trying to find Bowie in the dark, Audrey," said Syd, sidling up to my mother. "You can't really see him if you look straight at him." Lifting the arm not holding our son, she pointed to the moon. "Look into the space just to the left of the moon. If you look long enough, you should be able to see movement to the left. Keep it in your periphery, though. If you try to stare directly at it, it'll disappear."

Several minutes went by, and I could see my mother's growing aggravation in the form of a red dot on her forehead, right between the eyes. This spot showed up only when she was angry, a clear signal to either shut up or get the hell away from her. But finally her brow relaxed and she smiled wide.

"I see it. Wow, how did you see that thing, Shane? It's nearly invisible."

I shrugged. "Just caught my eye." I shivered. The statement was true enough, but somehow it felt very wrong.

5

We observed the object move steadily across the sky. Soon its course would take it in front of the moon, hopefully giving us a chance to see it more clearly.

"It's like a moving black hole," my mom said.

My dad gave a reserved chuckle.

I raised my eyebrows, anticipating one of my favorite arguments.

My mother didn't disappoint me. "You always make some stupid comment or make some stupid noise when the topic of black holes comes up," she spat.

"That's because there's no such thing." The usual quick and certain answer.

"You're a stupid man," my mom said. "You have no problem believing in God, angels, Satan, and demons, but *black holes* you have a problem with?"

"I think when our technology reaches the point where we can see that far out into space, they're gonna see something in the distance that they'll call a *black hole* because they don't have a freaking clue what else to call it. They'll see farther and farther over the years, while the image gets clearer and clearer until one day they'll have a perfectly lucid visual on what's out there. And you know what they'll see?"

He waited for a few seconds. When he was satisfied with the number of heads shaking (my mom and I were not amongst them) he continued. "They'll see God smiling and waving into the camera. Then the world will end."

My mom huffed. "Like I said…stupid man."

I laughed with everyone else. It was amusing if nothing else.

But as the seconds passed, the laughter dwindled and our eyes returned to the sky. While we listened to my parent's banter, the object had moved to the edge of the moon, and the night seemed to have grown darker.

I lifted my hand to point Zoe in the right direction, but my arm went limp and fell back to my side. My daughter inhaled a long cache of air and held it. The Argo had gone still, and I realized I wasn't breathing either. The dogs had ceased to chase and wrestle one another, not a single pant escaping their jowls, their heads bent raptly to the heavens. I felt around for Sydney's hand, not taking my attention from above, and when I found it, I grasped it tightly. Something wasn't right. We all felt it.

I expected the light from the moon to provide enough contrast to be able to view the object as it passed. Instead, a swirl of darkness preceded the thing, like the ink of a squid in the depths of the sea. It blotted out first a small sliver of the moon, then a quarter, and then, as fear gripped me, the sky went black. The spotlights from the house had been turned off in order to view the thing more clearly, and we now stood in absolute darkness.

A low growl issued from behind us, and I turned to see Bowie, body low and snarling, his hair standing straight along his spine. The other dogs bared their teeth and growled in the direction of the forest to our right. Northwest. The direction the thing in the sky was headed.

"Jax?" Devon whispered, taking a step toward her dog. She halted as the intensity of his snarling increased. "What is it?"

A faint sound rose in the distance, a high pitched wail...

Another erupted from the woods to the west, this one much closer. The dogs burst into a harmony of yelps and barks, moving between us and the forest from which the cries came. Several more joined the first, until my ears vibrated from the din.

My ears... I spun to my son. He had his face buried in his mother's hair, hands white against his ears, the tendons clenched high and tight on the back of his neck. I saw no blood seeping through his fingers, though, and felt a small amount of relief.

"It's like the screaming back home," Haley said. Her hands held her ears as well, and I saw most of the others doing the same. "We left our homes because of this, and now we're right in the middle of it again?"

I stepped closer to Haley and she backed away. I tried to think of something to say...some explanation, but there wasn't one.

Devon and Jordan wrapped their arms around their mother and stepfather. My mom and dad stared into the forest, holding hands, faces like stone. Haley's shoulders slumped, scared and defeated, as Dean stood beside her with his hands in his pockets. More shrieks echoed through us, their points of origin impossible to distinguish. The dogs had stopped barking, content to growl and stand sentry before us.

This was my fault. I led and they followed. Jordan nearly raped by thieves, my family nearly killed by road bandits...all to get to this place.

I looked to Sydney for help, but she crossed her arms over Faris, as scared as the rest of them. I turned to my dad, but he gazed into the woods. "I'm sorry," I said, the words tasting stale in my mouth. "I thought we were escaping this...not running toward it."

6

The dark, slithering orb completed its pass across the face of the moon, and it was suddenly light again. The shrieking in the distance ceased as abruptly as it started, and the canines relaxed somewhat.

My gut wrenched suddenly. I set Zoe down and hurried to get as far away from the group as possible before I threw up. I made it about ten feet. Doubled over, I heaved for several minutes until it hurt, and then plopped onto the damp ground far enough away from the mess that I didn't have to smell it. My realigned nose ached.

An arm hugged my shoulder and Sydney hunkered beside me, tears streaming down her face. And a smile. "I love you, Shane," she said. It was all she needed to say. I put an arm around her waist, drawing on her strength, and was then whacked in the eye by my son's little hand. I felt the corner of my mouth twitch upward and I kissed his forehead.

Faris giggled soundlessly, though the lines on his brow showed he was still in pain. *What have I done?* My gut turned again as I staggered to my feet, but I thought the urge to vomit had passed.

Jordan's phone rang. She answered quickly, fresh tears pouring from her eyes. It could only be Johnny.

After several minutes, she turned to me, and with trembling hands passed me the phone. "Your brother wants to talk to you. Be quick, the reception's bad."

I took the phone, aware I was taking up time she could be having with her husband. "Judah?"

"-ey, br-" was what came back. Poor reception indeed. "Did - ou see -at shit?"

"Yeah, I saw it. Where are you?"

A pause. "-ust got off 75, heading -orth on 129," his broken voice finally answered. I'm sure more got lost in static.

"You'll be here soon. Right?"

"Should be. Johnny's going -ike 100. -o one's on...road."

No, there wouldn't be, would there.

"That's a lie. Johnny can't physically go faster than 70."

"-ah, that -as ... lie." I heard a broken laugh. I couldn't understand anything he was saying.

"Judah. Look out for roadblocks and guys in *lucha libre* masks."

"-ook out -or what?"

"R-o-a-d-b-l-o-c-k-s," I said clearly and slowly.

"What kind of cocks?" *Oh,* that *gets through clearly.*

"Roadblocks, Judah! Roadblocks!"

"Hold on, -ane. -ere seems to be some kind of -oad…ahead."

"What do you see, Judah? Stop your car." I was getting frantic. They were driving right into those bastards.

"A …block. No, it's -ot far ahea-"

"Judah? Judah!" He was trying to say something, but I couldn't make out a single word. Then the line went dead.

"Sonuva whore!"

"What happened?" at least three people asked at once.

"The reception was bad and I couldn't warn him of the roadblocks. I'm pretty sure they're heading straight for them." I paced the yard, trying to think of something I could do.

"Try texting him," Sydney said from somewhere behind me. Of course the text queen would come up with that. And it was a good idea.

I punched in a short message: AVOID ROADBLOCKS!!!! MEN WITH GUNS!!!! SHOOT FIRST IF YOU SEE GUYS WITH MASKS!!!!

I read it over quickly. Satisfied, I hit SEND and took another deep breath. If this didn't get to them, they'd have no warning.

Even more disturbing was the thought that after half of their posse being wiped out by Dean and I, those assholes were *still* out there. The phone had no signal, but the message said it had been sent. Guess I got the word out just in time. But that didn't mean they received it before losing reception themselves.

"Signal's dead," I said as I gave the phone back to Jordan. "I don't think it's a location issue either. I think it's because of that." I pointed upward in the direction of the object creeping steadily across the sky.

"How can *that* mess with cell phone reception," Dean said, "when *that* is nowhere near us yet?" A murmur of agreement went through the group.

"I don't know, Dean," I snipped. "I don't even know what that thing is, let alone know what it can do. But I'm pretty sure those shrieks are related, too, and the ones we heard back home."

Zoe tugged on my hand and yawned. Faris nodded off in Sydney's arms. "Come on, honey, let's go to bed," I said to my daughter and started for the house without a backward glance. I couldn't care less if they followed me or not.

7

The slam of a car door startled me from my sleep and I jerked, kicking Sydney—who liked to sleep with her back to me—right in the butt. The sun gleamed brightly through the burgundy drapes hanging over the room's solitary window, casting a warm hue of light pink over the room. I felt good…until Syd's hand smacked smartly across the back of my head. I snorted and kissed her good morning despite our morning breath.

"I heard a car door," I said, jumping out of bed and going to the window.

"Me too," Syd said through a yawn as I pulled the curtains back.

"Man, I forgot this window faces the back."

"Dork. Go see if it's your brother. I'll check on the kids. I can't believe they're still asleep." I was already to the door. "Put some pants on first."

"Thank you, my love." I took a second to get dressed, kissed my wife again, and raced down the stairs.

Zoe and Faris hadn't slept in. My mother, granting us a much appreciated favor, had gotten up with them. They wrapped their bodies around both of Judah's legs, who was attempting to give his dog a hug.

"Did you kiss your dog or your wife first?" I said as I pried my kids off him.

"You know how much I love my dog," he said, then grabbed Devon around the waist and pulled her close.

When they were done hugging and kissing and kissing and hugging, I let go of the kids and they reattached themselves to his knees. "You had me worried." I hugged him. "Did you get the text?"

"We'll talk about it later, alright?"

80

I agreed and went over to talk to Johnny. "Good to see you, buddy."

"You too, man," he said, and we embraced as my brother and I had a moment earlier. His hair lay flat under the leather wide-brimmed hat he wore, and his horseshoe mustache appeared in danger of being taken over by the unkempt scruff on his cheeks and chin. Johnny was tall and fit with calluses on his hands and old scars on his knuckles. "I guess we need to exchange stories, huh?"

"You got that right." It wasn't until then that I realized a new arrival lingered in the parking lot. Someone I did not recognize. The stranger stood in the background, trying to make himself invisible and coming very close to succeeding. His left arm hung in a sling made from what I recognized as my brother's Lynard Skynard tee shirt. It had been torn at least once and tied around his right shoulder. I could imagine Judah's anguish as his favorite shirt was rendered unwearable.

"Who's he?" I asked, not bothering to lower my voice to soften the bluntness of the question.

"He's part of the story. For now I'll just say he's an extremely lucky, yet cheerfully vulgar bastard by the name of Patrick Fitzpatrick. He and Judah hit it off right away."

"Huh." I rolled the description around. "Patrick Fitzpatrick?" I said, more to say the name out loud than to make sure I'd heard him correctly. "Seriously?"

Johnny smirked. "Exactly my reaction. Nice face, by the way." With that he walked off to find his wife, leaving me alone with Mr. Patrick Fitzpatrick.

Lucha Libre (Part 2)

1

Respectfully, I gave Judah and Johnny as much time with their wives as they needed. I waited patiently outside, smoking cigarettes and allowing my heartbeat to slow down from being over anxious. Outwardly, I exuded a picture of calm; inside I raced like a junkie on PCP. But there was nothing for it. I could only stand there and wait. Unless...

True to form, neither Judah nor Johnny had introduced Patrick Fitzpatrick, so I took it upon myself to break the ice.

"I'm Shane," I said, approaching with my best welcome-smile and extending my hand for a shake. Closer up, I could see he had a nice gash along his graying hairline (which was *not* receding, by the way, lucky putz) above his right eyebrow.

"Patrick," he said quietly and took my hand in his. His grip was practiced, not too tight, not too light; the kind of shake one would associate with a public servant that greeted both men and women, young and old. He had to be at least 50, but he handled himself like a much younger man. In the few moments I stood with him, I got the strong sense he was a man with many stories of his own. His deep blue eyes portrayed a sense that they'd seen many places and things, perhaps some he wished he hadn't. But they also betrayed a healthy sense of humor.

"Patrick Fitzpatrick," I said with a grin.

"Just Patrick if it pleases ya." He had a distinct southern drawl.

"Um…if you don't mind, I kinda like the way Patrick Fitzpatrick rolls off the tongue."

He laughed easily, the kind of laugh that said he didn't take himself too seriously. That being the case, he should fit right in.

"So be it then," he said with a nod and a smile. Then motioning toward my cigarette, "Can I bum one a them fags?"

"Yep." I produced my half-full pack, from which he removed one and put it to his lips. I lit it and said, "The more the merrier."

"Actually, I'm supposed to be on the wagon," he said between a drag and an exhale, "but my nerves're strung tighter than a virgin's…" he paused and smiled, "well, they're strung pretty tight."

I guess our relationship hadn't quite reached the point of crude analogies yet. "Tell me about it, Patrick Fitzpatrick, but I believe you may have picked the wrong time to quit smoking."

"Judgin' by last night's business, I believe you may be right."

"So what's your story?" I said.

"Not much to tell, really…my step-kids called from Knoxville two nights ago sayin' their mama, my ex, was missin', so I headed up there and got caught up at that roadblock. "

"Where were you coming from?"

"Pensacola. Had a buddy was lettin' me stay with him 'til I got my feet on the ground. Since the divorce I've been broker than the Tooth Fairy on Viagra in a room fulla Meth addicted hookers givin' out $10 bangs."

"Nice," I said. "Any luck getting hold of your kids?"

He kicked a pebble off the walkway and shook his head. "Only talked to 'em the once. Don't have my phone anyhow."

"Wouldn't do you any good, anyway." I peeked at Judah, who was yakking away with Dean. "I wish my brother and Johnny would dispense with the pleasantries so we can get down to business."

"Ah, so you're Judah's brother. A strong name, that one has…Jeez."

"What?"

"I just sounded like Yoda."

"Yeah, but I've never heard him done with a southern accent." I heard the front door open and turned. "Speaking of…"

My brother slouched in the doorway and called us in. They were gathering on the back patio. He waited as we caught up and then led us through the house.

When we arrived, Sydney motioned toward the kids who sat quietly on the ground next to her feet, and asked if she should take the kids elsewhere. She was seated on one of the four concrete benches that circled the patio and I took my place beside her. "Let them stay," I said. "Faris won't understand this anyway and Zoe should hear what's going on. They're part of whatever's happening here, like it or not."

2

"I'm thankful beyond words that everyone's here," Judah began. He appeared older to me somehow, and I realized with a bit of shame that wasn't quite right. I was seeing him for the man he was, without the subjective lens through which an older brother views his younger brother; those skewed glasses that saw a kid who had needed protection since the day he was born. A kid that I had dragged from the bottom of the ocean, unconscious and not breathing.

"First," Judah said, "I need to introduce Patrick Fitzpatrick." I could see by the shake of our new acquaintance's head that Judah and Johnny had been calling him by first and last name since they picked him up. "He's trying to get to Knoxville to check on his step-kids."

"Just Patrick, please." I could tell he was only feigning annoyance, though. "I'm pleased to meet y'all. And I wanna thank ya, Luke, for lettin' me borrow one a your trucks."

"Don't mention it," said Luke. "The farm hands that should be driving it disappeared a day ago. Better you take it than lettin' it just sit and gather rust."

"You've already met Shane, too," Judah said, "who I see has been very supportive of your struggle to quit smoking. A nun's less committed to her habits than my brother is to his."

"Be that as it may," Patrick Fitzpatrick said, "the fag was much appreciated."

"The what?" Haley and Devon asked in unison.

"Cigarettes. Pardon me if I slip into the old-fashioned ever so often. It's a habit I've never been able to drop. Much like smoking..." He paused and his expression turned solemn. "But Judah's got the floor, so on with ya." He crossed his arms and leaned back, giving Judah a marginal nod.

"We exited I-75, and pulled off the side of the road. We made it a good ways from the highway, Johnny actually kept his speed above the 55 limit—but not by much.

"It got really dark all of a sudden, and we got out to see what was going on. For a minute we thought the moon had disappeared, but then we realized it was being hidden by something. We stared at the sky until whatever it was passed and the moon was showing again. I was pretty freaked out, I admit, especially when the screaming started."

"You heard them, too?" Devon said, placing a hand into her husband's.

"We got back in the truck, and I had the strong urge to get in touch with you all. We hadn't been able to get through to you since I'd talked to Devon and told her to come up here without me. What a good decision that turned out to be." I couldn't tell if he was being sarcastic.

"We were getting worried," my mom said, an understatement to be sure. She had nearly pulled her hair out from worry.

"Well, it wasn't for lack of trying," Judah continued. "We tried to call almost every fifteen minutes at first. Every fifteen minutes turned into every thirty, every thirty turned into every hour, and still no reception."

"So what happened before you left?" asked Dean.

My brother groaned and nudged Johnny. "You tell it."

"We got called downtown. It was complete chaos. People were screaming and fighting. Others were trying to escape or attempting to defend their children. It was a freaking clusterfu—" he glanced at his mother-in-law "—uh, it was…crazy. The cops were tearing through the rioters, but they wouldn't stop. It was like they weren't even feeling it when they were hit. Tasers did nothing but make'em mad. I spent the time trying to revive two little kids who'd been hit by a car. I got one of them breathing, but the other one…"

He took a deep breath. "Things got really bad after that. The cops were being overrun and there were way too many injured people for us to help. After the kid I was working on died, I went to find Judah."

"He found me underneath a pile of psychos," said Judah. "If he hadn't come looking for me, I don't think I'd be alive right now. And if I didn't have riot gear on, they would have chewed my arms off."

"They were biting you?" my dad said.

"They were all like the guy from your yard, Shane. Nothing stopped them. We put them down and they kept getting back up. I can't even remember how Johnny got me out of there, but next thing

I know we were running for our lives."

"We got to my truck and just drove," said Johnny. "I didn't want to but…we had no choice." He put his palms to his eyes and let his hands slide down his face.

"No one blames you for leaving," my dad said.

"Maybe no one here, but I took an oath and so did Judah. And then we abandoned everyone."

I shifted in my seat. I hadn't even thought about the people they were sworn to protect. I just wanted them with me. Was that so selfish? To want my brothers alive where I could see them?

After a minute, Johnny finally composed himself. "We stopped at Judah's to get his stuff and then at my house. The front door had been wrenched off the hinges, though, so we just kept driving."

Jordan caught my attention and shook her head slowly. As far as anyone else knew, we'd been attacked and I'd killed a man to get away. That was all. We'd omitted the near rape, and it seemed that was the story we were sticking with.

"So anyway," Judah continued, "we tried calling all day, but couldn't get through. And now my phone was dead and Johnny's was getting close. Like I said, the urge to call got really strong so I asked Johnny for his phone. I remember him saying it was a new phone so he didn't have anyone's number saved but Jordan's.

"I looked at the phone not expecting to see any reception bars, but there they were. I dialed Jordan and you actually answered, so I gave the phone to Johnny. They talked while I sat in the passenger seat, staring out the windshield as the car swerved between lanes, thinking Johnny couldn't talk and drive at the same time.

"I told Johnny I needed to talk to you, Shane. The same feeling that had made me try the phone in the first place was bugging me again. I was starting to fear we'd lose reception before I could talk to you. He finally told Jordan to give you the phone and handed it over.

"I thought you said something about cocks, but I'm pretty sure you were talking about roadblocks."

"Uh, *yeah*," I said.

"Well, anyway, Johnny saw the roadblock about a second later and then the reception cut out. I had a small tantrum and told Johnny to pull over. So he did and cut off the lights. That was when your text message came through."

From there, my brother recounted the things that happened at the roadblock. The men we had flown passed had discarded their masks and most of their clothing, now no more human than the freak wailing outside of my house a day ago. They stalked between the cars, only stopping to bend over and gnaw on a dead body.

Judah spied Patrick Fitzpatrick stumbling out of the last car through the scope of his .30-30 and nearly shot him until he realized the man was attempting to sneak away. He panicked and began to run, but the ex-*luchadores* closed in around him. One grabbed his arm and pulled. Judah shot the attacker in the head, but Patrick was already screaming. Johnny, irascible as ever, charged headlong, spraying his shotgun at the group surrounding Patrick who had fallen to the ground.

"Probably a good thing, too," Judah said to Patrick Fitzpatrick. "Johnny was just as likely to blast you the way he was flinging that shotgun around at everything that moved."

My brother swapped his hunting rifle for his M16 and followed after Johnny, picking off as many as he could. There were eleven altogether. Every one that Johnny blew away got back up a second later, and it wasn't until they'd gone through each of them at least twice that Judah realized the one's he shot through the head actually stayed down. It didn't take long after that.

"Should of known," said Johnny. "We've seen enough zombie movies to know you have to shoot'em in the head."

"These aren't zombies," I said.

"How do you know? They looked like zombies to me."

I lifted my bandaged arm. "If they were, I'm pretty sure I'd be one by now."

Johnny considered this for a moment and said, "Well what are they then? Zombies I can wrap my head around, but if getting bitten doesn't turn you into one of those things, what does?"

I had no idea. But the thought frightened me. If they couldn't turn you then what could? Something you ate? Something in the air?

Something in the air…

For the first time since I stepped outside that morning, I remembered the spot moving steadily across the sky. Except it was no longer a spot. It was a black hole on a sheet of white, just like my mother had suggested, and it seemed to suck the light out of the surrounding atmosphere, like a virus that absorbed what it touched rather than spreading the infection outward.

"If I had to guess, Johnny, I'd say your answer is up there."

3

"They're fast," my brother said. "Whatever people are turning into. It wasn't hard to kill them because we caught them by surprise, but when they figured out where we were they moved like animals…like predators chasing after prey."

My brother concluded their story, telling us how they had to dig Patrick Fitzpatrick out from under the pile of bodies that had fallen on him. His shoulder had been yanked out of its socket, and Johnny had to jam it back in even though he'd never done it before. The muscles in our new companion's jaw tensed as he listened, his hand moving to the injured area as if the memory had brought the pain back anew. It had taken three tries.

"Hence the sling made out of my favorite shirt." He glared at Johnny, clearly still incensed about the incident.

"Sorry, 'bout that," Johnny laughed. "It was the only thing I could find. Maybe if you didn't just throw your clothes all over the bed of the truck, I wouldn't have grabbed it."

"Maybe if you actually thought about things before you did them, retard, I would still have my Skynard shirt. You could've used any other shirt."

"I think you should hit him, Johnny," Dean said from his seat across from me.

"Freaking instigator." My brother threw his empty beer can.

I hadn't even noticed Judah held a beer until it bounced off the top of Dean's neatly sculpted head. And Johnny had one, too.

"Hey, where'd the beer come from?" I said.

Johnny twisted and pulled one from a cooler sitting behind him, the bench hiding it from my view. "Got it from a van parked by the roadblock. There were two cases of it. Got you a little something, too, Shane." He tossed me the beer and motioned around for any more takers. I hoped what they got for me was cigarettes.

I cracked open my beer and when I looked up Judah was burning a hole through Johnny with his eyes. Johnny clamped his mouth shut quickly as if reminded of something. Something he wasn't supposed to be talking about.

I was about to address this, but Dean beat me to it. "I saw that," he said. "What aren't you telling us?"

Judah made a momentary grimace, as if a sharp pain had passed over him, and then his lips smoothed into a forced smile. His eyes briefly met Johnny's, then Patrick's, and ended staring at the white concrete of the patio between his feet. "I'll show you some of what we found. Then I'll tell you the rest. But not in front of Zoe and Faris."

He rose to his feet and trudged slowly to the sliding door. I got up and thought of my kids. I wanted Syd to hear what my brother had to say, but someone had to stay out here with them.

"I'll watch'em if you and Syd both want to go," Johnny said and shrugged. "I was there. I know what happened."

I thanked him and Sydney and I made to enter the house, but Zoe grabbed Sydney by her pajama pants, almost pulling them down. She caught the waistband an instant before they fell to the ground, depriving Johnny and me of an excellent morning strip show. "I wanna go with you, mommy," Zoe said, her adorable voice nearly collapsing my resolve.

"You're not going, Zoe," my wife answered. "And let go of my pants before you show everyone what I got."

A groan of disappointment escaped my mouth. I'm pretty sure I heard a similar noise from Johnny.

Zoe let go reluctantly and gave it one more try. "Can I go with you, daddy?"

"Your mom already said no. You know better than that."

"Fishpaste," my girl said. At least she wasn't using the words I normally spouted after a disappointment.

Faris took Zoe's hand and guided her back to their chairs.

That settled, we followed the rest of the group through the house. Judah stopped at Johnny's red Chevy Silverado and threw back the blanket covering the bed. I moved to where I could see over the side—Johnny had his truck lifted last summer and I had to rise off my heels to peer into the back. It was no wonder Judah opted to show us rather than attempting to describe what they'd found. In a word: *munitions*. Two AR-15 assault rifles, a number of handguns of different makes and calibers, a couple shotguns, several military cases of ammunition, and...three compound bows. My heart leapt with excitement.

"Please be a lefty, please be a lefty," I murmured as I reached over the side to snatch the closest bow. Righty. I strained further to grab the one next to it. Also righty. I stretched higher, resting my stomach on the bed rail to reach the third bow. I closed my eyes as my hand grasped the bow's upper limb, knowing the chances of a left-handed bow being there was slim to none. Hopping down, I opened my eyes and breathed out with relief. It was a lefty. And since I was the only left-handed person here, with the exception of Zoe, it was all mine.

My brother was showing Mr. Argo and my dad how to lock and load the AR-15's and he smiled. "I thought you'd like that, bro."

"No doubt. Were there arrows?"

"There's a few quivers in there and about 50 shafts with broad-heads."

"Niiice."

I noticed the women (my mom and Anna included) standing together with their arms crossed, eyebrows high and not amused. I put the bow back into the truck bed and went to see what was up.

"I'm assuming there's a problem by your hostile body language," I said, trying to get a smile from Sydney at least.

The desired response was achieved. They dropped their arms and made a conscious effort not to smile. I saw through it though.

"Can the girls get in on this," Sydney said snidely, "or is this a boys only meeting?"

"Umm, Judah, you'd better include the wives here or we're all gonna have some problems," I said, then added, "you're probably gonna have problems anyway though."

"He's not the only one," my wife interjected. Then all the women laughed at me.

My brother halted his tutelage and strode over to where we stood, a couple yards from the truck. "Come on, pumpkin," he said to Devon, with a pouty smirk on his face. "I was just showing the dad's how to use the rifles. I'll show you, too." The last part came out as more of a question.

She gave him a fake, closed mouth sneer complete with raised eyebrows and slight attitudinal head shake. Looked like I was right about him being in trouble anyway.

"Alright, alright," I said, trying to bring the focus back to the items discovered in the *luchadores'* van. "Can you show us—" I glanced at the ladies, "—*everyone*, what you found. You said there was more."

The color drained from my brother's face. This was definitely something he didn't want to talk about, but he turned his attention to the contents in the truck and said, "In all, we found two AR-15's, two Remington combat shotguns, a few Smith & Wesson 9mm's, a couple Glock .45's, and three Ruger Blackhawk .357's. There's a butt-load of ammo in those cases—enough for everyone to practice their little hearts out. I grabbed three hunting bows. The lefty is obviously Shane's, but the other two are up for grabs and we'll be happy to teach anyone who's interested how to shoot them." He paused to reach into the bed and came back with a swaddle of blanket. He laid the bundle on the ground and uncovered its contents. "And we took these."

"Holy crap," Dean and I blurted. At least fifteen assorted knives lay spread out on the blanket. Some were folding blades, most were fixed. Others were large—the biggest being a long, curved blade called a kukri that would almost look like a boomerang if it weren't for the hilt. All had sheaths that could be attached to a belt. I had my eye on one of the two forearm-sized Bowie knives.

"Johnny already called dibs on the kukri," Judah said, "and I like the double edged fixed blade over there. I'm guessing you'll want a Bowie, Shane."

"Aw, you know me so well," I replied.

Some color came back to his face. "Other than that, have at it."

And we did. I knew what he was doing, occupying our minds with new shiny guns and knives, hoping we'd forget he had more to tell us. I wasn't going to be the one to remind everyone. If he got away with it, more power to him. He'd tell me later on.

The next ten minutes was spent divvying up the knives between us. I grabbed a Bowie and so did Dean. I snagged a five inch fixed blade for Sydney, knowing she wasn't going to take one herself. She was always a little standoffish when it came to guns and knives, but that was going to change.

I took a smaller folding knife for Zoe even though she wouldn't be able to have it for another year or two. It was engraved with detailed Celtic knot-work and simply too nice to pass up. No need to take one for Faris, there would be time down the road to fix him up when he got older.

Everyone present got at least one knife and they all seemed pleased with what they ended up with. That, at least, was a blessing. Pleasing everyone in this group was never an easy task. We took the time to examine our new toys, and when everyone had finished they converged on Judah. He hadn't finished his story, and it didn't appear he would be getting off the hook as easily as he hoped.

4

"Fine," Judah said through his teeth. "You people are like dogs begging at a dinner table."

"And you're like a kid with a bad report card avoiding his parents," Dean came back.

"Whatever," he spat. "This isn't for the faint of heart, so this is your last chance."

"Just tell us what happened, Judah," my dad scolded, "we've all seen Quentin Tarantino movies."

My brother threw his hands in the air. "So we found this van parked by the roadblock. Patrick Fitzpatrick was in a lot of pain, but we thought it would be worth it to check for supplies. In retrospect, I'm not so sure it was."

"He seems okay now," Jordan stated.

"Well, chalk that up to your hubby being a damn good paramedic. Plus, the man rode the whole way here hooked up to an IV. *You* should know how Johnny loves hooking people up to IV's."

All but the four older parents snickered, remembering a certain party where Jordan had way too much to drink and ended up needing an IV to rehydrate. Of course Johnny had given himself an IV on more than one occasion, too. He and my brother were borderline alcoholics.

Jordan bit her lip and then, probably feeling it wasn't enough to get worked up over, relaxed and conceded with a grin. "What can I say, I like mojitos."

"Apparently," Haley said.

"At least I don't get explosive diarrhea after two shots," Jordan said, pleased when Haley turned a dark shade of red.

"Anyway, if you could hold your comments to the end, this would go a lot smoother."

"Yes, professor," Dean said.

My brother ignored him. "The back doors of the van were wide open, and we could see inside before we actually arrived. There were guns, lots of them. These guys had an arsenal. It's a bloody wonder any of you made it past them. I doubt the cops could've stood up against that much firepower…"

He trailed off and focused on his boots, pulling on the end of his mustache. This was the part he was dreading. I'd never seen my brother unwilling—or unable—to talk about something. As far as Judah was concerned, nothing was off limits. Seeing him this way, the distance in his eyes, made my nerves twitch.

"It was too dark to see the blood until we were standing in front of the open back doors," he said, staring off into the woods. "It was dark and sticky and long streaks ran into the van like people—a lot of people—had been dragged through it. We later found more drag marks on the ground near both side doors, too. But we saw no bodies."

"None?" Dean asked. We had seen the slumped figures strewn about the line of vehicles as we raced past the very same roadblock. There had certainly been bodies then. "Not even in the cars?"

Shaking his head, my brother gestured to Patrick Fitzpatrick. The Southerner spoke up. "It was still light when I pulled up to the roadblock." Pausing briefly, he too gave his head a shake. "I don't remember much. I pulled up in the queue and put it in PARK. The car in front of me had probably been there a while 'cause I hadn't seen another car, going in either direction, for a long time. My window was rolled down and the next thing I knew, somethin' hit me in the noggin."

He rubbed the now treated crevice that jutted from his hairline. "I woke in my car, got out, and saw a bunch of naked men walkin' around. One of 'em grabbed me, and Judah told ya'll the rest. There'd been people in the cars in front of me 'fore I got knocked out. When I woke, there weren't none. Not a single car had a single passenger, dead er otherwise."

"Why'd they leave you?" I asked, finding it strange that he was the only person they found.

"It doesn't make much sense," Dean said. "To find no bodies except for Fitzy here? It's like they forgot you after they knocked you out."

"Uh." My brother cleared his throat. "I didn't say we didn't find any bodies. I just said we didn't *see* any bodies…at the time." His eyes welled, and I felt my nerves constrict tighter. "The blood trail led into the van and around both sides toward the front. The ones inside stopped at two big steel drums. Johnny opened the one closest to us, like we all didn't already know what was inside."

He stopped, not wanting to continue.

"The bodies had been butchered and stuffed inside," Patrick picked up with a thankful nod from Judah. "It was like a suitcase with too many clothes in it. They hadn't been there long enough ter reek, but the smell a…fear, and…I dunno know…loss…was rank. I only peeked in for a sec and lost my stomach when I saw the head of a little girl starin' up at me." He appeared as if he were about to lose it again. "Just the head shoved in there with the cut up bodies of all them people. I could've easily been inside one a them drums, and the thought brought up fresh puke. I had to get away from the van, and that's exactly what I did."

When it became clear Patrick Fitzpatrick wasn't going to say anything further, my brother said, "There were six more drums around the front of the van, all surrounded by blood and gore. We didn't open any of them. Those mask wearing freaks had taken their time and enjoyed themselves..." His voice faded and he took another deep breath, relaxing his fists. "I don't think they skipped Patrick. I think they wanted their victims aware of what was happening to them. So they were waiting for him to wake up. Looked like they lost their minds before he did though."

Patrick gasped and hunkered with his head in his hands. "I never even thought a that," he said once he'd calmed down. "I owe you a great deal of thanks."

"You owe us nothing," my brother said with a dismissive wave. "The world's gone mad. We'll take all the sane company we can get." He plodded back to the house and then turned, remembering something. "By the way, any of you notice where that thing was headed?"

"It's too far off to even try to guess where it will land," I said. "If it lands at all."

This brought a haughty curve to one corner of Judah's mouth. I hated that lopsided smirk sometimes. He was being smug and I hated that even more. His idiotic mustache taunted me.

"It's getting bigger, which I take to mean it's getting closer," he stated, satisfied with himself that he'd thought of something I hadn't. "Now I'm not a brilliant man, but with all the coincidences that have been going around and the weird stuff that's been happening it wouldn't surprise me if that thing touched down right in our backyard."

Again, he started for the house and came back. "Almost forgot." He opened the door to the truck and came out with a duffle bag. He flung

it to me and said, "Don't say I never gave you anything."
As he waltzed away, I unzipped the bag. Inside were ten cartons of cigarettes.

A Glimpse of Madness

1

Nearly twenty hours had passed since seeing the dark object, and we found ourselves bored and nervous in what the Argo's called their Oh Shit Shelter. Hidden below their barn in the northwestern most point of their property, the dark hole sank twenty feet through hardened clay and rock to open up to a spacious room almost the size of the barn itself. Supported by true 4'x6' lengths of hand cut oak, the shelter resembled an underground WWII bunker, complete with low wattage bulbs strung efficiently along the center ceiling beam. The walls were the earth itself, the Argos feeling no compulsion to spruce up a place they hoped they'd never have reason to use.

Luke's grandfather Jacob had begun the excavation of the shelter upon returning home from the Second World War sans one leg and three fingers. Hobbling on the remaining good leg and a makeshift prosthetic, he and his brother Jonah, who had been too young to be drafted, spent the next three years digging and dumping, digging and dumping. Both men had nearly been killed when a portion of the hollowed out room collapsed while fitting one of the beams to the ceiling. Luke's grandfather had the forethought to post a bell outside the opening of the barn to which he tied a long rope. The opposite end he fastened around his waist.

The collapse knocked Jacob and Jonah unconscious, and when they woke, they found themselves trapped in complete darkness. Jacob yanked the rope with all his might, hoping the soil blocking their way was loose enough to allow the thin cord to pass easily enough to ring the bell. He knew once he pulled the rope tight, the dirt would likely shift and would no longer provide enough slack for the bell to be rung a second time. He also knew if no one heard that single toll of the bell, they would likely die there. The small space had maybe half a day's worth of air. So Jacob pulled, but he heard no bell. The cave-in locked out all sound, and Luke's grandfather and his grandfather's brother were trapped without even the surety of possible rescue.

In the darkness, one loses all sense of time. Or so I'm told. It seemed years slipped slowly by before the *shoosh* sound of shovels could be heard from the other side of the cave-in. By then the brothers had all but fainted from lack of oxygen, and when dim shafts of light drifted through the newly made opening to hit their faces, the two men could manage no more than a weary smile. They were dragged to the safety of the barn and given water. Luke's Grandmother Isabel—a blessedly light sleeper—had been awakened by the sound of the bell, and upon waking realized her husband was not in bed beside her. Now it was not uncommon for her to retire without Jacob by her side, he being known to work well past dark, but when she looked at the clock next to her bed the hands read 11:36, far past the time Jacob usually came in. She leapt out of bed, not taking a bother to put on slippers or a robe, and tore down the stairs, out the back door, and to the barn. To make an increasingly long story short, Isabel assessed the situation and drove to her nearest neighbors who lived close to 3 miles away. Banging on their door, she woke them. The Olsens were a family of eight; four boys, two girls, and of course Mom and Pop. Poppa Olsen and his sons drove back to the Argo farm, shovels ready, while the women and girls went to muster more help. By 1:00am they had twelve men sweating in the nighttime heat to get the Argo brothers freed. By sunrise the next morning, Jacob and Jonah were lying on their backs on the surface.

The Olsens and others who had assisted refused to allow Jacob and Jonah to continue the work alone—which they were likely to do—and so, with the additional man-power, the shelter was completed six months later. This was 1949, and the bell that saved the lives of Jacob and Jonah Argo still stands proudly beside the barn. Although the bell's clapper has since been removed, the names of those who came to their aid have been added.

Luke graciously told us this story only *after* we had congregated inside the shelter. Laughing as our mouths dropped open, he said, "Don't worry, we've taken extra precautions." *Precautions*. Like the steel reinforcements on the half-century old lumber would make us feel any less nervous about the fact that two people had nearly been buried alive down here. I did have to admit, though, that if I ever had any doubt about the concept of American ingenuity, I had none now. Luke's grandfather had built this thing by hand on one leg and three missing digits. Sure he had help, but only for the final portion of the project. That was impressive.

And the story did help to pass the time.

The Argos added some minor luxuries over the course of years: a food pantry stocked with canned goods and other imperishables, a small water pump that flowed from the well outside the barn. This water wasn't generally consumed by humans, but if it became necessary, we'd have no qualms about drinking it; the livestock lapped it up just fine. There was a rickety table with several chairs, a few cots and enough bedrolls to be fairly comfortable—not that anyone was ready to make themselves comfortable yet. But my brother's idea that the dark object was drawing closer to us proved to be true. Over the past several hours, it had grown large and much more visible. In a few hours, it looked like it would be hitting us dead on.

And so there we were, huddled together below a ton of dirt, a few hours from impact. No, we weren't ready to make ourselves comfortable yet, but a growing unease was taking a foothold as the time drew nearer.

2

Don't panic, don't panic.
An hour crept past.
Don't panic. Don't panic. Don't panic!
Another slipped by.
DON'T PANIC! DON'T PANIC! PANIC! PAN—
"Alright, we need to talk," I blurted, startling everyone, most likely from the same thoughts I had been plagued with. Zoe and Faris had fallen asleep out of sheer boredom about an hour ago, having grown tired of the ancient army men they found in a box in the corner.

"Whadda we need to talk about, Shane?" Judah said, tugging his mustache. "The fact most everyone has gone insane and that stupid thing hasn't even hit Earth yet? Why would we need to talk about that?"

"We need to talk about *something*," Dean said, "or I'm about to go crazy from the tension." There was a murmur of agreement.

"Well, Johnny's already crazy, so we don't have to worry about him," Judah said and most of us at least grunted a nervous chuckle despite not really wanting to.

"It's called getting things done, pig," Johnny replied. "And mark my words; you'll need someone like me before this is all over."

"Blah blah blah," I said. "The world's crazy, Dean's going crazy, and Johnny's already crazy. So what do we do now? Judah just said that thing hasn't hit yet, but it should hit in—" I grabbed Judah's arm to consult his watch, then shook my head "—any time now. If we survive, life as we know it is likely to be history. We might have electricity for a little while longer, but there's no telling how long. We'll have gas for as long as we can find it, and I don't intend on getting in anymore gunfights over it. We're gonna be left to fend for ourselves. And trust me, there're gonna be a lot of other people doing the same thing. So I'll ask again. What do we do now?"

I looked around, stopping when I met my dad's gaze. He rolled his eyes, seeing something in my face. "You already know the answer to that question, don't you?"

"Maybe."

"So why don't you just tell us?" Jordan said.

"Because, Jordan, I want to hear what you all think," I said. "Believe it or not, I don't like talking that much."

"Yeah, right," my brother, dad, and wife muttered in unison.

There was a moment of silence, and when no one else spoke up, Johnny finally did. As I hoped he would. "We've had enough drunken bonfire conversations for me to know what's on your mind. Hell, it's been on *my* mind since we took out those effing son-a-bitches at the roadblock. The answer's pretty simple. We become self-sufficient. Actually doing it, though, will be a lot harder."

"Shut the front door," Judah said, distraught. "That sounds like it'll require me to do actual work."

"We all know that will be tough for you," Dean said.

"Seriously," Johnny said. "We'll need to grow and harvest our own food, accumulate our own supplies, and build our own defenses."

Dean's face brightened. "I'll take charge of that one. I'll come up with some ballin' traps and fortifications." It was unlike him to get overly excited about much of anything besides the prospect of hooking up (which he always needed Judah to help him accomplish; even Haley took a crap-load of wingman support), so I was encouraged at his interest.

"Alright, good," I said. "Whatever you need, Dean. Volunteers for the other things Johnny listed?"

Haley's hand popped up immediately. "We're not in school, Pudge," I said. "You don't have to raise your hand."

"Yeah, yeah. I'll help with the gardening, though I've never actually done any."

"Me too," said my dad. "I had a pretty *ballin'* tomato plant growing back home."

My mom cackled. "Yeah, *a*, as in *one*, tomato plant. He killed the other four."

"Live and learn, my dear," my dad sang.

"Your problem isn't the living part. It's the learning part that gets you."

He cocked his head to the side, resigned. "When she's right, she's right, Pops," Judah said. My father was never very good at the hands-on type of stuff. He was more of a supervisor. He was excellent at telling people where to put things and overseeing hard work like the time he, Johnny, and I had helped Judah put in new paving blocks for his back patio. He picked up a few blocks, sure, but mostly we just heard him saying things like, "That's not very straight" or "Anyone want a beer?" He was good company though. And he always had plenty of beer.

Luke had been sitting quietly as we hashed out our plan, and finally he decided to make himself known. "In case you haven't noticed, this *is* a farm. I can grow crops, raise livestock, harvest and butcher, then replant and start all over. I'll show you how to do it all, 'cause it's extremely hard work and I'll need everyone—even you, Judah—to play your parts. We use the manure from the cows to enrich the soil, and we'll save some of everything we harvest to plant during the next season. It's harder that way, but buying seeds and fertilizer might become impossible, like Shane said. We'll have to recycle as much as we can."

Everyone besides Luke and Anna sighed with relief. "At least one of us knows what they're doing," I said.

"What about showers, and water for washing clothes and dishes?" Devon said, obviously concerned about keeping herself pretty.

"We can probably get the old water tower behind the house to work," Luke said. "My grandparents used to use it to pipe water into the bathroom…after they had one installed in the '50's. It'll be cold, but it will be better than wiping off by the well."

"Sounds good," I said. "Now let's talk about defenses. Dean will oversee most of that, but we need to stock up on guns and ammo."

"We might not have to do as much of that as you think, Shane," Luke said. He was grinning from ear to ear, clearly pleased with what he was about to say. "I've been stocking up on munitions for the better part of a decade. Ever since that last Fascist bastard took office. I always hoped we wouldn't need them, but now I'm glad I listened to my gut. I have thousands of dollars' worth of ammo in the cellar. Everything from .22 rimfire to .30-06. Plus I got all the guns to go with it. Combined with what Judah and Johnny took from those *luchador* fellas, I'd say we already have quite an arsenal."

"Well, stick it in my rear, Luke," Johnny said. "I never knew you were a revolutionary."

"I do my part," Luke said humbly, but still grinning wide. "It's nice to see you guys are willing to do yours. But I'll keep away from your backside if you don't mind."

This was turning out better than I could have hoped. Dean and Judah whispered to each other, most likely about some of the defense tactics Dean had in mind. Johnny may always have been the one starting fires as a kid, but Dean was the one who enjoyed blowing things up. I cringed as I attempted to surmise what he had rolling around his brain. Haley, Sydney, and the twins discussed with my mom and Anna how excited they were to start growing vegetables. *As long as they keep the tobacco growing,* I thought suddenly. Cigarettes would eventually become scarce in the marketplace if things panned out the way we were talking. I'd have to ask Luke about that one.

Johnny and my dad listened intently while Luke told them about all the guns he had stored. Eager beavers ready to get their hands on some weapons as soon as it was safe to leave this hole.

Patrick Fitzpatrick, who hadn't said a word since descending into the shelter, continued his silence. Like me, he observed a little of each conversation.

I thought about my children pushing a plow or butchering a cow, and

I could envision it easily enough. Zoe was an extremely bright girl and not a bit squeamish when it came to blood and guts. She hadn't quite developed much of a work ethic yet, but she was still young; those types of things came in time. Faris liked to do anything and everything Zoe did, so if I could get *her* working…

Then we felt the rumble.

3

Dull thunder rolled in the distance and silence fell like a guillotine onto the room. A second later the earthen walls, ground and ceiling of the Oh Shit Shelter began to quake. Chunks of compacted dirt fell from above, giving me chills. *What if it collapses?* The thought entered my mind, and I pushed it away quickly.

"Don't worry. It'll hold," I heard Luke say.

No one responded. We just sat, still as art, waiting as the thunder grew louder. Miraculously, Zoe and Faris kept sleeping.

Then the ground began to shake, lurching slightly like a ripple in the water, knocking shelf-loads of canned goods from the rickety pantry and sending larger chunks of dirt raining down on our heads. Zoe jolted awake and immediately began to cry, dust and grit clinging to her hair. Sydney stumbled over to her and picked her up; comforting her in a way only a mother can despite the terror that she herself was experiencing. I followed behind her to hold Faris who, unbelievably, continued to snore.

I stood over him, protecting my son's head from the debris. Our eyes had all turned upward as if we could see through the layers of dirt and clay, through the barn roof above, and directly into the night where a globe of darkness hurtled down upon us.

We waited in fear for what seemed like eternity. In reality it was no more than thirty minutes, but the time was excruciating. I'd never felt so stressed in my life. Fumbling in my pocket, trying not to wake Faris, I pulled out my pack of cigarettes and lit one. Sydney immediately swatted it from my lips and glared at me. "Really? While you're holding Faris?"

I thumped my head with the heel of my hand and passed off my comatose son to my mom. I lit another cig and felt an instant surge of calm flow through my nerves. Patrick showed a sign of life by lighting one for my dad and himself with a single match. He'd been eager to leave, worried about his step-children, but we'd talked him into staying at least until this thing passed.

"You mind going to the other side of the cave to do that?" my mom said, scrunching her face in the same way she would if she had just gotten a whiff of one of my dad's farts. We obeyed without a word.

After a few minutes I snuffed out my cigarette and joined Sydney around the table. We stared for a moment, passing our fear and assurances silently to the other, and then I shifted my attention to my brother. He gave me the finger, and I burst out laughing. Everyone else stared at me in wonderment. When I regained control I said, "Maybe that was the en—"

Just then a violent tremor shook us. The ground heaved, throwing us all to the ground in a downpour of dirt and rocks. Jordan's head was tossed into the wall behind her with a thud. Johnny scrambled to get to her, but lost his footing and went down hard. Patrick and my dad, who were still standing in the smoking section, clunked heads and ended up sprawled on the ground. I saw these things happen before my face was thrown into the table with a crack. New agony flared up my already broken nose as blood splattered across the dirty table and down my shirt. I fell to the floor in a ball, the pain causing me to forget everything else. Shaking my head to clear it, the situation came back into view and I remembered my kids. I saw two of everything, but I couldn't tell if the cause was the impact of my face on the hard wood table or the vicious shaking of the shelter. The urgency to get to Faris increased and I searched the room for my son. Chairs, cots, and food items were strewn everywhere. I spied Sydney under the table, covering Zoe with her body. My eyes moved frantically through the chaos until they came to my mother. She had hit her head when she fell and did not seem to be completely lucid. I crawled to her, heaving two chairs from my path, and arrived beside her a moment later. Faris sat upright next to her, not crying at all, his eyes wide as saucers. His hands said, *it's here*, and then I was holding him in my arms, covering his head.

"Is everyone all right?" I yelled into the thunder. I barely heard my own voice, and when my mouth opened a stream of blood poured in.

"Sound off. Sydney."

"I'm okay."

103

"Mom, Dad."

"Okay!"

"I'm alright."

I went through the list, receiving answers immediately until I got to Jordan. *"Johnny, where's Jordan?"*

"She's unconscious. She hit the wall hard, but she's breathing steadily."

This all happened in a span of two minutes, and when the convulsions lessened seconds later we were able to properly assess the damages. It appeared Jordan and I got the worst of it. She was just coming to and Johnny held her head in his lap. The Argos hovered close, concern for their daughter plain on their faces. A roll of paper towels had fallen from a shelf nearby, and I stuffed a wad against my nose to try and stop the bleeding.

"Um, I'm getting out of here," I stood and said to anyone who wanted to listen.

"I second that," said my brother.

"You sure that's a good idea?" Patrick said, rubbing his head. There was already a goose egg rising on his head from where it had collided with my father's. "It may not be over yet."

"It's probably not over," I conceded, "but I'd rather not stay in here and wait to be buried alive." I could see we were far from a consensus. "Look, I'm not telling anyone what to do. I'm just saying that I'd rather take my chances in the open air than in a hole. After feeling that last shake, I'm pretty sure it's not gonna be any better down here when that thing hits."

"Again, I second that," Judah said.

"I concur," Dean said.

"Of course you do," Haley said to her husband. "You do everything Shane tells you. I guess I'm going, too."

"Syd?" I said, unsure which way she was leaning.

"I'd follow you anywhere, baby," she said.

In the end, everyone but the Argos, Patrick Fitzpatrick, Johnny, and Jordan went back up. Johnny stayed with Jordan because she was still dizzy and couldn't climb the ladder. Patrick Fitzpatrick stayed because "he felt like it". The Argos said they were staying with Jordan, but I think they really stayed out of sheer principle. It was their shelter and they were gonna use it.

I don't blame any of them for staying—especially Jordan who

couldn't even walk—but they definitely missed a spectacular show.

4

Topside, the wind swirled cool and harsh, sweeping across the trees with mild force, bending them to the east. The dogs sluggishly came to meet us (a nine to four vote—children excluded—won out on leaving anything on four legs outside; which greatly disappointed Johnny, Judah, and I) tails between their legs, heads low. They were scared to death and I didn't blame them.

"We never should have left them out here," my wife said.

I gave no response. Neither did the others. It was clear she believed she had made a mistake and the silent consensus said there was no need for an I-told-you-so.

Zoe and Faris wrapped tightly in the blankets we had acquired from the shelter and seemed warm enough. The others stood cross-armed, bundling themselves against one another, and stared into the night that loomed darker than ever. The nearly invisible object formed an immense web of shadow across the sky like a blanket of black that weighed down upon us; a descending ceiling intent on crushing the life out of all below.

It was no longer necessary to look to the side of the object in order to view it for it now filled the sky. As it neared at frightening speed, I expected to be able to make out features, possible contours, cracks, canyons, a face…*anything*. However, I beheld nothing but a moving hole, an indescribable void.

We watched as it flew over our heads, an immense darkness the size of a city block, blacking out the view of the moon and stars as it made its way to the fields north of the Argo. It came fast—moving past almost as quickly as it arrived—and shot over the tree line, disappearing from view.

In the seconds after its disappearance, I heard several gasps. Sydney cringed and clutched Faris tightly, who held his ears. I gripped her shoulder—to brace myself for impact as much as it was to support her—and seized Zoe to my chest. A sharp inhale came from Judah on my left, and then complete and utter silence. Not a cricket or dog made a sound; no one breathed. A faint ringing began, like the kind people inflicted with Tinnitus are plagued with, and rose to a deafening pitch in a nanosecond.

The explosion came next, setting the ground heaving. We were flung every which way like startled seagulls, some smacking into others, all ending on the ground in scattered heaps. Most of us had gained our feet when a blast of hot air hit us, bringing with it chunks of forest debris—mostly small rocks and branches…and one unfortunate opossum—that pelted us painfully. The wind gusted strong enough to push us backward a few feet as we lost our footing once more.

The worst of it was the sound. The explosion bounced off the hills and faded, but the incessant ringing never stopped. Its decibel level rose and rose, and when I thought it could not reach a higher note, it rose again. Lying on the ground, it felt like my head was going to burst from the sheer pressure of the unearthly noise. The windows of the Big House blew out simultaneously; oddly, the stained glass of the chapel remained intact. Hands still over my ears, I had an unfocused thought to clamp my elbows over Zoe's for added muffling. I ventured to open my eyes and witnessed the others sprawled out, hands grasping their ears, their mouths agape. They all screamed, and I realized I was too. I heard neither them nor myself, but I knew we were screaming. Tears poured down my face as the sound increased again, and something warm seeped through my fingers. I felt my eyes bulge, the pressure threatening to push them from their sockets. Bowie balled up beside me in an unnatural position. I turned to see the other dogs lying in twisted lumps, and the last thing I thought before the red cloud took me into unconsciousness was: *My God, the dogs are dead.*

5

I woke with a start to something nudging my arm. Then a warm tongue splashed over my face. I groggily pushed it away and sat up. Peeling my eyes open—it was hard at first, the quick accumulation of moisture had sealed them shut—I was startled to see Bowie breathing excitedly into my face. It was still dark. My head hurt, and my twice broken nose bled again, but that horrible sound had stopped. Zoe stirred beside me, and I noticed the others beginning to move as well. I picked up my daughter and held her in my lap, and as I did so I noticed semi-dry blood had streaked down the sides of her face from her ears. I looked at my own hands and realized they were stained a dark crimson.

What was that sound?
Sydney, the same red lines trailing from her ears, attempted to sit up and I scooted across the few feet of grass to help her. Faris sat at her side, wide awake. I kissed them both, then sat still to catch my breath, which came in weak, uneven gasps. The others were now either sitting up or lying on the ground not far from where they had fallen, and great relief swept through me.

I was about to ask if everyone was alright, when I heard voices coming from behind me. I turned to see the Argos and Johnny helping Jordan out of the barn. Patrick Fitzpatrick followed at a meager distance.

When they reached us, Johnny said, "You 'tards still glad you came outside?"

I, along with a couple others gave an amused chuckle, then grimaced at the pain it produced in my head. When it had passed I said, "You guys alright? I see the shelter didn't cave in."

"Looks like plenty of dirt came down, though," my brother said in a stronger voice than my own. "You guys are filthy."

"At least we're not bleeding out the ears," Jordan said, concerned.

I studied the blood on my hands, on Zoe's ears. "Did you hear that down there?"

"Hear what?" Luke asked, clearly perplexed.

"You didn't hear that high pitched ringing?" Dean exclaimed in absolute disbelief. "How could you not hear that?"

"Don't know what you're talking about, boy, but I believe *you* heard something. Your ears have taken quite a beatin'." Luke scurried over to Devon, who sat with her head against Judah's shoulder and knelt beside her. "You okay, honey?"

She smiled unconvincingly. "I'm a delicate flower, but I'll be alright." She sighed and rested her head again on Judah. "Is it over?"

I surveyed the early morning sky. It was still pitch black, but all I saw were the moon and the stars. "I hope so. How long were we out?"

Johnny checked his Timex and gave a calculating expression. "Judging by the moon and the position of Polaris, I'd say almost two hours."

"Geez," my mom said. "I feel like I was hit by a truck. And Polaris is always in the same position."

"Huh?" said Johnny.

I laughed, knowing he had no idea what she was talking about, but impressed he even knew there was a star named Polaris. I ran my hand back over my short hair—a habit I rarely realized I was doing, like biting my fingernails—and pushed it forward again. "Anyone feel like exploring?"

"I feel like going to bed," Sydney said.

"She's right," Dean agreed, "we should get some sleep and check out the damage later."

I nodded my consent and rose to my feet. The others made their way up as well and we meandered back toward the house. "I hope you all have enough blankets though, 'cause all the windows are shattered."

"What?" both Luke and Anna yelped.

"I told you it was a *really* high pitched sound. We'll board up in the morning, which should be in about an hour."

"Then we'll board up in the afternoon," my dad said. "By the way, did anyone else see that possum fly through the air?"

6

I couldn't sleep. Thoughts of what had occurred and dread of what was coming flashed through my mind like a projector on steroids. Sydney snored next to me, content in her wild dreams. The kids had fallen asleep as soon as we'd cleaned the blood from their ears and their heads hit the pillows. I gave a frustrated moan and got up with the intention of going out for a cigarette. Clothes on, mind a mess, I left the room and bumped into Johnny who had just left his. "Can't sleep either?"

He shook his head. "Think I'm gonna start putting up the shutters."

I smiled. Johnny was restless; tireless even. He needed sleep less than anyone I'd ever met, and he spent his waking hours he wasn't working busying himself with various projects and hobbies—the most recent being an endeavor into beer making (unfortunately we had to leave the four kegs of his latest batch in Florida due to space requirements). "Think I'll join you." As long as I was awake, I might as well do something useful. "Is there any beer downstairs?"

"You read my mind."

The beer, what was left of the horde Judah and Johnny had found at the roadblock, served as medicine for my troubled mind. My brother was going to be pissed when he discovered we'd drunk the last of it. And considering we both downed one during the short truck ride to the barn, I saw that as a real possibility. How did we go through two cases of beer in two days?

"You look like shit, Shane." Johnny blurted as we began pulling the large wooden emergency shutters from their place behind a stack of hay. A spider scurried across my hand and I let out a minor yelp. "And you sound like a girl."

"I hate spiders. And I haven't been sleeping well. I keep having these dreams that I can hardly remember. I wake up in a panic just about every night."

"That sucks, man," he said, not overly sympathetic, but then that wouldn't be very Johnny-like. "I have this recurring dream where I have a gun and I try to shoot someone that's trying to kill me but I can't pull the trigger. I squeeze as hard as I can, but it just won't budge."

We had loaded most of the wood into the back of the pickup, and I deemed it break time. I lit a cigarette and popped another beer, my fourth. "I'm sorry to hear you can't shoot anyone in your dreams, Johnny—"

"I can sometimes."

"Ok. I'm sorry that *a lot* of times you can't shoot people in your dreams. Better?"

He pursed his lip and nodded.

I continued, "These dreams are about Faris. That's the only thing I can absolutely remember. And my pops had one about him, too." I finished off the rest of the beer and took a drag of my cigarette.

"Your dad did? That's weird. An older man dreaming about a little boy…"

"Very funny. Toss me another beer." He did and I took a long gulp. "It might be better than the dreams I usually have, though." Conversation came to a halt as we loaded the remaining shutters into the truck.

By the time Johnny hit the brakes in front of the Big House, I was six beers in and feeling pretty good. We hauled the shutters out of the truck bed and started sorting them by size. The shutters, styled to look like thick blinds, were of the sort that had holes designed to fit over thick bolts jutting from the house's walls. All it took to install them was to align the holes with the bolts, slide them on, and screw on the wing-nuts. They were heavy though. And lugging them up a ladder to the second story was no picnic. The project took a little more than two hours, over which we had nearly finished off the case of beer, and almost fell off the ladder twice each, laughing wildly in our intoxication. Surprisingly, we woke not a soul.

The sun rose as we finished. Watching the pink and yellow sky from the orange roof of the house, we sat quietly sipping the last two beers. Johnny, though, was never much for silence, and when he had had enough of it he said, "So you're still having that dream about Sean, huh?"

"I shouldn't have even mentioned it."

"You need to talk about this sometime."

"I let him drown, Johnny. I found him first and I left him. What else is there to talk about?"

"Ugh. How 'bout the fact that you saved your brother's life…"

"I was forced to choose between my brother and my best friend. How can an eight year old kid be expected to live with that? How can I not question every decision I make? And here we are, things are going to shit, and I've already had to make more decisions than I ever wanted to. I've killed…I can't even keep track of how many people I've killed—"

"People that were trying to kill you."

"Regardless." I rubbed my eyes and my vision came back foggy. "I don't want this, Johnny. The others turning to me for answers. Having to make the hard choices. What if I get someone killed? What if it's you that dies because of a decision I make?"

Johnny adjusted his hat and flashed his teeth. "Then I die," he said. "I won't be around to be pissed at you."

"Your wife will though, and she'll probably kill me back."

"That's true. I would try not to get me killed if I were you. Jordan can be a vengeful little cuss when she wants to be." He clapped me on the back. "But seriously, I trust you and everyone else trusts you. Not to make the right decision all the time, but to make the decision *you* believe is right. Whatever happens from there happens. You ever realize how lucky we are?"

"You mean how fortunate we are to have each other? You, me, Dean, and Judah?...and the girls, of course."

"Yeah. How many people can say they have friends like ours? People have close childhood friends; sure, but how many of them stay close?" I lit a new cigarette from the butt of the one I just finished. I had another close childhood friend once, but I'd talked about that enough for one day. "We're more than close, Johnny," I said. "And I'd definitely say we're more than just friends. I'd die for any one of you, and if you had kids, I'd die for them, too." I took a drag. "Speaking of which…"

"We're trying, man. The girls in Jordan's family take a long time."

"You sure it's not *your* problem?" As I said this I slugged him in the nuts. He balled up on reflex, laughing and cringing, and nearly fell off the roof. I was laughing too hard to be of much use to him, and if he was a weaker man, he would have fallen two stories. Instead, he palmed the roof's shingles, using the toes of his boots and callused hands to slide to a stop just at the edge of the drop.

He scrambled back up—I flinched away, expecting some form of retaliation, but instead he just sat down, grinning and shaking his head. "I think you're right about us being more than just friends. Anyone else that did that would be falling to their death right now."

"We're only two stories up, Johnny," I said, not doubting for a second that he meant it. "I highly doubt it would be to their death." I lit *another* cigarette and turned to Johnny, putting a hand on his shoulder. "You're mellowing out in your old age."

"I know," he said. "What's wrong with me? You wanna go in?"

I took a moment to view the horizon—the sun had poked its head out more than halfway now—and nodded. "You going to bed?"

"Actually I was thinking of waking Dean and Judah up. My gut is telling me we shouldn't take a big group down to the crash site. Maybe we can get gone before anyone else wakes up."

"Our wives will be pissed when we get back."

He shrugged. "If it wasn't this, it'd be something else."

"Agreed."

Johnny made for the ladder and I crab-walked behind him. The roof had at least a 5/12 pitch and didn't make for easy walking.

He went down first. When he reached the bottom, I swung my leg over and began my decent. Halfway down I had a disturbing revelation and whipped my head toward the ground. Johnny was getting something from the truck several yards away, and I dismissed the thought. I climbed the rest of the way down, sure in my safety, and as my right foot touched the ground a sharp pain tore through my groin and into my abdomen. I fell in a moaning heap, banging my head on the ground repeatedly from the agony. And I heard laughter. That son-of-bitch racked me in the balls. I had suspected he'd be waiting for me at the bottom, but when I saw him fiddle-farting around in the truck I let my guard down. *Idiot!*

He was still laughing, but his hand stretched down to help me up. I took it, struggled to my feet, and hunched over with my hands on my knees. The pain was subsiding, but I was still far from comfortable.

"Payback's a bitch, ain't it?" he said.

I waved him away. With an amused grunt, he shuffled into the house. I followed a few minutes later when my stones dropped back into the proper place.

7

We almost lost Dean that day. And Johnny's insistence on going on our own turned out to be well founded.

The truck ride north turned into an annoying combination of grumbling and complaining caused by two sleep-deprived wussies. Not to mention I had to pee like a racehorse from the twelve beers I consumed a half hour before. Dean and Judah were still half asleep, each antagonizing the other as much as possible, making me turn back from the front seat more than once to break them up like a father threatening to turn the car around instead of continuing on to Disney World. Johnny and I had quietly snuck into their rooms, and after admiring their sleeping wives in their skimpy underwear, we simply picked them up and hauled them into the hall. We dropped Dean on top of Judah, who had been thrown out first, and as they lay there like two dazed homos, Johnny attempted to explain what we were doing. They didn't quite comprehend the situation then, and they didn't get it now.

"Why aren't we still in bed again?" Judah whined in a cranky voice.

I felt like slapping him and Dean. We'd been over this at least four times already. "We are going to the crash site. We are leaving everyone else at home because Johnny has a bad feeling. You have your guns because of that bad feeling. You are not still in bed because you would piss and moan more than you already are now if we had left you at home. Are we clear, you effing morons?"

"Well, when you say it like that, it makes me feel stupid," my brother said. "Devon's gonna kick my ass when we get home."

"You need to get your wife under control, Judah," Dean said. "That girl is running wild."

"She is, isn't she? Maybe I should beat her more."

"You should," Johnny said from the driver's seat. "Jordan doesn't tell me what to do anymore since I started."

"I haven't had to hit Sydney in a while."

"Please, Shane," Judah said. "Syd would beat you down and we all know it."

I couldn't argue with that. Syd could certainly give me a run for my money.

"You know where you're going, Johnny?" Dean asked, though he didn't sound very interested.

"Just following the smoke."

I leaned forward to peer over the trees. Indeed, a long wall of smoke billowed up in the not so far distance. Johnny drove us by the most northerly road until it began to veer off to the west. At that point he said, "Screw it," and turned off into the field on the right. We were able to make it about a mile before the forest halted our progress.

"Guess we huff it from here," I said as I hopped out of the truck and opened the rear half-door to let Judah out. He and Dean got out from opposite sides and secured their pistols. I had just finished strapping my gun belt on when I saw my rifle floating toward me in a short arc. I barely caught it. Judah stood by the truck, whistling to himself, pretending nothing happened.

I made for the trees in the direction of the smoke, throwing the gun over my shoulder by its leather strap. Weaving our way through the brush, we made it about a mile without talking. The dawn was cool, sending unexpected shivers up and down my arms, legs, and back. A mild mist hovered six inches thick on the forest ground, making it hard to see where our feet fell, but the trees and flora weren't close enough together to make it much of a worry. What did bother me was the sense of peril that flooded my mind almost immediately upon entering the woods. This time of morning, a number of sounds could generally be heard: crickets chirping, birds talking, and squirrels making a ruckus, just to name a few. This morning, however, there wasn't a single chirp, tweet, or broken branch to break the disquieting silence that surrounded us. The feeling was like the power going out in the middle of the night; the air stops circulating, the clocks stop ticking, and the completeness of the silence is often enough to bring you out of sleep. This silence was like that, only deeper than any I had ever felt.

Judah, as usual, was the one to speak up. "How big do you think it is? It looked huge when it passed over last night."

"I wouldn't know," Johnny said, sounding a little irritated.

"Oh yeah. You were hiding underground with your in-laws. That must have been so awesome."

"They're your in-laws, too, shit for brains."

"I would have thought it would be larger considering how far away it was when we first saw it. It's like it receded into itself or compacted as it got nearer." I realized how dumb the idea sounded out loud. "Anyway, I'm more interested in seeing *what* it is. In the meantime, I'm thinking we should be as quiet as possible. The lack of movement in these woods is starting to creep me out. Think you can handle that?" My brother gave me the bird, twisting his face in a gesture of mock disdain, but kept his mouth shut. He felt it too. By the way Dean and Johnny shifted their eyes, fingers near their triggers, I'd say we all felt it. My rifle no longer hung by its strap over my shoulder, but in a fire ready position, safety thumbed halfway. We were approaching some menace we could not begin to imagine. Whatever it was that had fallen from the sky the night before was unnatural, making whatever we found when we arrived potentially very dangerous.

The trees opened into a large clearing another mile later, but it wasn't until we had cautiously broken cover that we realized it wasn't a natural clearing. The trees that had been here mere hours before were now nothing more than charred gray mounds lying this way and that like a newly poured game of Pick Up Sticks; the ground smoldered black ash. From where we stood, the opening widened to roughly three hundred yards and stretched beyond our range of vision (which wasn't very far—the ground itself, along with the flattened foliage, was sending off continuous streams of dark grey tendrils, fogging our perception as if we were peering through a soap-scum caked shower door). In the center of the clearing was a deep black rut that ran off into the distance. We couldn't see the bottom.

Giving an added fifty yard berth, we made our way along to the eastern shoulder and began following slowly. The trees on either side of the canyon had been hewn down by the object's passage, but for now at least the right edge would give us a wider walking path as well as a more gradual decline into the gorge. The eerie silence of the woods became impossibly deeper as we walked, and I found myself wondering if the absence of noise could become so thick that it could actually be grasped, much like how the Florida heat can be so thick you can almost wrap your arms around it.

As we made our way north, my unease morphed into fear. The haze of fog and smoke thickened dramatically to the point it became difficult to see further than an arm's length ahead. We moved roughly four hundred yards before we halted in our tracks.

"Do you feel that?" Dean asked.

I nodded. *I feel it alright. But what am I feeling?*

"It's like a vibration…but more…," Judah said, trying to find the right words, but couldn't finish. It *was* like a vibration but you didn't feel it shaking your body. It was in your head. A soundless buzzing.

Suddenly, a thought occurred. "It's like the high pitched sound we heard when it flew over our heads. Except it's in my head not my ears." I knew Johnny couldn't compare this feeling to the sound, but Dean and Judah could. Lights went on in their faces and I knew I was right. Whatever the feeling was, it came from the thing at the end of the canyon.

8

Though the sensation in our heads became increasingly uncomfortable we pressed onward. Visibility diminished to within a foot, and we were forced to progress onward like newly blinded men; arms feeling about for obstacles, feet tapping the ground before taking a subsequent step. It was as we traveled in this manner that we heard the twig snap. The sound came from the mutilated tree line to our rear and was quite unmistakable in the silence. Not unlike grazing antelope, we stiffened abruptly, becoming perfectly still; our breath held. For what seemed like an hour, the only sound was the click of my thumb setting back the hammer of one of my revolvers. The others held their rifles or shotguns at the ready as we hiked, already prepared for action. But nothing came. After some time, my muscles released their tension and the adrenaline pumping through my bloodstream began to subside. I felt like I had to take a dump. I turned my head toward the others and was startled to find I could only see shadowy silhouettes through the scrim of haze.

"Let's move," I whispered. "But quietly."

We inched forward for several minutes and again heard a snap, this time directly behind us, much closer.

"Back to back," I said quickly. "Judah, on me."

My brother and I stood against each other; I could barely see Johnny and Dean doing the same a few feet away from us, a few feet closer to the edge of the gorge.

"It's an animal," Dean said, though I hadn't heard another sound other than our movement. "And it's clo..."

Dean was cut off suddenly and then Johnny was yelling his name. We felt our way toward the sound of Johnny's voice as swiftly as possible, but the chasm was close and we couldn't see. I could hear Johnny's frantic shouts, his shuffling feet moving further away, closer to the edge. And then the mist lifted. Slowly at first, then more rapidly until Johnny could be easily seen lying prone on the degrading ground. He was struggling, that much we could see, but Dean was nowhere in sight. And we could no longer hear Johnny.

Judah and I rushed to the spot where Johnny lay, and were once again stopped in our tracks. The first thing to pop in my mind was Han Solo being dragged into the sarlacc's pit as Lando Calrissian tried to pull him up. Except this wasn't some sci-fi fantasy, and Dean—although quick with a come-back—was no Han Solo. Johnny held onto the butt of his rifle with one trembling hand, his grip slipping fast. The rifle's business end was a tangle of flesh and hair as Dean struggled against his assailant. And he was losing. The thing on his back—a wild canine of the likes I'd never seen—had sunk its jagged teeth into the top of Dean's shoulder, attempting to drag him into the crevasse less than a yard away. The wolf was easily as large as Jax, my brother's overgrown Labrador. Its hair, matted and mangy, ran thick along the ridge of its spine. But the thing's most striking feature was its eyes. They were insane, rimmed in red, and as they met mine the wolf released a sharp snarl that made me step back. I realized I was retreating just as it sunk its teeth into my friend's flesh and became suddenly cognizant that it meant to take Dean with it into the gorge.

Judah made the first move to rescue. Not daring to fire at the beast for fear of hitting Dean, my brother charged, dropping his guns and diving headlong over Johnny. He collided into the dog with an audible smack, undoubtedly produced from a breaking bone, but from which party remained unclear. They rolled dangerously close to the edge, Judah's hands clamped around the beast's neck, keeping its snapping jaws at arm's length. He would not be able to protect himself for long. My brother's movement jerked me from my stupor, and I acted on pure instinct. Hands trembling with the surge of adrenaline, I yanked Dean up. Blood poured from just above his collarbone and his upper back where the wolf's teeth had sunk in deeply. There was no time to investigate, however. Judah was now the main concern.

I drew and fired.

9

We nearly lost Dean seconds after my first shot blasted into the side of the beast.

It was a safe shot, careless as it had been; clean to the center torso, a shot that would have dropped any other animal of comparable size. But instead of falling off of Judah, or even staggering slightly, the thing released a howl of rage and turned its malice from Judah. Its burning eyes locked onto Dean—who had not moved since I helped him up and remained a couple feet closer to the wolf than I—and leapt. In one pounce, it closed the gap, clamped its jaws over Dean's side, and flung him like he weighed no more than a child's doll. One moment, Dean was standing dumbfounded a yard away from the cliff, and the next he was sliding past Judah and into darkness. My brother flung out his arm, grasping at Dean as he tumbled by. He caught hold of something, was yanked onto his stomach, and dragged to the mouth of the pit.

A shotgun erupted from my right, and the beast no longer stood between me and my brother. I dove into the space, landing painfully on my stomach and balls, but acquired a firm grip on my brother's legs with both hands. Two more blasts ripped through my ears as my brother came to a stop, dangling over the side from the waist. "Shu-aaaaane!" Johnny called.

I rolled onto my back, producing a cry of pain from Judah as his legs twisted in my grip, in time to see the dog bounding toward us. It pounced again, and I brought my legs up in an attempt to soften the blow. The beast landed with its heavy midsection squarely on top of my upturned boots and I kicked. With all my strength I kicked. I felt its weight shift over me and with a burning flair of pain across the side of my face it was gone.

My teeth gnashed against the vibration in my skull and the strain on my arms, both hyperextended from the awkward angle of my brother's legs, and then the weight was lifted. For a panicked moment I thought I'd dropped them both. But when I forced my eyes open, Johnny and Judah were pulling my limp friend to safety. I breathed, the smoky sky whirled above me, and I nearly joined Dean in unconsciousness.

10

The pit held only darkness. Black and unending, the thing was an empty void, inviting me in. Its summons was warm, promising, undeniable. I imagined giving in to its call, relinquishing my hold, and slipping into its embrace. But it was not a bottomless abyss I fell into; whatever was sinking into that inky hole was tangible, substantial. It reached into my mind. Icy black fingers pierced my eyes, my nose, my mouth, stretching into my heart and lungs, into the very core of my being. It gently took hold, and there came the sensation of being separated, torn in two. I pulled back, and the delicate grip tightened. I yanked again, and the force of its pull intensified, thrashing, tearing; its desire clear to me now. I released my hold, and felt myself laugh. Something flowed through me as the fingers were pried open and dispelled into the gorge from which it came.

I stood, peering over the ledge, seeing through my own eyes, hearing with my own ears. The buzzing in my head was gone, and I could think clearly for the first time since stepping into the misty field. I turned my focus to my surroundings, visible now that the fog had lifted. The impact had created what looked like a gigantic old-fashioned thermometer, the initial collision and subsequent canyon ended at the spot where the thing now swam in its pool of darkness. I could barely see the opposite end of the crevasse, and what I glimpsed made me jump.

"What is it, brother?" Judah asked.

I pointed a shaky finger across the pit at the figure I had seen standing against the backdrop of trees on the other side. But my hand faltered as well as my voice. It was no longer there. "A…man," I managed. "He was there."

"Are you sure you saw something?" Johnny asked. "It's foggier over there than a drunk's memory."

"I saw it," I said, but now I was unsure. "He didn't look…right."

"Didn't look right?" Judah said. "What's that mean?"

I shook my head. I had no idea what I meant. I just knew I had seen a figure on the other side of the canyon. And I had felt his stare even though I hadn't seen his eyes. "Never mind," I said. "Let's just get outta here."

There was no argument there.

It was slow going, taking turns carrying Dean over our shoulders, but it was also a bit easier now that we could see farther than an inch in front of us.

As we neared Johnny's truck, I stopped and said, "I think that thing is…intelligent."

Johnny flopped Dean onto the ground. He was still bleeding, but the flow had begun to subside. He'd still need stitches, though. Reminded of my own injury, I wiped some blood off the left side of my stinging face.

"I won't say you're crazy, Shane," my brother said. "Not after what just happened." He threw a glance in the direction we had come, a paranoid motion that was unusual for him. "What'd you think, Johnny?"

Johnny slung Dean over his shoulder again and we resumed our hike. It wasn't until we arrived at the truck ten minutes later that Johnny answered the question. He laid Dean into the truck's backseat and finally said, "I think something drove that four-legged sumabitch mad, that's what I think. I don't think Shane's crazy, but I'd bet my wife that wolf was."

More silence as we hopped into the cab. I lit a much needed cigarette, and my heart wrenched in my chest. Out the truck's windshield I saw a middle-aged woman standing under the forest canopy, just off the path we walked down minutes before. She faced my direction, but gave no indication she realized I had seen her. The figure—like the one I had seen earlier—gave me a start, but there came no sense of wrongness to go along with it this time. Then the truck reversed and the woman was gone. Like she had never been there.

"That vibrating in my brain came from the pit; of that much I'm sure," Judah said as Johnny put the truck into drive and we headed back to the road. "And there was nothing good about it. If the wolf was hearing the same thing, it could explain why it attacked us."

My mind circled back on the woman in the woods, but I decided to keep it to myself.

"And the mind-shake ended when Shane heaved the wolf over the edge," Johnny added.

Or did it end when I resisted its pull?

He adjusted the rear-view mirror so he could see me and raised his eyebrows. I shrugged, but said nothing, deciding to keep that to myself as well.

John returned his eyes to the road. "So if it stopped when the wolf died, it must have been meant for the wolf, not us?"

Judah, who had no real investigative abilities despite the badge he wore said, "So what does that mean?"

"It means that thing sent that wolf after us, dumbass," Johnny said.

He was half right.

We pulled into the Argo's main drive. Our families gathered outside, and I could already see the scowl on my wife's face. "Try to wake Dean up," I said.

Judah slapped him a couple times and Dean was startled back into consciousness just as Haley came up to the window.

"Wha' happened?" Dean said in a groggy voice.

"You passed out like a girl," I said. "For now, not a word about what you do happen to remember. That goes for everyone. Especially to your big mouth wife, Judah." He flicked me off. "Tell 'em we went to look for the crash site, but couldn't find it. We were in the woods and a wolf attacked us."

"That's true enough," Dean said, hauling himself into a sitting position. "Everyone knows I do everything you tell me to do."

The others nodded their agreement…of both statements.

We stepped out of the truck and into a barrage of questions. I gave them the story I came up with, and Luke rushed Dean to the house to take care of his wounds. He'd be back for me, he said.

I was sitting by the truck smoking, waiting for Luke to get done with Dean, when I noticed one of our group members was missing. "Where's Patrick?"

My dad shrugged. "Haven't seen him this morning. But one of Luke's trucks is gone." He pointed to the vacant spot where the white 1960's Ford should have been parked. "Probably left before we could talk him into staying longer."

"Hope he makes it alright," I said and took the last few drags of my cig.

A few minutes later I was in bed. A clean white bandage covered the whole left side of my face. The slice from the wolf's claw went deeper than I'd thought and required three stitches. Dean's puncture wounds took fifteen so I hadn't complained. I closed my eyes and the events of the past few hours flashed through my head. Then there were only two images: the darkness in the pit and the woman. The woman I would see again several times over the next few years; I would see the thing at the bottom of the abyss again only once.

I thought about what Judah said on the way back to the Argo. The vibrations in our heads did come from the thing in the pit. And as Johnny rightly guessed, they had driven the wolf to attack us. But Johnny was wrong when he said they weren't meant for us. The truth I felt in my gut said the mind-screw was meant to either drive us insane or put us under that thing's control. I didn't know which, but it hadn't worked. So it sent the wolf after us. And there is only one reason for it to do that: it feared us.

The thought brought little comfort as I lay in bed. I couldn't think of much of a reason it would have to fear us, but I could think of plenty of reasons to fear it. As I floated off to sleep, one of those reasons drifted off with me. The silhouette of the eerie figure beyond the abyss. And it was laughing.

The Wretched Refuse of a Teeming Shore

1

The year that followed came and went like the ebb and flow of a tide, each month worse than the one before. The country was in chaotic disarray. People's homes were abandoned or destroyed. The world's tired, poor, and tempest-tossed, all migrated inland in homeless, huddled masses, searching for a lamp beside a golden door that had been extinguished and sealed shut. Brutal skirmishes, some all-out wars, erupted in the name of property rights, a place to lay one's head. This had been mere days after the darkness had fallen to earth...when we still heard talking on the ancient ham radio Luke had brought in from the cellar. At first, the reports of localized attacks were widespread, on every channel. But the volume of voices diminished quickly, their tones morphing from terror to despair. Only static speaks from it now.

They came upon us in that time of confusion—some in search of sustenance and shelter, others on a mission of usurpation and murder. We greeted all with open arms at first, for we had the means, and more working hands meant more work being accomplished; more food being gathered and stored.

Naivety is a fine tool of learning. It's also a condition that can only be afforded once, and never if it can be avoided. But kind hearts are often ignorant, indiscriminate. Open arms leave the heart vulnerable for malicious intentions. Such was our plight. The lesson began as the roaming masses descended upon our peaceful existence. It was learned at the expense of one of our own; it ended with the loss of our innocence.

Patrick Fitzpatrick was the first of many vagrants that came to us that first year, though he only stayed a couple of days. The initial wave of refugees arrived in the twilight of what we estimated to be a chilly November evening. The days had grown shorter somehow; noticeably and increasingly darker, though not enough to hinder outside work. The moon had taken on a red hue and hung like a voyeur in the east. It had been visible since early afternoon, and I wondered more than once if it was actually the eye of some supernatural entity that had taken an interest in our daily activities. The idea gave me a shudder. It was under this moon that a group of travelers happened upon a sign on a stretch of road over which they had walked uncountable miles.

2

Haley was first to see the visitors. She had decided to use the cool fall evening to get her hands dirty and pull the weeds that threatened to overwhelm the Big House's front flower garden. In a happier time, Haley had been an avid farmer—at least as far as Farmville went. Much to her husband's amusement, she would spend time each day planting and harvesting pixilated crop-bytes for the benefit of no one but the game studio that created it. Upon settling down at the Argo, the newly named Mrs. Gerard—she had married Dean little more than a year before trading the Florida heat for the beautiful, yet technology-deficient, state of Tennessee—decided to see if her thumb could actually be green or if it was only good for moving around a mouse. As it turned out, not only did she have a knack for planting, growing, and maintaining all types of vegetation, she also discovered that it provided an enormous release from stress.

So it happened that Haley was working in the front garden when she heard soft whispering coming from behind her. I was chopping wood and flew around the side of the house when I heard her cries.

"Dean! You need to get out here!" Haley backed toward the front door and opened her mouth to yell again, but Dean was already behind her, engulfing her in his arms. Judah and I were right on his heels.

"What's wrong, Hales?" Dean asked, trying to strain his neck in order to see his wife's face. They were fastened onto something straight ahead of her, however, and when she didn't respond, he followed her gaze toward the front drive. "Oh," he whispered.

Standing behind them, I also found the objects of Haley's concern. The sun had all but set, and the moon provided a rear illumination that silhouetted a small cluster of people huddled at the point where the drive meets the front lawn. My first thought was, *Finches. They look like a bunch of finches.* The birds were abundant in the area where I grew up, and they had the habit of moving their heads in quick jerks. Up, down, left, right, up again. The shadowed outlines before us moved theirs in much the same fashion, just as jerky, not quite as quick. It creeped me out a little.

I turned to Judah to tell him to get Johnny and some guns, but he was already headed for the front door. My revolvers hung from my hips as they always did when I left the house, but I kept them in their holsters.

Judah and Johnny burst through the front door, distracting me from the group of strangers. "Stay here, Haley," Dean said, taking a rifle from Johnny as he passed. Judah marched right behind, and Dean and I had to jog to catch up to Johnny's gung-ho power-walk.

"It's really nice to see your security measures are working, Dean," Judah said as we caught up.

"Yeah, you might as well have put a sign by the road that says, 'Come on in,'" I jabbed.

Dean shook his head, frowning. "You both know I haven't gotten to the front yet. But, hey, I don't really *need* to take my time with those explosives."

Johnny halted five yards away from the strangers, almost causing the rest of us to run into him. We hadn't even discussed what to do. *Ok, John. What now, turbo?* This was nothing new, of course. Johnny, was all go-go-go; never *plan*-go-go-go. It usually worked out though, so I let him do his thing.

"Welcome to the Argo. If you come in peace, then peace you shall have."

"Very poetic," my brother said with a low chuckle.

"Just trying to be polite."

"Well I think your politeness is a little scary."

The newcomers looked at one another; the tense bird-like quality eased some. Up close, they were less like finches and more like frightened deer.

When they didn't respond, Johnny spoke for them. "Y'all lost?"

Now a thin man stepped forward. He held the hand of a very rotund woman who I took to be his wife. She wore black spandex, her stomach and rump folding just far enough over the tops of her thighs to make her resemble an overweight action-figure. Her husband wore a tattered pair of jeans and a tee shirt. They all, in fact, wore ragged clothing. They had to be cold. I could see the shivering gooseflesh even in the failing light.

"Excuse us if we appear frightened," he said softly. "But you're the first gun-toting people we've seen in months that haven't shot at us on sight. We've lost more than one person that way."

His despair appeared genuine, and it was difficult not to let sympathy overcome my caution. "We assure you, we'd rather not shoot *anyone* if we don't have to," I said. "We will have to search you, though, before taking you any further onto the property."

"Your property?" A stout man standing toward the rear asked. "How have you been able to keep such a large area of land? Without it being taken, I mean."

The four of us exchanged confused glances. "Taken?" Dean asked. We hadn't even seen anyone else for over six months, let alone been in danger of having our property stolen.

It was the thin man that spoke: "You mean *no one* has tried to wrest your land from you? How long have you been here?"

"We've been here over a year," Judah said, getting a little impatient as he tended to do. It was the nature of being a cop, I think. He liked being the one asking the questions, not the other way around. "And no one has tried to *wrest*"—fingers making quotation signs—"our land from us."

There came gasps of surprise and—*was it hope?*—at that, and they began muttering amongst themselves.

"Uh hmm," I cleared my throat to gain their attention. "In case y'all have forgotten, we do have guns, and we have yet to decide whether or not to let you come any further."

"Good use of *y'all,* bro." Judah again with his useless comments. Johnny had said it seconds before without harassment.

"Shut up and frisk them like a good pig," I grinned at him.

He snickered as he slung his rifle over his shoulder and strolled around to the rear of the group. Johnny and Dean did the same, beginning on either side. I drew both revolvers just to be safe. I didn't want any surprises, and if they *had* guns, they outnumbered us two to one.

"They're clean," Judah announced once they had felt up all eight. "Not even a knife among them." He began herding the group up the path toward the house.

"Those were already taken," the stout man who had spoken up earlier said.

"Taken by who?" I stopped.

"By the hunters," he said, receiving a sharp glare from the other man. I shivered. "Who are the hunters?"

His eyes shifted to the thin man's, then shook his head. "If you don't know already, you soon will."

3

We took them to the barn, which had more space and was warmer despite the draft that swept through the front door and out the back. There wasn't enough room for them in the house. Johnny, as always, made a roaring fire in the barn's center; the smoke billowed upward through the opening in the roof we had cut out earlier that year. As our guests warmed themselves by the fire, Anna and the girls brought out a small truckload of homemade sausages that Luke and my dad made a few nights ago. They shoved them onto the ends of slender sticks, held them over the fire, and ate in huge ravenous bites. They were starving animals and ate everything. Everyone except the chubby, stout man, that is. He refused, complaining of an upset stomach.

When they had their fill, we all reclined by the fire. I offered cigarettes (another luxury that was soon to come to an end; it becoming increasingly difficult to find them) to our guests; only a few accepted, much to our relief.

"We haven't eaten like that in a long time," the thin man, whose name was Alex, said. He was one of the few that smoked. "We thank you all beyond thanks for your hospitality."

"We give it as we can," said Luke. "But you're welcome."

"Can you tell us what's going on in other parts of the country?" Sydney asked. She sat on the ground with the kids and me.

"We haven't heard any news for almost a year," said Haley, who sat snuggled against her husband. "Actually, we haven't had any form of communication at all."

It was true. The cable went out before we arrived, Luke's radio became useless a month later, and our cell phones hadn't worked since the night Judah and Johnny encountered the highwaymen. For some reason, the house's landline refused to operate without electricity.

James, the stout man, turned to Alex who nodded. Alex was obviously the one in charge of the small group of vagrants, though by the look of annoyance on James's face at having to ask permission, that title may be up for discussion soon. James didn't strike me as one who liked being told what to do. He didn't strike me as overly intelligent either. He said, "We can only tell you what we've experienced, and I guar-un-tee you won't like much of it."

"We don't like much of what's going on as it is, buddy," Judah said. "What you have to say isn't gonna change our moods much, I don't think." He thought wrong.

"Right," James said, "'cause you're all cozy in your secluded mansion." He gestured toward the Big House with disdain.

"You're welcome to leave our 'cozy mansion' anytime you wish, fat man," Dean said, not angrily.

Judah's attitude was different. "Why not just make him leave now?" He stood up and moved toward a now frightened James. I grabbed his shirt-tail to halt his progress as he passed. My brother hardly noticed. "We feed you, and then you insult us? I should shoot you in your rotting teeth. We're secluded, as you pointed out. I don't think anyone will take notice."

He drew his gun, and Dean, Johnny, and I scrambled to get between him and James. Judah resigned himself easily enough, but I was glad the glare he threw James as he stepped back hadn't been directed toward me.

"I recommend ya'll show these boys a higher lever of respect," said Luke once things calmed down. "Or you're apt to find yourself with a few extra holes." He gazed across the fire at James. "And they stick together."

The air grew tense. It took much longer to get Judah to sit back down than it did to stop him from shooting James. It was Jordan that broke the ice. "Yeah, they stick together, but they argue like five-year-olds," she said. "No offense, Zoe."

127

"I'm six," my daughter said through her missing front teeth. It came out sounding like *sith*. Our family chuckled a bit, but the newcomers were still too frightened to find humor in much of anything.

"Actually," my dad said, "I'd say Zoe's got more brains than any of 'em."

"And she can shoot as well as any of 'em too," Sydney added with pride. Zoe turned red.

The joking around did little to alleviate the stranger's fears. Luke must have seen this for he stood up suddenly and spoke. "The point, I think is this. We are all normal everyday people that have been put in a difficult situation. The difference between us and you is that we have a place we can call home, while you're still trying to find yours. I can certainly understand anger, and even a reasonable amount of jealousy.

"But I warn you to reign in that jealousy, and direct your anger toward those more deserving of it. These boys will do anything and everything to protect their family and their home—any of us would. And I would think twice before saying or doing something else that could bring their anger down on you. If not, next time there will likely be four or more guns pointing at you."

Luke's brow, which had taken on a serious scrunch as he made his speech, relaxed, and he spoke more softly. "For now, you remain our guests, and you may remain so as long as you wish, under the condition that you do nothing to risk the safety of this family. If you wish to stay, we will help you build shelters, and in return you will work the fields." He turned to Alex, then to his followers. "What say you?"

Alex smiled. "We accept your offer with great thanks. I'm sorry our relationship began on rocky ground, but I hope we can move forward as friends." He stretched out his hand and Luke took it.

"You can sleep in the barn tonight," Luke said, and we all stood. The hour grew late. "We'll make preparations for your shelters in the morning. Sleep well."

We left them to talk amongst themselves. But I glanced back and didn't like the glower on James's face.

4

The morning came too soon, as most mornings do. In the kitchen, Syd and my children waited for me with a plate of eggs and toast. I wasn't hungry, but I ate it anyway because Syd said Zoe and Faris had made it. I didn't want to go on our morning stroll either, but again I did anyway. Mornings were about the only time we had to ourselves since everyone tended to wake up at different times. We took the opportunity, which I normally loved, to walk the paths surrounding the property as a family. Quality time, Sydney called it.

Today, though, my mind swelled with anxiety. I had a troubled feeling in my stomach that centered on James, that fat tub of goo. The feeling said we should have let Judah put one between his eyes.

We were on our favorite path that ran up and down the tree-covered hills to the southwest of the property. The trail, now covered in the orange and brown leaves of autumn, snaked its way along the southern and western edges of the main property, far enough into the woods that the vast plots of farmland were barely visible. Branching off from the southern driveway, the path wound to the west through the thick tangle of trees and turned north after about half a mile. From there, it entered a stunning wilderness kept untouched by the Argo family. Hills and valleys, streams and rock formations, never altered by human hands, stretched for miles in nearly every direction.

By the time we reached the first turn, I felt my spirits lifted. I was hard pressed to continue brooding in a place like this. Zoe and Faris busied themselves picking flowers that grew along the path. It always surprised me that there *were* any flowers to pick since Zoe was obsessed with plucking them whenever she saw them. And she wasn't at all picky. Flowers of every sort and color (as well as weeds that looked like flowers) got picked. Then they were all given to whoever happened to be closest to her at the time. I'm sure every room of the Big House was filled with withering bouquets. I know mine was.

"So what do you think of the new people, Zoe?" Sydney asked.

She didn't answer so Sydney asked again, this time more loudly.

"Don't ask me that," she said. This was her default response to something she didn't want to talk about. It usually came in reply to a question about spelling, reading, or math, but was not limited to academic queries.

"You can tell us how you feel, honey," Sydney said. "It's alright."

She hesitated for a moment. "He's creepy."

Faris nodded furiously.

"What's *creepy* about him, Zoe?" I asked. "Do you feel that way because of what happened last night with your uncle?"

Again she locked eyes with her brother as if exchanging thoughts. Finally, she said, "No, it was the twitching."

"The twitching?" Syd and I asked.

"Yeah, the twitching!" she exclaimed as Faris nodded his head enthusiastically. "Like this." She and Faris proceeded to move their heads in quick, jerky motions: front, side, front, up, other side; eyes rolling, teeth gnashing. They looked…

…*Like retarded finches,* I thought, remembering the way the strangers had acted upon their arrival yesterday evening.

"I think I would've noticed that, Zoe," my wife said, but her face became worried.

"When did you see this?" I asked.

"Last night. Through the window. Me and Faris watch the moon sometimes, and last night we saw that man down by the barn. He was sneaking off into the woods—" she and Faris began tiptoeing around in circles "—but the dogs cut him off before he got far from the barn." Now Faris was acting like a dog, silently yipping and bouncing around on all fours while Zoe pretended to throw her arms up in surprise. "Bowie and Shelby started growling and that man growled back." Zoe snarled at doggy-Faris and jerked her head sharply; Faris feigned a whimper and took a few steps back. "Jax came up from behind him and bit him on the leg—"

"Don't even think about biting your sister, boy," I said quickly as Faris circled around behind Zoe. He sat on his haunches and panted, grinning.

Zoe continued. "But the man turned and kicked Jax and he let go." She turned toward Faris, but then thought better of it. "The dogs backed up and the man ran into the woods."

Syd and I were speechless. I would have clapped for the performance my kids had just put on if it hadn't depicted something so…*off.*

"Can you tell us where he went into the woods?" I said.

"That's easy, daddy. He went in on the other side of the field across from the barn."

I considered the geography. That would have him crossing the end of the path we were on. My gut seized. I wasn't enjoying this walk anymore.

5

I went down the path alone. Sydney had taken Zoe and Faris back to the house, and was supposed to return with one of the guys. My mind spun again; my daughter's story gave new life to the bad feeling I'd woken up with. I strolled to the point where the path took its turn north before I heard Sydney and Judah talking a few yards behind. Slowing, I could hear my wife detailing what Zoe and Faris had so expertly described, and I felt sorry that Judah had to settle for Sydney's description instead of seeing it acted out by a four and six-year-old.

"You bring guns?" I asked them both when they caught up.

Judah lifted his shirt to expose his Glock .45 sitting in its police issued holster. My wife's shotgun rested on her shoulder. *Why did I find women with guns so attractive?*

"Who has the kids, Syd?"

"They're with your mom. I couldn't find anyone else. Judah just happened to step out of his room when I went in to get the shotgun."

"What do you expect to find out here?" Judah asked as we took the path north.

"I hope nothing, but my insides are telling me otherwise." I felt as if we were in a horror movie and this path was leading us to something unworldly.

We covered the next mile or so in silence, listening for anything out of place. But what we heard in return was more silence.

"It's like it was when we passed through the woods on our way to the crash site," my brother whispered. "Too quiet."

The only sounds were our footsteps on the leaf covered ground and the low hiss of our breathing. I gave my brother a severe glare, and he buttoned his lips, realizing my wife was listening. What we experienced a year ago—the wolf, the dark figure, the woman, the general unease, all of it—had not been discussed outside the group of four that experienced it. Even now, the others (my wife included) believed we could not locate the fallen object, and Dean had merely been attacked by a starving wolf.

"I saw that, Shane," Sydney said suspiciously. "What's going on?"

"Nothing, babe," I answered in a whisper. "I just want Judah to shut his fat mouth."

"You're the one having a conversation," he said. He was the epitome of a little brother.

"Both of you quit acting like children," Syd interjected, shaking her head in not-quite-disbelief. "And *both* of you shut your pie holes. This is serious."

We hiked for over a mile and were only now approaching the place Zoe described as the point James had entered the forest. "Alright, alright," I said. "Power down. We're getting close."

Sydney found a few footprints crossing the path another yard down, leading deeper into the trees. To the right, I located the entry point marked by broken undergrowth and crushed flowers. Through the tangle of trees, I could scarcely make out the open field and the red flash of the barn beyond.

"This is it," Judah said quietly. "He entered here and crossed at a sprint from the distance between these footprints."

"Yeah, that's a pretty brilliant theory, bro," I said. "Do you think he went into the woods on the other side, too? Or do you reckon he just floated off into the night?"

He gave me a closed-lipped smile and scraped the tips of his fingernails under his furry chin.

"Do you smell that?" Sydney said, sniffing the air and moving toward the west side of the trail. She always had a better sense of smell than I did, and my brother had a deviated septum caused by several fight-related broken noses, so it was no surprise when we both shook our heads in the negative.

"It smells rotten, and it's coming from over there." She gestured in the direction James's footprints led.

We made our way as silently as possible through the thick brush, and I had to wonder how a pudgy moron managed to fly through here with what appeared to be gracefulness. The prints we were able to make out were still a decent distance apart, meaning James had been moving at an incredible pace—incredible because of his body mass as well as the thickness of the forest. And we could find no prints leading out of the woods. Whatever he was doing, he certainly didn't return to the barn the same way he left.

The stench became stronger the deeper we ventured through the trees, and it wasn't long before my brother was vomiting uncontrollably, which in turn resulted in me emptying my stomach contents shortly after. Sydney rolled her eyes, unaffected by the horrific reek that now engulfed us. She did, however, cover her nose and mouth with the collar of her shirt. Judah and I mimicked.

We came to a small, carved out glen a few minutes later. Eyes watering from the stench, I cautiously stepped out from the trees, approaching what appeared to be a large puddle of blood bubbling in the center of the opening.

"That's a lot of gore," Judah said, his voice muffled through his thick sweatshirt.

I had to agree, though there was no sign of its source. We searched the perimeter of the hollow for any sign of a carcass, but found nothing.

"So where's the body?" Sydney asked through her teeth. The smell was starting to get to her now.

Judah twirled slowly and said, "Maybe there isn't a body."

"What do you mean?" I asked. "Like whatever did this ate everything? Bone and all?"

He shrugged. "I don't—What the…?" He wiped his hand at the nape of his neck. "Something just dripped on me."

I didn't wait to see the blood on his hand. I instantly looked up, expecting to see an animal hanging from the branches above. What I saw made my stomach heave. My attempt to speak came out as a garbled gasp, but Sydney and Judah followed my eyes.

A mutilated body hung above, lashed to the overhanging branches by strips of its own skin. It was human, but just barely; its flesh had been cruelly peeled from the fat and muscle beneath to reveal shredded innards and entrails. The head, the only remnant of the victim's humanity, had been severed completely and impaled upon a sharp branch high above the ravaged carcass.

Judah started to retch. I was too shocked to vomit, as was Sydney who stared at the figure above us with tear-filled eyes.

There was movement across the clearing. I squinted and made out a dark female figure that disappeared as soon as my eyes locked on.

"Judah," I said quietly once he had composed himself. "Judah, go find Dean and Johnny. Secure the Argo. And take Sydney."

"You're not…staying here alone, Shane," my brother protested through another full-bodied gag.

"Go, Judah," I said sternly. "Take Sydney and make sure the kids are safe. There's something I have to do. Lock down every one of those strangers in the barn."

He stood there a moment, weighing what I had said. Without another word he prodded Sydney on the arm and they headed to the farm.

When they were gone, I moved to the other side of the clearing and combed the trees where I'd seen the old woman. I knew irrefutably it was the same woman I saw in the forest a year earlier as we fled the crash site and the insane wolf.

I searched everywhere, but found no sign of her. Could it have been my imagination? I was starting to think it was, but as I slumped back, all doubt washed away like a flash flood. The woman stood with her back to me at the edge of the bloody puddle, gazing at the body overhead.

6

She appeared to be in her mid-sixties, hair a tangled, white weave that fell just below her shoulder blades. She stood with a small hunch, and when she turned, I beheld a face webbed with deep crags, far past the point of mere wrinkles. Still her eyes gleamed bright silver, and she smiled in a way that made me think she had once been remarkably beautiful.

I hesitated before stepping into the clearing. This person before me was half my size and many years past her prime, but I became suddenly very aware that I was alone. My friends would not likely hear my calls for help.

"Hello, Shane," she said sardonically, like I was an old acquaintance that's been avoiding her. The voice creaked, but again the remnant of youth lingered, and I could sense no ill intentions.

"Hello…whoever you are," I said. "What are you doing here?"

"You may call me Sara, and I am here, against my calling—as well as my good judgment—to aid you."

"Aid me? Seriously? How?" I was beginning to believe she was a tad on the side of crazy. After all, she was roaming about the forest, hanging around dead bodies; not to mention the smell didn't even seem to affect her. If she wasn't as old as my grandmother—hell, my great grandmother—I would have been inclined to suspect she had mutilated that body.

"How indeed," she said and laughed. It was a disturbing, yet pleasant sound, and would have set me off guard had I not been determined to keep it up. "Perhaps instead, you should ask how I have aided you already."

Her smile disappeared, and I suddenly felt an overwhelming power hidden within her. "How have you helped me already?" I asked more cautiously.

"An earnest question, but not nearly as significant as the why. You must be more prudent with your questioning, for we have little time before you must return to your brothers. But since I did lead you to ask, it was I who lifted the fog the day you were set upon by the wolf. My first act of intervention after a millennia of scrutiny, and I must say, it felt glorious to utilize my gifts for something other than observation."

I took a step back. "What do you mean you *lifted the fog*?"

"Another useless question," Sara said with a hint of impatience. "Things are changing swiftly, Shane McCall, and it would behoove you to begin accepting the things you see as impossible, rather than wasting time analyzing them." Here she glanced briefly at the carcass above us. "What you see is only a taste of the evil that has taken a foothold in your world. So I shall answer the question you should have asked. I helped you and your brothers because it is imperative you survive what is coming. Getting killed by a wild animal would hardly have been beneficial."

A trillion questions swarmed my mind, many more than I had time to ask. According to this woman who called herself Sara, a great evil was here. An evil we must survive. Only one question seemed pertinent now. "What must I do?"

She smiled. "You are catching the drift, I think is the phrase you use these days. What you *must* do, what you *must not fail* to do, is protect your offspring. Your son is of great importance. Zoe will be a great asset to him, but it is absolutely essential that Faris lives. Upon his shoulders the fate of humanity rests. And so it rests on yours as well. If he is lost, all hope is lost with him."

This revelation was not at all what I'd anticipated. I expected Sara to give me a task, something that would ensure our safety. Instead she gave me a vague direction that I thought I was already following.

"I would die before I let anything happen to my children."

"And you almost certainly shall, Shane McCall. The chances of your survival are slim."

"Oh that helps. Can we stop speaking in riddles and start

speaking plain? What is coming?"

Her smile faltered. "What comes is an ancient darkness capable of destroying your world. It has already begun and it will not stop until every living thing on this planet is either dead or under its control."

It was my turn to show some impatience. "I can see something has begun. What happened here? I came to find a man named James and I find this instead. What's going on?"

"What you sought after and what you have found are one in the same." Her eyes flashed again to the body in the trees, the pity—or was it condescension?—plain on her face.

"This is James?" I said. "What happened to him?"

"The answer to that, Shane McCall, lies with his people, those you so graciously allowed into your haven. Do be careful." Her head turned sharply in the direction of the Argo and she made to retreat into the forest. "Your brothers come. I must go."

"Wait," I called after her. "What are you?"

When she reached the trees, she stopped and said, "What I am does not concern you for the time being. Beware strangers at your door. This is my final warning. Be brave, Shane McCall."

Then she was gone, and Johnny and Dean were crashing through the trees.

"Who were you talking to?" Dean asked, panting, then threw his arm over his nose and mouth. "Mother of God, what is that smell?" Dean began heaving almost at once, but Johnny only stood staring at the sickening display in the trees.

"What the hell?" Johnny said.

"That would be our friend James," I said, and then panicked. "If you're here, who's guarding the Argo?"

7

"So that woman was the same one you saw a year ago?" Dean asked as we sprinted over the already trampled underbrush. I could strangle my brother for letting them come out here. I only hoped we weren't too late.

"The same." I breathed heavy, the decision to quit smoking once again at the forefront of my thoughts. I had recounted my conversation with

Sara while we bounded back to the Argo. Johnny wanted to cut James down and bury him before we left, something we'd certainly need to do eventually, but my urgency to get back pressed too strong. I wasn't looking forward to that gruesome task.

"And she said James's people did this to him?" Dean asked before stumbling over an exposed root. I pulled him to his feet as Johnny came up beside us.

"She said the *answer* lies with his people. Not that his people did it." But I knew they probably had, or at least one of them. "Did Judah and Sydney mention what we found out there?"

They both shook their heads, and I gave a sigh of relief. It would be easier to investigate if no one knew we had found a body.

"Right," Johnny said as we resumed our pace. "So how do we find out who done it?"

"Find the one with the dirty fingernails," Dean said.

When we arrived on the Argo main grounds, I immediately went in search of my kids, and found them in the one place I least wanted them to be: in the barn with the finches. At least Sydney, Judah, Luke, and my dad were with them. My mom, Anna, and the other girls made their way from the house with a plateful of sandwiches.

"Zoe, Faris," I said in a tone that I hoped didn't sound stressed. "Go with your Grammy back to the house." My mom must have heard it, though, because she led the kids away without her usual tirade of questions.

"Anyone seen James lately?" I said to the newcomers once my children were out of sight. They looked more like finches than ever— turning this way and that, searching for an answer, but not receiving one—as my brother, Dean, and Johnny flanked them on each side and the rear, hands on their guns. My last intention was to spur more violence, but if it came to that I would not hesitate.

"No one?" I said incredulously. "No one has seen James?" I paused for effect, then continued. "Because I've seen James. My brothers and my wife have seen James. And judging from his…condition…it stands to reason that *someone else* has seen him as well."

They continued to gawk at one another, frightened and confused. Except Alex stared right at me. The hair on the back of my neck stood on end, but I restrained the shiver.

"Alex," I said in a conversational tone. "Have you seen James?"

He continued his stare, emotionless. The edge of his mouth twitched once, twice, and he grinned so that his teeth were bared. I drew my gun and held it at my side, tapping the barrel against my thigh, returning the stare and giving him a grin of my own.

"What're you doing, Shane?" Luke stepped forward, concerned at the direction this was going.

"Stand back, Mr. Argo." My eyes remained on Alex, and his on me. "James is dead, and someone sitting here killed him. Mutilated him. Personally, I'm leaning toward Alex here."

Luke retreated a step, and I glanced at him for a fraction of a second. It was all the time Alex needed. He leapt to his feet, threw Judah against the side of the barn, and twisted around Luke in a flashing movement I wouldn't have thought possible. *It would behoove you to begin accepting the things you see as impossible.* Sara's words came back to me and I suddenly understood.

Not human. Like the wolf. The hunters.

As the girls screamed, Alex backed away toward the rear of the barn where a small door would lead him onto the grounds and into the forest. Using Luke as a shield he crept further from us, snarling, his eyes never leaving mine, but keeping his hostage between himself and those with guns. Blood ran in thick streams from his nose and ears, the corners of his eyes.

When he reached the back door, he kicked it open and stepped out, positioning Luke in the doorway. He let out a familiar shriek and reached his hand around Luke's face. With a powerful snap he separated Luke's head from his body.

Screams and gunshots filled the confines of the barn, deafening all who were present. The shocked faces of Anna, Devon, and Jordan were enough to bring me to my knees.

What just happened? The thought raced through my mind as other less productive thoughts attempted to take prominence. *This is my fault. I should have cleared the barn before I started questioning them. I thought* more *people would be safer.*

"Did anyone hit him?" Johnny's voice brought me back to the matter at hand.

"I don't know," Judah said.

"I didn't even shoot," said Dean in a low voice.

"Get the girls out of here," I yelled to my father over the chaos.

They were just beginning to move toward the twins when Haley's voice rose above everything else. *"Oh Shiiit!"*

8

All eyes turned in the direction she pointed. Blood spewed from the noses, ears, and eyes of the strangers. They twitched awkwardly, sniffing the air in short gurgles as the blood was sucked back the way it had come. The sniffing ceased a second later when they found what they were hunting for.

I realized their target a split second later and drew my other revolver. *"Kill them all!"* I bellowed, pulling the triggers. Two of the…whatever they were…stumbled sideways from the force of the slugs, but were otherwise unhindered as they joined the dozen others in their scramble toward Luke's decapitated body. Gunshots again filled the barn. I saw one go down to my right, but the others kept moving despite being shot several times each.

"Aim for the head!" Judah's voice was barely audible above the guns' reports, but we heard enough.

One by one the others went down, but not before they had reached Luke's body and began devouring it. Shreds of flesh flew in every direction as the creatures tore into him, oblivious that they were being gunned down. Systematically we took them out; closest first, then those behind as we moved nearer the back of the barn. The last one came up from his meal realizing he was now alone, and pounced at Dean who stood closest. Every last bullet was emptied into the thing and it dropped dead at Dean's feet.

Utter silence held sway as our adrenaline and shock wore off. I felt sick, and I rushed out of the barn in desperate need of fresh air. Judah came up beside me, covering my back as I recovered.

"We need to find Alex," he said.

I nodded and we paced around to the back of the barn where my dad and Haley covered Luke's remains with a dirty tarp. Johnny and Dean joined us at the edge of the grounds, staring out into the trees.

"He's bleeding from every hole," I said, pointing at a splattered trail of dark blood leading into the forest. "We should be able to track him."

The blood trail led past the place where James hung and off to

139

the northwest. We all had the same idea where he was headed because we had all been there a year prior. If we continued in this direction, there was no doubt it would lead directly to the pit.

An eerie gloominess hung around the trees as we struggled to follow the spots of blood that were becoming more and more sparse. They finally disappeared altogether an hour later. We searched to no avail for another hour, but we knew where he was headed. It would take another couple hours to get to the canyon. By then it would be dark, and no one had to voice their objections to being in that place after nightfall. To fuel our unease, soft rustlings began in the brush around us, keeping a good distance, but closing in on our flanks.

"I think it's time we got out of these woods," Judah said below his breath.

As if in response, a chorus of ear-splitting wails rose from the darkness; a chilling sound, somewhere between the cry of a large bird of prey and a child's high-pitched scream.

We high-tailed it. Alex was far from the only thing in these woods. The screeching faded off into the distance as we hurdled our way back to the Argo, allowing us some relief that we weren't being pursued.

My dad had already buried Luke in the chapel cemetery by the time we returned. He was slumped over the shovel, clearly exhausted.

"Wanted to get Luke out of sight of the kids sooner than later," he said.

It was pitch black, much darker than usual. I scanned the sky, but could not make out a single star. The moon appeared very large, but its light did little to alleviate the suffocating darkness that had fallen over us.

"James will have to hang out in the woods till tomorrow," I said. "There's no way I'm going back out there tonight." *And there's no way I'm dragging what's left of him through the yard.*

Syd and Haley lit a few lamps as the family gathered around Luke's grave, and my father said a few words. My mother comforted Anna as she sobbed; my brother and Johnny wrapped their grieving wives in their arms; and I stood holding Sydney and Zoe's hands, unable to banish the certainty that this was all my fault.

Twitching

1

I was target shooting with Zoe on the West Hill when we heard the bell. More than a year had passed since we lost Luke, and we all felt the impact. Heeding Sara's advice, strangers were forbidden on the property. Certain measures had been taken to secure the Argo, and some of them were about to come in extremely handy.

We kept to the main grounds as much as possible, the threat brought on by Alex and his finches ever present in our minds. Alex kept his distance following his escape, but he wasn't the only thing roaming the forests that bordered the Argo. Shrieks could be heard in the dark. Sometimes only a few from far off. More often it would be a chorus that sounded much closer. Still other times the forest would be completely silent. That was somehow worse. Faris always seemed to hear them whether anyone else did or not. His hands would go to his ears nightly, beginning an hour or so after dusk, and Sydney and I began to take turns rocking him to sleep.

Dean spent the year tightening security, which meant it was hazardous to enter the woods in most places for fear of being blown up by jerry-rigged landmines, or falling into deep pits that never caught anything but the occasional deer or rodent. The paths and trails he left alone, and since I insisted on going to the hill with my kids, Dean created a certain route that bypassed the traps.

The hill rose a mile and a quarter southwest of the Big House; an easy walk out, difficult climb up, but altogether perfect vantage to hone one's aim. Its ridge stretched 400 yards to the north before dropping off into a gully that wrapped itself three quarters of the way back around the hill's eastern side and then on to the south. This, along with its steep slope, contributed to the West Hill's cumbersome climb, but after two years of trekking back and forth to practice with various guns and hunt whatever deer and hog remained, we all but conquered the exhaustion that had plagued us in the first year. Of course, Zoe never seemed to tire.

My daughter had become nearly proficient with her .22 caliber rifle thanks to our weekly trips to the hill. Tuesdays were one of my two favorite days of the week. At least I thought it was Tuesday. We left the calendar tracking to Haley a year and a half ago when the power died permanently. I know she missed days because the chalkboard in the kitchen tallied the same count two days in a row on more than one occasion. She remembered most of the time though, and since one day was basically the same as the next, it wasn't a catastrophe when she forgot.

Most days followed the same monotonous routine. But the days I *thought* were Tuesday and Friday were special. Tuesdays I practiced shooting with my daughter; Fridays I shot with my son. Now the warning clanged from the chapel bell tower, and Zoe hadn't even gone through a quarter box of ammo.

"Lying prone will give you the most accuracy with your shot," I told Zoe, "but you hit the target at 100 yards every time in that position." She grinned, her resemblance to her daddy unmistakable. "Actually, you hit the target in every position except for standing, but that's just because the gun's too heavy for you to hold long enough to aim."

The seven-year-old beamed at me. "So what now, Daddy?" She opened the action and popped out the last cartridge, catching it with a fluid grace, then quickly slid the bolt back into place and flipped the safety on. It was my turn to beam. Heaven help the fool who thought of her as just a cute little girl.

The bell tolled six times. Fear set in with the realization of what it meant. "I think it might be time to see if you can shoot something other than targets," I whispered.

My daughter made no reply. From this height, the orange roof of the Big House peeped through the dense forest of white oak, maple, and pine, but I was more interested in what was happening to the south of the mansion.

Situated in the center of the Argo's property, the rickety, yet tall chapel served as our extended family's lookout tower. The bell was an added bonus, and the one manning it was supposed to ring it twice every twenty seconds for a threat coming from the north, three times to the northeast, four times to the east, and so on around the compass. Six lay to the south of the Big House where the Argo's main entrance wound its way through the trees.

I could make out the place where the forest ended and the mansion's front yard began. Another advantage of being on the West Hill: you could see at least part of everything north, south, and west of the Big House. No movement there yet, at least from any possible threat. My family would be going through their long practiced and perfected routines, taking up their defensive positions. This wasn't our first confrontation, but it was the first one we were prepared for. We learned from our mistakes.

Things happened quickly from there. To my right, Zoe locked and loaded her rifle with eerie speed, bringing my attention back to our own surroundings. She sat on her butt, using her knees as rests for her elbows as she sighted in at something I couldn't see. I knew something, or someone, was there though. I knew it was there because Zoe knew it was there. Her uncanny ability to tune into movement and sound at her age was the reason she had already killed twice as many deer as I had in all my thirty years. She could keep still as a statue, and be aware of everything around her at the same time, a trait she certainly didn't inherit from me. I was way too fidgety.

Whatever or whoever lurked out there had better come in peace, or they were about to get their head blown off—if they didn't trigger an explosion first.

2

At first, I considered standing our ground. That changed when the rustling and cracking started beyond the tree line. Moving fast…and there were a lot of them. Too many to handle on our own.

"Run, Zoe," I whispered. She didn't budge, and I had to raise my voice in order to penetrate her focus. *"Zoe, run. Now!"*

My command registered and she bolted for the trail as several sets of orange orbs appeared through the trees. A few strides and I was running at my daughter's side. The first explosion came a second later, nearly knocking us to the ground, but I kept my feet, grabbing Zoe's arm to help her keep hers. We were moving too slow.

I hauled her over my shoulder, and her rifle banged painfully into my spine. I hissed and risked a glance behind us. They poured through the trees, at least ten of them, emaciated and crazed. I would have thought them animals if they weren't tearing after us on two legs. And they only tripped one Claymore. I wondered how many more there would've been if not for Luke's illegal stash of explosives.

We had to make it to the trail far enough ahead of them or we'd get caught up in any explosions they'd set off once they made it across the clearing. I forced my legs to pick up the pace and took the first few yards down the east side of the hill in one leap. The weight on my upper body pulled me forward, my abs and lower back screaming as I strained to keep balance.

The narrow path swerved like a snake through the mine cluttered woods. Unlike the Claymores set on the far side of the hill, there was no danger of setting these off by mere proximity, but a single errant step off the trail could mean the end of both of us. We made it around the second bend when the next explosion shook the trees. Another followed, this one much closer, and chunks of pale blue debris rained down on us.

I puffed along the winding trail, fully aware our pursuers followed in a straight line. I heard their snarls escalate into ear-splitting screeches as they closed in around us. My daughter's screams to hurry buzzed like a gnat in my ear compared to the intensity of the clamor at my back.

The detonation of several more mines drowned out the wails, prodding me forward. I could see the opening in the trees ahead and the smooth grass of the Argo. The chapel beckoned like a guardian angel, guiding us to safety from its lofty height. The forest erupted as I hurdled onto the treeless expanse of the main property, ears ringing painfully from the blasts. I spun around as a man tumbled through the space I'd just occupied, and I sent a bullet through his forehead. His body fell at my feet.

I swung Zoe from my shoulder and thrust her in the direction of the chapel. *"Get in the tower,"* I shouted, the words barely registering through my blaring ears. I hadn't even heard my gun's report. My daughter hesitated, backed away, and then ran with all her might for the white building.

144

I drew my other revolver and waited for them to come.

3

"I got Zoe," my dad hailed when I approached the tower. "Get to the front." I struggled to make out what he said, glad my hearing had returned enough to decipher most of it.

I'd taken down two more of the pale people after my daughter's retreat, the rest disintegrated in the chain reaction that had leveled half the forest. I reloaded as I ran, nervous about what I would find at the front entrance. I heard no other explosions, but that didn't mean much considering my temporary deafness.

What I encountered as I barreled around the house was the farthest thing from what I'd expected. Two Hummers parked at the foot of the lawn, less than a yard from the end of the tree-lined driveway, and eight soldiers in army fatigues stood before them, armed with assault rifles. Judah, Johnny, and Dean approached them, guns drawn, their faces grim.

I made to join them, panting, the energy I'd exerted running for my life increasingly apparent, when Johnny suddenly lunged for the closest man in the opposing group, his fist plowing into the middle of his face. I darted to my brother's side as the man crumbled under the impact, unconscious.

His men, and one woman, took a step back, raising their weapons.

"We're not try'n ta pick a fight, lads…an' lass," Dean said. "Leave now an' there'll be no bloodshed." He winked at the woman. "Ye can stay if ye wish, lass. Yer a looker ya are."

I cringed. *Is he really doing his William Wallace impression?*

The woman blushed—at least Dean would swear she did later—before another man took control of the troops. He wore a hard face under his helmet, clearly not amused by Dean's ultimatum. A series of parallel scars ran from his forehead and over the bridge of his nose, like a large cat had taken a swipe at him. "Shut your mouth," he growled. "You're outnumbered at least two to one. Either drop the weapons or we open fire."

Judah laughed, bringing confusion to the man's face, but didn't so much as lower his gun. "He thinks we're outnumbered," he said. "I love to tell you this, you arrogant prick, but not only are we not outnumbered, but we have you surrounded." He raised his voice loudly when he said the last four words. Immediately, the sound of several actions pumped, levered, slid, and cocked to life from the cover of trees to the sides and rear of the cluster of troops.

The expressions on their faces were priceless. Like a bunch of bullies confronted by an overwhelming army of nerds. At least my brothers remembered *most* of the plan. Although it definitely didn't include decking an armed man or using ridiculous accents to hit on equally armed woman.

Scarface clenched his teeth and peered at us through squinted eyes. The rest of our family, including Faris with a .22 caliber handgun, had set an ambush, cutting off their means of retreat. The man's head shuddered and released a *kaghk!* from the back of his throat.

"As you can see," my brother said, lowering his voice to a threatening level, "you're the ones who are outnumbered."

But the guy with the scars, along with half of his men (and the woman), no longer listened. Their heads jerked and twitched like meth addicts with serious cases of withdrawal. It wasn't unintelligent movement, however. Their focus was sketchy, unorganized, but it was *searching*. They scanned the trees to the sides and rear.

"Uh, you guys have itchy assholes or something?" Johnny said, not really expecting a response. We had all seen behavior like that before. The end result had been the death of his father-in-law.

He got one though. In unison, the twitching men snapped their heads forward from whatever uncomfortable angle they were in. They glared at us with such venom, I felt my insides tremble. I was exhausted, barely able to hold my revolvers, but Judah, Dean, and Johnny leveled their rifles at three of the enraged troops.

"You have five seconds to drop your weapons, remove your vests, and walk away," Judah said. "If I get to five, we're opening fire and I promise you, no matter how much body armor you freaks have on, not one of you will survive." He paused to let it sink in for a split second and began the count loudly enough for those in the forest to hear. "One!"

No movement.

"Two!"

Nothing.

"Three!"

Not a sound. Not a motion.

"Four!"

Still nothing.

"Fi—"

The scarred man released a growl and threw down his rifle. His face twisted like a rabid animal. I could actually feel the heat radiating off him. The vest came off next, then his side arm. The rest copied, strewing body armor and M-16's on the lawn. He pointed to their unconscious commander and two men took hold of his legs and dragged him down the drive. He stood scowling at the four men who had stood up to him, and said, "You've done well today." It was not the same voice that he spoke with earlier. This voice was raspy, unsettling. "But you have things you can no longer be allowed to keep." As he said this, he scanned the tree line a final time. "See you soon."

He gave a half-assed salute, spun on his heels, and marched off to join the others. They were about to climb into their vehicles when I heard a voice.

It said, "Wait."

4

The voice was mine. It just came out, as if something else directed my tongue…something within me. I'd heard the stranger's final speech, known what it meant, but it wasn't until now, now that I'd called him back, told them to wait, that it sunk into my bones, stirred through my nerves, ground at my intestines, my bowels, my heart.

The man halted, one leg propped upon the Humvee's running board. His head swiveled deliberately on his thick neck, and faced me, his mouth a lipless white line. He said nothing, but his eyes said everything I needed to know. In that instant I heard the screeching of creatures streaking through the trees, my daughter's screams as they swept down on us. I heard Luke Argo's stunted inhale as his head was torn from his shoulders, the shocked cries from Devon and Jordan as he slid to the floor, the anguished sobs of Anna as the dirt buried his mangled body. I heard the wolf snarling, Johnny shouting Dean's name through the mist, the moaning agony of the masked man I'd shot through the leg, the shrieking of the maniac that bit me on my front lawn. I heard my brother's gasp as the air finally filled his lungs and my best friend's parents wail as Sean's bloated body was dragged to shore. I heard a child's soothing chant penetrate a nightmarish vision. I heard my son's silence.

 In that moment, in the time it took for the man to lower his boot from the steel step-bar to the grass, I glimpsed the divergence of a path. One way rolled easy, and smooth, curving out of sight. And I saw another, the course I was meant to follow; uneven, ragged, and steep. Straight. They approached with slow steps as I placed my foot on a rocky path of my own.

5

"You're not going anywhere," I said. My gun raised, firm in a hand that only seconds ago could barely bare its weight, and I squeezed. The man before me, he who swore to return to finish what we had prevented, fell to the earth dead. My revolvers swept over the others as they backed away, their armor and weapons no longer protecting them, and I pulled the triggers until they clicked empty. I hobbled to the Hummer where the man Johnny had knocked out had been placed. I yanked him out by his leg, loaded a single bullet, and sent it into his skull.

Before me, seven men and one woman lay in scattered disarray, slain by my hands. I returned the smoking guns to their homes on my hips and knelt to one knee. My brother's voice and those of my friends faded to faint mutterings beneath the beat of my heart.

I rose and staggered, suddenly dizzy. Six hands steadied me, pulled me from the mess I'd created, and then I was buried in a cloud of red hair.

6

"A distraction," Judah said, nudging at the corpse of one of the creatures with the toe of his boot.

It was difficult to withdrawal from my wife's embrace; the scent of her skin so intoxicating I hardly remembered moving to the west side of the property. Besides my wife and brothers, the rest of our family gave me a wide berth. I didn't blame them.

"We weren't meant to survive this onslaught," I muttered, running a hand through my hair. "The soldiers kept us busy while these things swarmed from our flank. If it weren't for the mines…"

"Damn, I wish I could've seen that," said Dean. "How many were there?"

"Around twenty, I think." I was beginning to feel more like myself. Talking helped. "The traps got all but three."

"Damn, I wish I could've seen it," Dean said again, his voice nasally and slightly more somber.

"You would have gotten guts in your hair," I said. Only then did I notice the greasy blotches covering my clothes. Most of it was dried, but my shirt stuck to my skin like I'd been in a wet tee shirt contest; a putrid reek wafting off me.

Maybe that's why they're keeping their distance.

"There's no blood," said Sydney, brushing something from the middle of my back.

I checked my shirt and jeans. She was right. Not a single drop of blood.

I hunkered beside one of the corpses and pressed a finger to its upper arm. "It's soft…like memory foam." I removed my finger and the dimple I made rose slowly.

"There's no density," I said. "And you can almost see through the skin. All the blood's been drained."

"Don't surprise me," Judah said. "Remember how the blood ejaculated out of them people in the barn?"

"What's jakelated?" Zoe said, and my wife about slapped my brother.

"It means to shoot out, Zoe," said Syd.

"I jakelated out of my nose yesterday," my daughter said, "when I was drinking milk and laughed."

I couldn't restrain my smile. The others laughed openly, and Zoe got a confused look on her face. "What's funny?" she said.

"Nothing, goofball," I said. "Don't use that word anymore."

"Can I touch it?" she asked.

I shook my head, not wanting her anywhere near those things.

She crossed her arms and stomped off to where Faris stood with my mom and dad, her forehead scrunched and lips pursed like a duck.

The mood lightened by Zoe's ignorance, but now the tension returned somewhat. Dean and Johnny began prodding the corpse with their fingertips, as I had done, gawking as the skin sluggishly returned to its original form.

"How is this even possible?" Judah said, joining the other two beside the body.

I remembered what Sara had said in the woods where we found James hanging from the tree. *It would behoove you to begin accepting the things you see as impossible.*

"I'm not sure, brother," I said, "but I think things are about to get a lot worse."

I took Zoe and Faris by the hand and led the way back to the house, my footfalls coming to rest upon a surface that seemed rougher and steeper. But it stretched straight as an arrow.

Missing

1

A week went by without incident, though the chapel tower remained occupied with round-the-clock lookouts. Our unease grew with each passing day, the bell expected to toll at any moment. Guns, bows, and equipment stayed loaded and on standby, and emergency responses were rehearsed three times daily.

By all reasonable means, we were prepared for the retaliation we knew was coming. But nothing could prepare us for Anna going missing.

Her behavior—her demeanor—had begun to spiral slowly downward in the year following her husband's murder, and the charming and kind woman I had known for close to three years now took to skulking aimlessly around the grounds with little or no purpose besides accumulating flowers and weeds to be placed on Luke Argo's grave. She seemed to favor no flower in particular, but rather randomly picked things from the garden and about the grounds regardless of their often undesirable appearance. This bothered Haley less than the rest of us, probably because Anna regularly cleared her garden of weeds and thorns.

Anna's behavior became commonplace over the course of several months, but when she disappeared three days after the military confrontation, panic spread like wildfire through the Argo. Every inch of the compound was searched; Jordan and Devon slept less than an hour in the two days that followed, and then only because they passed out from sheer exhaustion. The fear of attack was put on the back burner as we scoured the forest, and it wasn't until twilight had fallen on the third evening that we picked up on a trail.

Johnny discovered a sparsely placed line of flowers leading off into the woods to the northwest. The direction was well known to us by then, and no one felt eager to follow.

"My mom is in there," Jordan stated after we had laid out our fears of entering the woods that we were now sure harbored shrieking ghouls. We each waited for someone else to respond.

"If it was one of us, you'd be in there in a second," Devon exclaimed, exasperated. She moved to stand with her sister, her big eyes pleading.

I sighed. "No one said we weren't going in. We're just saying it's not safe in there. You didn't hear the screeching."

Sorrow stared back at me, and I resigned.

"Okay, one person goes with me," I said. "Who's it gonna be?"

After a second, Dean stepped forward. "I'll go," he said. "Judah and Johnny should stay with their wives."

I nodded. "After you, then," I said with a small bow.

"Uh, how 'bout no," Dean replied. "This was your decision."

I grinned and led the way into the steadily darkening forest.

2

My tracking skills were much better than they'd been upon first arriving at the Argo, thanks to Luke's expertise and patience. Two and a half years ago, I never would have been able to follow Anna's trail in the middle of the afternoon let alone in the dark. The flowers leading through the trees were sporadic at best, like they'd merely fallen from her grip rather than being purposefully dropped, and the idea that Anna did not intend for us to follow her became steadily more apparent.

She took almost the exact route James had taken a year before, and when Dean and I passed the weather-smoothed mound that we had buried him under, a severe shudder broke my skin out in gooseflesh from my head to my toes. I could still smell the stench of his mangled corpse clinging to the trees.

A half hour later, the darkness around us grew alive with faint rustlings, and we drew our guns, ready to sprint back at the first shriek. We traveled at least two miles into the forest when a shadowy figure appeared before us. I halted Dean, who covered our rear with his shotgun, and pointed into the darkness. The wood screamed silence. I tapped my ear, motioning for Dean to listen. The rustling had ceased. I almost wished it hadn't.

The figure remained, as still as a statue, but before we crept more than ten feet closer it darted to the left and out of sight.

Certain we had been seen, uncertain of what had seen us, we moved to the spot the figure had stood moments before. A branch broke in the direction the figure had gone, so we made our way after it as my stomach made its way into my throat. I couldn't see a thing, and there was no way I was turning my flashlight on. We slinked a few yards further and a second branch broke behind us. I whirled around and caught a glimpse of a shadowy shape to my right. Leaves rustled to my left.

Fear drenched me like a wave. This continued for what seemed like an eternity. We were getting turned around, which wouldn't have been a problem in a different situation, but I didn't think we'd have the opportunity to consult the compass in my pocket if we had to make a quick escape.

Something snapped behind us, this time much closer than the others. Again we found nothing. I heard Dean let out his breath, and I turned to put my back against his.

"Ohgoodgod," I gasped, nearly firing my gun. Anna stood less than five feet from me, stark naked and filthy. Blood leaked from her nostrils and ears in thin rivulets, her chest rose and fell in rapid heaves.

"Mrs. Argo?" I said. Dean came to my side, gawking in disbelief. "Anna? Are you alright?"

Her eyes met mine, but nothing was there; only a blank, emotionless stare.

"She's bleeding like Alex and the others," Dean whispered.

I nodded, risking a step forward. She remained still, her eyes rimmed in red.

"We're taking you back to the house, Anna," I said, as calm as I could manage. "We'll get you cleaned up."

I took another step and something cracked under my foot. She straightened to full height, lifted her gaze to the sky and let out a cry that nearly deafened us. Thinking only that Anna's wail would arouse whatever else was in the forest, I dashed forward and clubbed her in the head with the butt of my gun. The sound ceased abruptly and Anna collapsed to the ground.

3

I knelt down, grabbed her beneath the armpits and hauled her up, lugged her over my shoulder, and tried not to dwell on the naked ass of Devon and Jordan's mother bouncing mere centimeters from my face.

Shrill shrieks lit up the forest to our right and rear, and we ran. I had no clear idea which direction the Argo was in, but heading the opposite direction of the screams felt like a decent plan. Things crashed through the brush behind us as we picked up speed. Dean twisted around and fired off a shell from his shotgun, and I heard a cry that sounded slightly different from the others.

"Got one," he puffed.

I was already running out of breath. Despite my smoking, my stamina was pretty darn good, but Mrs. Argo was heavier than she looked. Dean sent off round after round into the darkness behind us as pain-filled squeals bounced of the trees.

"Are they...that close?" I gasped, impressed that he hit something almost every time he pulled the trigger.

"Yeah, but they keep getting back up," Dean yelled, reloading as he ran.

"The head," I panted. "Shoot for...the head."

"You try shooting something behind you in the head while running flat out."

I turned to my left and fired once. The head of one of our snarling pursuers exploded. "Ha!"

"Lucky," he said, blasting off a few more shots.

We had to be nearing the Argo by now, but a terrible thought occurred to me. What if we were running in the wrong direction? There was no way I could keep this pace up much longer, not without dropping the dead weight I carried. And the twins would never forgive me if I left their mother behind. Dean could take a turn carrying her, but in the time it would take to transfer Anna to his shoulder these lunatics would be on us.

So we struggled forward, step after exhausting step, until something awful happened. My foot caught under a root and I fell headlong onto my face. Anna's limp body tumbled through a few rotations and settled in a lump a yard away. Panicked, I turned onto my back, drawing my second revolver, and opened fire.

Three heads exploded less than ten feet away. They were closing in fast, Dean and I firing into a mob of at least twenty shrieking people. At least they used to be people. Their faces twisted with unbridled rage; their bodies, mostly naked, had taken on a pale semi-transparent quality. I could see dark blue veins and strips of muscle through the portions of skin that weren't covered in blood and filth. A few were missing arms, thanks to Dean. One had a large hole in his abdomen, and another actually hopped on a single leg as the other dangled at the knee from a shred of tendon.

Then they were on us. The front runner lunged at Dean. He removed its head with a roar of the shotgun, blood and gray matter splattering us both.

Blood? I pushed the thought away, and yanked the triggers until both pistols clicked empty. I heard the same from Dean's shotgun, and despair overcame me. There was no way we could reload before being ripped to shreds.

But gunshots continued to echo around us. Two more lunatics dropped at my feet. I rolled to see over my shoulder and almost cried with relief. Judah, Johnny, and my father fired into the mob. Sydney and Zoe called to us, frantically waving their arms. Once they saw they had gotten our attention, they both raised their rifles and began taking out our assailants one by one.

Dean and I wasted no time. I got to my feet, helped Dean sling Anna over his shoulder, and we hustled for the rescue party as bullets whizzed past us. We didn't stop when we reached the others, but raced on until we broke the trees and crossed onto the Argo's main grounds.

I reloaded quickly and rushed back in, while Dean stayed with Anna. They had thinned the mob to almost nothing by the time I got back to them, my daughter disintegrating the head of a rather obese creature right as I stepped in line next to her.

"Good shot, Zoe," I said through wheezing breaths. "Now get back to the Argo."

"One more, daddy," she grunted and shot the head off the last of the mob.

4

Devon and Jordan huddled next to their mother, bundled beneath a patchwork quilt, when we returned. My mom stood at the edge of the tree line waiting for me and gripped me in an embrace so tight I felt my vertebrae crack. Haley wiped the blood and chunks of bone from her husband's face, telling him over and over again that she loved him. "You're not going to want to hear this, girls," I said once everyone had calmed down, "but we'll have to restrain your mom until we can figure out what's wrong with her." She was turning into one of them, but I was exhausted and in no state of mind to take on that discussion. "What do you mean, restrain?" Devon asked, obviously about to put up a fight.

"I mean chain her up, Devon." I tried to be as sympathetic as possible. "Sorry."

"But she's just in shock," Jordan argued. "She needs a bath and time to sleep."

This was unavoidable, I realized. "She's not in shock, Jordan. She's bleeding out of every hole in her body. Same as Alex."

"They hurt her, Shane," Devon pleaded. "That's why she's bleeding." I didn't have the patience to argue so I pulled Johnny and Judah out of the twin's earshot.

"Are we on the same page here?" I said, my voice harsher than I intended.

For a few moments I couldn't read their faces, but then Johnny glanced furtively toward his wife and said, "She's definitely out of her gourd, but I'm not quite ready to start shooting family members."

"Uh, no one even suggested that," I said. "All I said was she needs to be restrained. I'm not exactly advocating we start shooting everyone that starts acting weird...although I'm pretty sure Anna's no longer with us."

We observed the slouching figure that was once Mrs. Argo. Her daughters sat close with their arms around her, trying desperately to extract a glimmer of recognition from their mother's dead eyes.

"How did this happen?" Judah said, tugging at his mustache.

"I don't know," Johnny said. "She hasn't been out of our sight until tonight. She's been depressed since Luke died...but that was over a year ago."

"These bled when we shot them," I said, pulling my stained flannel away from my chest as proof.

"They must've been newer," Johnny said. "Turned more recently."

My brother yelped and held a few strands of facial hair up to his face before flicking them away. "Replacements...it's spreading."

I nodded, stealing another glance at Anna. "I don't understand why she's infected and we're not, though."

"She does everything we do," Johnny said. "Except get drunk and break stuff. Set things on fire...throw knives at small animals...play naked Olympics in the middle of the night—"

"We should do that again soon," my brother interjected. "We can add naked hurdles this time—"

"*Shane!*" Dean's frantic voice cut in.

We spun around in time to see him yanking Anna away from Devon by her matted hair as she attempted to sink her teeth into her daughter's neck. Thrashing wildly, she clawed at Dean, but he flung her away from him and the others that now massed together like frightened children in a tight huddle. Anna hit the ground and was on her feet again in a flash, teeth bared. Her feral eyes searched the group until they rested on Zoe. She seemed to grin, but it was in no way the smile that had illuminated the once beautiful face of the woman before us. A deafening screech issued from her mouth and she sprang.

"*Dean,*" I shouted, cursing myself for not keeping between my children and that thing. Her speed was astonishing.

Without hesitation, Dean swung the butt of his shotgun and the creature that had once been Anna ran into it face first with a sickening smack. She fell to the cold grass unconscious for the second time.

"*Mom,*" the twins cried in unison as they rushed toward the sprawled body.

Judah and Johnny were ready to intercept their wives, not wanting them anywhere near their mother. Embracing them both in bear hugs, they whispered to no avail that the body lying naked on the ground was no longer their mother. The scene was disheartening to say the least, and through accumulating tears I watched as Sydney and Haley approached, enveloped Devon and Jordan in their arms, and led them away sobbing.

5

"What now?" Dean asked, once the still unconscious body of Anna Argo had been dragged into the cellar. Judah and Johnny had gone to console their wives; my mother had taken Zoe and Faris back to the house, which left myself, Dean, and my dad to figure out what to do with Anna. She bled heavily, and a dark trail led the way from the edge of the yard, down the outside steps, and into the basement where my brother's handcuffs now restrained her in the corner to some obscure but solid array of pipes.

"There's no way you caused that much damage when you hit her, Dean," said my dad. He had already attempted to stop the bleeding, but as it now poured from every outlet in her face, he had given up.

"It's just like the others," he said, wiping his hands on his pants.

"So we agree she's definitely turned into whatever it is they are, right?" I said, and they each nodded.

"Like I asked before," Dean said, "what do we do now?"

No one had a good answer.

"I wish Sara would show up," I said under my breath.

"Who's Sara?" my dad, who was clearly not as deaf as he sometimes made out, asked.

Dean laughed loudly. "Oh, she's a figment of Shane's imagination that apparently pops up whenever he's alone."

I hadn't told anyone beside my wife and the guys about Sara, and I was now very sorry I had let her name slip in front of my dad.

"Oh really," said my father. "Does Sydney know you're meeting strange women that no one else can see?"

Irritated, and not wanting to have this conversation, I said, "She just shows up. I don't know where she goes or what she does, but I know she's already saved our lives at least once. So let's drop it for now and figure out what to do with her." I pointed at Anna who had begun to stir.

"Alright, take the intensity level down a bit," Dean said with a sneer. "Is it just me or can anyone else kinda…see through her skin?"

We peered more closely at Anna's body, which we didn't bother to cover up again. It was indeed becoming translucent. Dean bent his head closer and I saw her eyes snap open just in time. I pulled him back by the collar as snarling teeth clamped over the space where his head had just been. Then the screeching began again.

Dean hunched over with his hand over his heart. I felt mine beating hard in my chest as my head began to pound from the high pitched noise.

"We have to shut her up," I bellowed.

"We need duct tape," yelled my dad. He sounded extremely far away though he stood less than three feet from me.

He began to rummage amongst the shelves that lined the cellar's back wall. The intensity of the screaming rose impossibly higher and I felt like I was going insane. I yelled for him to hurry up, and then all fell silent. I turned back to see Dean shrugging, shotgun in hand; Anna once again slumped over, out cold.

"Found it," my dad said a second later, holding up a roll of silver tape. "At least we won't get bitten or anything now," he said. "Hold her head up, Shane."

I did—reluctantly—as he wrapped a thick layer of tape around her head, covering her mouth completely, and half her face.

My dad went inside the house, bolting the door from the inside. Dean and I left through the outside stairway, padlocking that door behind us.

"I think we have another problem, Shane," Dean said, suddenly more serious than I had ever seen him.

I lifted my head, aware I had momentarily been on auto-pilot, my mind still being in the cellar.

"I think Haley is starting to crack up." He stopped walking as we reached the front garden that his wife had painstakingly resurrected over the last two years. He ran his hand over the blue plumbagos Haley had recently planted. "I guess it's a good sign she's still planting new flowers."

Dean, who normally needed no prodding to disclose problems he and Haley were having, said no more. I allowed a minute to pass, giving him the opportunity to continue on his own, but when the silence became awkward I asked, "How has she started to crack, then?"

He frowned, shook his head, and sighed. "She's…she's been saying things like, 'All hope is lost,' and 'We're not gonna live through this.' It started a while ago, and it wasn't a big deal, but now it's every time we're alone together. She's depressed, doesn't talk to me anymore…hardly ever smiles. Her telling me she loved me when we got back with Anna was the first thing she's said to me all day." He paused, and then said hopefully, "Has Sydney said anything to you? Maybe Haley is talking to her."

"They *are* besties," I said, trying to lighten the mood. "But Syd hasn't said anything to me about—"

"I just feel like I'm losing her, Shane," he interrupted, speaking quickly. "She's drifting away again, just like before."

I didn't know what to say. Dean hadn't spoken about his wife's depression since she left the care center she had been Baker Acted to four years ago. So if Haley's behavior reminded Dean of that miserable time in his life, it was something to be taken seriously.

"I don't know," I said after some time. "I guess just watch her and keep me updated." We climbed the house's front steps. I stopped suddenly and faced my friend. "But if her head starts bleeding, Dean, you don't screw around."

His eyes shifted nervously away from mine.

"I mean it, Dean. That's not Anna Argo down there anymore," I said, pointing around the side of the house toward the cellar. "And it won't be Haley anymore either if she changes. You were right next to me in those woods, Dean, and I'm sure all those psychos that were chasing us used to be someone's something."

"Do-do you think she's turning?" His voice was almost nonexistent, tears threatening to fall.

I put my hand on my friend's shoulder. "I don't know. But if she does, it means we're all in *a lot* of trouble." I grabbed his shotgun, pumped it and shoved it back into his chest. "If she does, Dean, you do what you have to do."

Escape

1

The nights grew longer. The darkness would linger throughout the waking hours like a parasite, until the days were nothing more than an extended twilight. Like the sun, Anna's humanity continued to deteriorate. Her skin became nearly transparent. Hundreds of pale blue veins snaked visibly just below the surface like so many sub-dermal spiders' webs. She refused to eat, although we placed three hot meals within her grasp each day, her hands now unrestrained in exchange for strong chains around her ankles. The bleeding ceased abruptly two days following her capture; however, the floor around where she crouched retained the evidence of the steady flow that had issued from her nose, mouth, ears, and eyes due to the inability to get close enough to mop up the dried black puddles.

She did not sleep.

I spent countless hours in the cellar over the course of her imprisonment, staring into the eyes of what was once one of the most caring individuals I had ever met. But there was no love there now; a rage the likes I had only seen in the faces of an insane wolf and an equally insane mob burned back and I would be forced to turn away. The tape over her mouth had to be changed daily, her teeth so sharp and jagged they would wear through, and once unhindered, the screeching resumed.

How could she have become something so horrible? Was it despair that allowed whatever evil stalked the woods to enter? Or was it random; something that could not be defended against? What if it was *my* mother sitting there? These questions swirled through my mind as I sat and watched her change. I did not believe it was random, that there was no way of preventing this curse. But how was it that virtually every person we had met in the years following our move to the Argo had turned so? Everyone except Patrick Fitzpatrick. But he'd been gone for over a year, and there could be no certainty even in that. I thought of the depression that had taken hold of Anna in the months following her husband's death. The wandering, forlorn way she moved. Was it emptiness? Or was it apathy? Why had I not succumbed to this? Why was Anna chained to a wall in a dark basement and not me?

My mind turned to Haley and the hopelessness Dean had described. I envisioned blood pouring from her screaming face, and I wept. For a long time I cried before a sneering, inhuman creature in a cold cellar. I cried for Anna and Haley; for Dean. I cried for my parents, Sydney, and the others. But most of all I cried for my children who would never have a normal life.

The outside door creaked open as I wiped my eyes with my palms, sniffing the snot back up my nose. By the time my dad and brother descended the stairs, there was no evidence of my sobbing.

"What are you doing down here, son?"

They approached quietly, and my dad laid a rough hand on my shoulder as he spoke. They had grown hard calluses over the trying years we had been at the Argo. I could remember when they had been as soft as Sydney's. But even hers were now coarse and scarred.

Judah took a can of snuff from his back pocket and flicked it against his middle finger.

"Where'd you find that?" I said, truly curious. Chewing tobacco had become a lost luxury within the last six months.

Stuffing a pinch between his gum and bottom lip he muttered, "Foun' it at da boddum a one a my bags." A glob of drool dripped over his bottom lip and soaked into the scraggly soul patch below.

"I find it easier to think about what we're dealing with if I'm face to face with it."

They glanced at Anna and turned away just as quickly. I lit a cigarette, silently thanking Luke for his obsession with hording things. I found several cartons in the cellar freezer a few days ago while searching for the chains Anna wore. They tasted stale, but I was way past the point of complaining. Judah had gone a year without dip.

"Any conclusions?" my dad said, holding his hand out for a smoke.

I lit him one and shrugged. "It doesn't happen through interaction. If it did I would've been a goner when the first one bit a chunk out of my arm back home. We've been breathing the same air, eating the same food as Anna since we came here. Her husband is butchered, she mopes around for a while, and then she turns into this." I pointed to Anna, forcing them to look. "She hasn't eaten or slept in four days. She's bled out every ounce of blood she has. For all intensive purposes—"

"Intents and purposes," my dad said.

"What?"

"You said, 'intensive purposes', but it's 'intents and purposes.'"

"Whatever. For all *intents and purposes*, she should be dead. And…I think she is."

"You think she's dead?" Judah said, spitting a brown stream into the cup he carried.

I locked both hands behind my neck and stuck my head between my knees. "Ughhh," I groaned as I came back up. "I have no freaking idea."

Judah laughed while my father frowned at the obscenity. I ignored both of them. My head pounded, and I was sick of having no answers. "I see that wolf every time I look at her," my brother said. "She's like a wild animal."

Suddenly a light went on, and I lurched to my feet. "What sets human beings apart from animals?"

My dad had jumped when I sprang from the chair, but he gave an immediate answer. "A soul."

"And the ability to reason," my brother added, putting a hand to his mustache.

"But what does a soul do?" A theory began to formulate. "Without a soul, the sense of right and wrong, good and evil, is nonexistent. An animal is neither good nor evil because an animal has no soul. They have instincts that are necessary for their survival. Gather food or kill for it, find shelter, breed, protect their young."

"You can train a dog to be good," said my brother.

But my dad shook his head. "You can teach a dog that if he behaves a certain way, he'll be punished. If he behaves another way, he'll be rewarded. This isn't teaching the dog good or bad, only what results from his behavior. The dog won't crap on the floor because he gets punished for it, not because he knows it's a bad thing to do."

"Whatever," said Judah. "Jax will try to protect me if I'm in trouble.

I'd say that's good."

"No, that's called survival. Jax relies on you for food and shelter. And you treat him well, so he would respond to keep the one who feeds and takes care of him safe."

"Maybe, but I'm freaking positive dogs go to heaven."

I peered back at the contorted face of Anna Argo. Soul or no soul? There was a second part to that question, however. According to my dad, not having a soul didn't make an animal evil. But what I saw in front of me, grinding and gnashing its teeth, was evil in the most primal sense of the word. Fury pulsed from its pores. If I were to set it free, it would tear me to shreds.

If Anna's soul had somehow been removed, what had taken its place?

2

The week that followed was filled with preparations. Gathering food from the gardens, farmlands, and livestock; stockpiling guns, ammo and clothing; erecting fences, rigging booby traps, and running through defensive scenarios. Tensions mounted as we worked closer together, well past the point of enervation. Judah and I had fallout after fallout—usually from a combination of my impatience and his general laziness—which escalated into countless arguments, almost always resulting in my brother quitting whatever we happened to be working on. This was followed by me apologizing or making fun of him, and ended with us being best friends again…until the next time we worked together on anything. With my mother acting as mediator, it only took five days to complete the fencing around the property. It probably would have taken a pair of non-siblings a day or two less.

Dean and Johnny spent the week riding around in Luke's rundown backhoe, digging trenches around the Argo. They had a great time, laughing and pointing while our blisters gave birth to blisters, until the tractor broke down and they were forced to finish the last hundred yards of the ditch the old fashioned way. My dad found close to twenty barrels of roofing pitch in the garage, some of them dating back further than Luke had been alive. We dumped it all into the trench. Dean raided the munitions cache in the basement for frag grenades, dynamite, and detonators. Anna's presence there caused some initial hesitation, but soon his love for explosives won out over his revulsion toward the creature chained to the wall.

My mom and the girls picked vegetables and slaughtered livestock, filling the Chapel storeroom and the Argo's freezer with canned-goods and meat, respectively. Their hands eroded to disgusting shreds of raw flesh by the end of the week, and Johnny set tubs of warm water in the living room for them to clean and soak their wounds.

Zoe and Faris migrated from one job to another, until my daughter decided she had a knack for supervision, and began following my dad around, shouting orders and correcting our mistakes. It was cute for a while.

Once the fence and ditch were completed, Faris spent every waking hour with Dean, stringing wire, rigging detonators, and setting traps. If he blew up my son I would feed him to Anna.

Through all this, Dean continued to update me on Haley's condition.

"She's regressing, Shane," he would say. "It's like I'm not even there. She doesn't talk to me anymore."

"But she seems fine," I would reply, flicking my head toward Sydney and Haley. They would be deep in conversation, Sydney laughing light-heartedly.

It was only later I realized Haley never even smiled in return.

3

The dogs were barking wildly. Sydney was already up and at the window by the time my eyes opened to the semi-darkness of the otherwise quiet bedroom. The nights were getting cool, and the fact that we didn't need it made me think of air conditioning; an absolutely essential part of my life in the near forgotten state of Florida. We hadn't had air conditioning, let alone electricity, for over two and a half years, and none of us seemed to miss it. I didn't miss cell phones or email either.

I pulled on my pants and shuffled next to Syd who hadn't bothered to put on hers. The moon trickled through the parted curtains, bathing my naked wife in a soft silver glow. She was a goddess. The particles of dust swirling around her shone like stars in the reflecting moonlight. I squeezed her butt cheek and peered through the glass. She sighed, but didn't remove my hand. A yelp came from one of the dogs, but I couldn't see through the haze that floated just under our second story window, thicker than it'd been in months. Growling rose from the mist, and I grabbed my guns.

My brothers were in the hallway, dressed and armed. "Shall we?" said Johnny with an excited grin.

"After you," I said, and followed him downstairs.

The yard appeared darker from ground level, visibility about ten feet through the fog. Like the morning we'd gone to the pit.

The intense commotion made it clear which way to go, though we were careful not to overrun our range of vision. We rounded the corner of the house, passed the open cellar door, and—

The open cellar door. I panicked, my mouth forming the word "stop", and then my head slammed into the stone wall, the warning lost in a burst of red sparks. I was conscious, but barely. I felt my body brush against someone, then thud against the hard ground as the rattle of chains swept by my head. I heard the dogs barking, one closer than the others, and I wondered why I was seeing fireworks, but wasn't hearing them. A shriek broke through the thought, slicing into the night and my mind like a dagger. The flickering in my eyes ebbed, and I could make out a shape crouching over me, someone yelling my name, the dogs barking, the shadow bending closer. Excruciating pain blazed up my arm. Then it was gone, the shape retreated, a dog thrashing at its heels.

I groped the wall and attempted to haul myself to my feet, but slid weakly to the ground again where Bowie hunched, still growling. He stood between me and the figure that could only be Anna, his hair and ears bristled, ready to defend his master. Shelby was nowhere to be seen, but Jax tore away at the creature in the fog. Judah's hand on my shoulder startled me as he climbed out of the cellar, rubbing his bald head with a grimace.

"The bitch pushed me down the stairs."

The struggle continued before us, Jax snarling and thrashing, Anna's chains clinking and clanking, Dean and Johnny nowhere to be seen. Suddenly, Anna's hand clamped around Jax's throat. There was a horrible gurgling sound, and my brother scrambled to his feet. A snap and a second later, the dog went limp, and Judah fired into the fog. Anna had disappeared.

"Cease fire, Cease fire," yelled Dean from somewhere to my right.

Judah holstered his gun and knelt next to Jax. Dean felt his way to me like a blind man, with Johnny following.

"She went into the woods. She was a few feet in front of us, but then she disappeared in the fog. You almost shot us."

"That was Judah, I think he lost his dog," I said, nodding to the hunched blur a few yards away. "Where were you two?"

They turned on me defensively, like I was blaming them for Jax's death.

"Dean saw something, so we went after it, alright?" said Johnny. "I almost tripped over Shelby. Alive but unconscious. Then we headed back when we heard the struggle, got lost in the fog, heard bullets flying by our heads, and saw Anna run into the woods. It seriously happened that fast."

"I'm glad you're alright," I said. "Play watch-out while I go talk to Judah."

I made it to my feet and hobbled to where Jax lay broken on the wet grass. The dog's head hung lifeless in my brother's lap.

After some time my brother said, "He saved your life you know." Tears streamed down his cheeks. "Through the doorway, I saw her bending over you, her nails digging into your arm, and then Jax attacked her and pushed her back."

I rubbed my bicep where fire still burned under my sleeve. Red blotches seeped through in four places on one side, a single spot on the other. "He was brave," was all I could give him.

"Remember when dad said dogs aren't good or bad?"

I nodded.

"How do you feel about that now?"

4

We gave Jax a hero's burial in the Chapel cemetery the next morning. His little dog friends were all present, though Bowie, Shelby, and Samson spent most of the service sniffing and urinating on random rocks and bushes. Haley dismissed herself during our moment of silence, and ambled her way into the house. Dean and I exchanged a glance, yet remained silent out of respect for the dog that had, at the very least, saved me from severe injury at the hands of the former Mrs. Argo.

I spent the remainder of the day with my wife and kids, playing in the yard with the dogs. Faris and Zoe discovered a renewed interest in Bowie after the loss of Jax, and they spent hours playing fetch and chase while Syd and I watched with a queer mixture of amusement and sadness. Preparations had been made for the defense and survival of our clan—shrinking though it may be—and so we had time to spend at our leisure. A whole day with nothing to do normally bored me to tears. This day, however, I reveled in the absence of work with the realization that a day like this may never come again.

A bonfire and cookout completed our somber afternoon. All were present and most came hungry. Haley slouched by Dean, never lifting her head from the bunless hot dog rolling back and forth across her plate. The others chatted casually with either real or faux happiness, I couldn't tell which. Especially when it came to my brother.

Three hot dogs and five mildly cool beers later, it was time to put the kids to bed. We went through the nightly routine—bath, jammies, story, and bed—once again with the budding sense this could be the last time.

Syd and I rejoined the circle, plopping into our lawn chairs like fat men exhausted from their trip to the refrigerator. The day had been an easy one, but I felt more tired than ever.

"Think she's watching us?" Jordan said. Devon squinted into the darkening forest to the northwest. Both were handling the second disappearance of their mother much more gracefully than they had the first. Perhaps it was finally sinking in.

"We could detonate the woods and find out," said Dean, and the twins shot him a scowl. "Too soon?"

My brother patted him on the back. "I'm dying to push that button."

"All the time Faris has spent with you, I'm surprised it hasn't been pressed already," Sydney said to Dean.

My mother laughed. "That boy can shoot a pistol better than you, Shane, but he's still a five year old. We always had to take the stairs when you and Judah were little, because you couldn't control yourselves in the elevator."

"Remember our one and only trip to New York?" my dad said. "Judah pushed half the buttons in the Empire State Building and it took almost an hour to get to the top."

"Now he just pushes *my* buttons," I said.

"Well, what kind of little brother would I be if I wasn't on your nerves all the time?" Judah's smile lit up his face for the first time since his dog was killed.

"The kind that got some work done, probably."

"Please," my father said. "Judah's never gotten any work done. Even as a kid he'd get side-tracked by some toy he hadn't played with for a year or was talking one of our ears off."

"Actually," said Johnny, "today was the first day I hadn't heard his voice rambling on continuously since we moved up here."

My brother stood up in false offense. "What is this, pick on Judah time?"

"The night we saved Patrick Fitzpatrick from those demented highwaymen, you talked so much on the way up here that I fell asleep and dreamed you were still talking, then woke up and you were *still* talking."

"Patrick Fitzpatrick and I were having a conversation, John."

"He was asleep when I woke up."

I laughed so hard I fell backward off my chair and into a patch of mud.

"That's what you get, chode licker," said my brother while everyone else pointed at me and laughed.

I was covered in mud. "Guess I'm calling it a night. I'm going in to take a shower."

Hoots and hollers followed as I headed to the house. At least Judah was back to his old self and not thinking about his dead dog anymore.

5

The house was dark and cold. I allowed my eyes to adjust before stripping down to my boxers, leaving the soiled clothes by the door. The moon shone dim tonight, but enough of it penetrated the front windows to cast eerie shadows on the walls. I clomped up the stairs and peeked in on the kids who slept soundly in their beds, then went down the hall to my bedroom. I snatched some clothes from the dresser and heard the front door open and quietly click closed. I called for Sydney, but no one answered. Shrugging it off, I stepped into the large community bathroom and shut the door. An oil lamp and matches lay next to the sink and the room was soon illuminated with orange light. The flicker of the flame danced over the porcelain figurines and silk flowers set about the counter, toilet, and small shelves. Anna had taken pride in her home and this bathroom was a stark reminder of the mother and wife she had once been. I pushed these depressing images from my mind, dropped my clean clothes on the toilet seat, and turned on the water.

I used to look forward to showers, but since the loss of electricity three years ago I no longer felt the same way. No electricity means no hot water. The Argo had two generators, but because gas was now in low supply, we reserved it for cooking and washing clothes. The small water tower had taken several months to repair, but once we got it working, it supplied a steady flow of fresh water to the house.

I washed quickly, barely rinsing away the shampoo and soap before turning the icy water off, and with shrunken balls and razor hard nipples I flung the shower curtain open. Horror movies like Psycho had prompted me to do this since I was a kid, but the curtains always opened to an empty room. Tonight was different. No one waited by the tub with a raised knife, but someone had been in here. The door stood ajar, and I could see into the dark hallway. I knew I'd closed that door, and I thought I locked it, a habit I developed long ago living with two children with no concept of privacy.

I reached for the toilet, but my clothes were gone, along with the dirty boxers I left on the floor. The cold air of the house blew over me through the open door, and my body shivered. Grabbing a towel from the linen shelf, I dried off and wrapped it around my waist as I stepped from the bathtub. On tip-toes, I crept down the hall, passing my own bedroom to check in on Zoe and Faris in the adjacent room. Still asleep.

Somewhat relieved, I passed silently to my room. This door gaped open as well, and though I couldn't remember whether or not I had closed it, I stepped in cautiously, scanning the darkness. Again I saw no one. My eyes stopped at the bed where my clean clothes were laid in a neat pile.

Am I going crazy? I moved to the bed, stepping on something soft, but before I had traversed the short distance I heard the bedroom door close behind me.

I whirled, my towel dropping to the floor, and saw Haley. She was as naked as I was, and my eyes went to the clothes I had treaded over on the way to my bed. Her body seemed to glow in the subdued moonlight much like Sydney's had the night before. She was stunning.

"You're smaller than I thought you'd be," she said, her eyes caressing me as she came closer.

"The water was cold," I said, feeling obligated to defend my manhood for some reason. Another shiver swept through me and fear followed. Nevertheless, her nakedness, the way her hips swayed from side to side, how her breasts bounced slightly with every step, aroused me.

"That's better," she whispered, gazing down at me once more. She stood only inches away. I could smell the smoke from the fire still clinging to her skin, but underneath hung a sweeter, seductive scent that reminded me of my wife.

Sydney...my wife... I stepped backward, but my heel bumped against the bed frame, blocking my retreat.

"You need to leave, Haley," I breathed, knowing I wasn't forceful enough.

Then she was kissing me. Her leg wrapped around mine, her breasts pressed hard against my chest. As my skin met hers, unbelievable warmth washed through me. I felt myself giving in, my arms engulfing her, pulling her closer, my fingertips descending over the slope of her back, up the curve of her cheeks. Her hand slipped down my stomach and she grabbed hold of me.

I vaguely remember the massaging movement of her hand, her tongue in my mouth, being pushed onto the bed. Then she was on top of me, moving against me; warm liquid dripped over my face and chest, the same heat covered my groin, and I was falling. I saw only darkness. I felt only pleasure. Haley was in control. Nothing else mattered.

Time ceased to exist. For days or seconds I writhed in the churning black, unable to separate a coherent thought from the desire for more. Haley groaned and suddenly my wife's face flashed through the darkness. *Sydney.* It disappeared, but that was all it took for the bonds to be broken. The frozen fingers loosened their grip as they had years before when I stared down into the inky blackness of the pit. It receded quickly, freeing my mind. The complete ecstasy that consumed me a moment earlier vanished, and shame swooped in to replace it. Immense shame…and something else. Something stronger than both the darkness and the guilt. Something I'd never experienced. Something new.

My body was again my own, and I blindly pushed with all my strength. Haley's weight lifted, and my eyes flung wide to see my friend's wife sprawled on the floor at my feet. Except she was no longer the beautiful woman Dean had married; her nakedness was no longer intoxicating. Her skin was drenched in the blood that poured from her nose, mouth and ears; from her privates. I realized I was also covered in it and nearly vomited. Haley righted herself on her hands and knees, and her eyes were terrifying. Like Anna's, they were bloodshot and feral.

Through my mounting fear I managed to whisper her name, but she merely glowered at me with wild rage. A truth dawned on me then: *Anna didn't escape from the cellar. Haley let her out.*

As if reading my thoughts, she flashed her dripping teeth, and sneered. Footsteps mounted the stairs and she twisted like an animal toward the door. I took the chance to scamper over the opposite side of the bed, gaining distance and an obstacle between myself and Haley. She snapped back at the movement, but uncertainty betrayed her face. The footsteps drew closer. She teetered between attack and escape. Naked and vulnerable, I braced myself for attack.

The door swung open and Sydney stepped inside. My wife took in the creature that was once her best friend…and me in the corner. A shotgun hung from her hand. Her expression morphed from alarm to confusion, and then it turned to stone.

Haley's savage eyes shifted from the shotgun to Syd's face. She sprang, clearing the bed in one fast, blurred movement. Sydney took aim, and I covered my face and cock with my hands, sure the shotgun's spray would pelt me as much as it would Haley, unsure that my wife was calm enough to care. But before she could pull the trigger, Haley had smashed through the boarded window. I watched in awe as she plummeted two stories to the hard ground, landed nimbly on her feet and hands, and disappeared into the black forest.

6

"What the ffff…" She faltered, wilting into the doorframe to keep from falling. A hand went to her drooping head, hiding her face from my view. The other clutched the shotgun, its barrel aimed at the floor, shuddering as waves rippled down the length of her body.

And I watched speechless, not daring to utter a sound.

What was there to say? She had found me, her husband and father of her children, alone and naked with her best friend. That we stood several feet apart and drenched in blood counted for nothing. I knew the truth of what had happened, the weakness I had succumbed to, and I counted myself lucky that she hadn't walked in a minute or two earlier. But even that thought shamed me.

We stayed like that for what seemed an eternity, helpless and alone, separated by a few feet and a chasm of betrayal.

Finally, my wife straightened, drew a steady breath and looked me in the eye. "Clean yourself up," she said, flinging my towel across the awkward expanse. Then, with great effort her face softened, if only by a small amount, and she said, "Are you okay?"

"No," I answered. It was weak and feeble. "I thought I was dead."

Her eyes studied me over and she shook her head. "Tell that to your dick."

I bent my head and was appalled to see I was still hard. I stuttered for an explanation, and finding none, sat on the bed in disgrace.

Sydney made for the door, but stopped with her back to me. "What do I tell Dean?"

"Nothing," I said, thoroughly depressed. "I'll do it."

And then she was gone.

I barely noticed the coldness of the water as I scrubbed the blood from my body. I wasn't as much worried about Dean's reaction toward me as I was about his reaction to the loss of Haley. She had turned, something he had suspected was happening for some time. But his fears were now a harsh reality. How could he possibly be prepared for this?

I dressed and came downstairs where the whole family waited in

173

silence. I avoided their inquiring eyes, though I was confident Sydney hadn't said anything.

"We need to talk," I said to Dean.

He rose and motioned to Judah and Johnny. "You two are coming."

Maybe it will be easier with them there.

I grabbed four beers from the cooler by the door, and lit a cigarette. Man, I didn't want to do this. The fire burned low, and I took in my friends' faces, but all were fixated on the glowing embers at our feet. I told them everything.

"I saw this coming," said Dean after a long silence.

"You saw what coming?" Judah said. "Your wife seducing my brother?"

"No, fudgenozzle. Haley turning."

"You should've seen her land on her feet when she jumped out the window," I said. "It was…inhuman."

"Are we going after her?" Johnny said. He picked at his fingernails with his knife.

"I'd rather not, considering what happened when we went searching for Anna," I said.

"You mean every psycho in the woods chasing after us?" Dean said.

"I'll go if you want," I said. "She's your wife. Your decision."

He thought about it and said, "And what if we do find her?"

I hadn't considered that. What *would* we do if we found her? Put a bullet in her head? The idea made my stomach turn.

I shrugged, and he nodded grimly. Whether we liked it or not, we all knew what had to happen if we saw Haley again.

"I'm sorry," I said, putting everything I'd done and everything we may be forced to do into those two words.

"You're lucky we've been friends for so long, Shane."

"I think I'm lucky to be alive."

"Anything else?" Johnny said. "'Cause I'm done with this beer."

"Uh," Judah said, "I know this isn't the best time, but I don't really see better times coming in the near future. Devon's pregnant."

"What?" I said. "I'm finally gonna be an uncle?"

"Yep. Heaven help that kid."

"Heaven help us all."

174

Being Human

1

Judah's head popped through the tower hatch, signaling the end of my shift, but I sent him back down, in no rush to return to the freezing downstairs couch or the dreams that would surely haunt my sleep. Sydney had moved into the master suite, and without her beside me, the nightmares rained down like a plague almost every night. Floating heads would peel their masks away to reveal the faces of my friends, and they'd twist into terrifying creatures with orange eyes and bloody teeth. Once I saw my brother as he had been as a child, drowning, bloated and lifeless in the murky sea. I reached for him and his eyes flicked open, but it was no longer Judah looking back. It was Faris, and he screamed, tiny bubbles soundlessly displacing the water as dark blood gushed from his ears, roiling around him until he was enveloped in a veil of red. I reached into the cloud, my hands searching frantically, coming back empty. Then laughter surrounded me and I woke.

I was utterly depleted. The distance from my wife and the barrage of nightmares created an impossible situation. I would close my eyes to escape the devastation I'd made of my marriage, only to have them flung open by the images in my head. I tried placing the blame on Haley, but in the end it was my own actions that were at fault.

It was during the hazy chill of my second three hour shift that Haley returned.

A flash of white streaked out of the woods to the northwest and then vanished behind the barn. It was foggy, as it was every night, and I squinted to be sure of what I'd seen before I risked rousing my family to a false alarm.

"It's her," said a soft voice from behind me.

Startled, I spun, backing myself into the tower's railing. Sara stood before me, though much younger than she had been a year ago. The sere, withered face of an ancient hag had been replaced by that of an angelic young woman; the hunched spine and sagging, spotted skin now straight and smooth and creamy white. Her voice had a gentler timber, but retained the confident power I remembered so well.

"What *are* you?" I managed to say. She must have been beautiful in her youth, but the woman standing here was so much more. She was shocking. Her hair was pale gold, her face and hands without a trace of blemish. Her eyes sparkled silver, her small nose sloped to a perfect point, her cheekbones high, her lips plump and pink above her narrow chin. The robes were the same grey she had always worn, but even they draped over her ample curves, swirling gracefully with every gust of wind.

"What I am is not important at present, Shane McCall," she said. "Your questions have not improved since last we spoke."

Still stunned by her appearance, I could think of nothing to say.

"Your brother Dean's wife has returned. Her attempt at seduction failed, and so her intentions have changed. You are more resilient than I gave you credit for."

"Haley was not the one who failed," I said, thinking of Sydney. "I was." Anger stirred in my veins, burning to be unleashed, but no one deserved this wrath more than I.

She studied me with her shining eyes. "No, Shane McCall, you have not failed. If that were so, you would be a shadow in the forest, hunting your own kin, and we would have naught to say to one another."

"My family is turning…*dying*, and you say I haven't failed?" I bit the inside of my cheek and tasted blood. "All I've done is survive…so far."

She moved closer and her robes swished about her bare ankles. "You've done so much more. Arriving safely at the Argo should be seen as a victory unto itself. You walked away from the pit, resisting its call. You destroyed the infiltrators you called finches, survived the onslaught on the hill. You rejected Haley's temptation. All this you have done and still you live. Its tactics change with every defeat, but you have overcome them all."

"You keep saying *It*, but never say what *It* is."

"*Ra'ah*." Her voice lowered to barely a whisper. "The consuming spirit, the beast of the darkness, eater of souls."

"What does it want?"

"The world…and your son."

"But he's a child," I said. "What could it want with a little boy?"

"Do not underestimate the innocence of a child. Tell me, have you ever seen a child enthralled by its power?"

I shook my head, unable to recall anything but adults chasing us through the woods.

"Their innocence protects them from its influence…but not from its wrath. Yet Faris is special not because of his innocence…" Sara paused, struggling to explain. "It's…because he…will remain so. Because of what he shall become." She closed her eyes and said, "I cannot see what will be, but this I know. The spirit senses a familiar threat within your son and fears him. But it is also curious as to why, and therein may lie your opportunity…and its weakness."

The streak of white darted from the barn and into the fog. I moved to pull the rope that would sound the alarm, but Sara stayed my hand.

"Where are your children, Shane McCall?"

"Asleep in their beds, Sara, if that's your real name," I said, mocking her tone.

"Then sound the alarm. They are coming for them. They may not know which one to take, not without their master present, so guard them both. Fair thee well, Shane McCall."

She stepped onto the railing, and I called out to her. "What do they become, when they turn?"

"They are the Enthralled. I've heard some of the others call them *thralls*."

"The others?" I said, but she stepped off the railing and vanished like a vampire into the mist. Her soft voice floated to me through the darkness below. "Faris is all that matters."

On that point I disagreed. We *all* mattered.

I rang the bell with all my might.

2

"When they gather at the fence, light it up," I said.

"Been waiting for this for a long time," Dean said holding up the detonator.

"Women and children to the Oh Shit Shelter." The shrieking had commenced, rising from the woods all around us. I could barely hear my own words. "Take the dogs with you."

Sydney, Devon, Jordan, and my mother led Zoe and Faris to the barn, and the dogs followed. Bowie, Shelby, and Samson…our last line of defense.

"Everyone ready?" I said to my brothers and my father.

They raised their guns—an assortment of shotguns, assault rifles, and pistols—and I double checked my AR-15. Their expressions revealed anything but confidence.

"*Go!*"

My dad took his post at the rear entrance of the barn. Dean and Johnny set up a little further out on the building's eastern end, while my brother and I took to the south. This way the barn was surrounded by guns.

They came from every direction, shrill screams announcing their arrival long before the first creature was seen. With a push of a button, fire erupted from each corner of the property. The small explosions ignited the gunpowder and tar that filled the trenches, moving along the Argo's borders until chest high flames created a protective wall on the outside edge of our newly erected fence. Sharpened spikes protruded like jagged teeth every few feet along the enclosure, waiting to impale anything that rushed through the fire.

More blasts sounded beyond the wall as Dean blindly detonated several chunks of Luke's C4. It was hit or miss, but the strategically placed explosives were sure to take out at least a few of our attackers.

Mounds of burnt flesh piled quickly along the fence line, but they were not slowing. Like insects to a porch light, the thralls swarmed. They burst through the flames. Those that hadn't been caught in the initial inferno were skewered on the stakes; those behind them scampered up their backs and over the fence, their skin blazing and blistering.

Gunfire pounded in all directions, but there was no time to worry about the others. One by one Judah and I picked them off as they came into range. The fog to the south draped thick, but the fiery thralls made easy targets. I blasted several, but for every one I shot, Judah took down three. Together we killed more than we could count, but still they came, faster than we could pull the trigger.

My rifle emptied and I snapped a new magazine in, leaving the expelled one where it lay. A series of clicks told me Judah had done the same. Another six hit the dust in front of us, blood and flames everywhere, neither of us knowing who killed what. Heads exploded in front of me, the fact these had once been people never crossing my mind.

Then we ran out of ammo. A bag of munitions lay at the outside corner of the barn and we rushed to it. Dean and Johnny did the same. I could see the litter of bodies to the east. It was nothing compared to the mob that still swarmed toward us. Judah picked up part of the slack at the front of the barn as the rest of us reloaded, laying low a dozen thralls less than twenty yards away. My dad's gun sounded over and over, and I prayed he was not being overrun. The wails were crippling, making it difficult to think.

"We stand here," I said, shoving a few clips into the pockets of my jeans. The others moved to the opposite side of the barn. They were too close now to push forward any further. I blasted a runner within arm's length of Judah.

"Thanks, brother," he said, shooting three more in quick succession.

We kept putting them down, but each dead body was replaced by two more, like the heads of a hydra. There were just too many. We retreated to the front entrance of the barn, and I heard my father shouting.

From there chaos erupted as our carefully constructed plans crumbled.

"Shane! Judah!" my dad screamed from the barn's opposite end and we sprinted. Johnny and Dean stayed in the front. My heart sank when we reached him. A single thrall we both recognized lay unconscious on the ground beside my father. He knelt in the dirt, sobbing and bleeding. Faris rocked with his arms around his knees in the corner, eyes clenched shut.

"She took her…Anna," my dad stammered. "I couldn't…stop them both. She bit me and I…swung the shotgun. Must've hit her when she ran…by with Faris. My arm…what's wrong with my arm?"

When my father's head lifted, his right arm came into view. I nearly passed out. It had been torn from the shoulder joint and dangled from his torso by a few bloody strips of meat. How he was still conscious and speaking was beyond all reason.

Judah glanced at our father, hesitated, and then dropped into the shelter to find his wife.

My mother's head poked from the hole a second later, and with a gasp, she rushed to her husband, forcing him to lie down, all the while whimpering the words, "Stupid man, stupid man", as she frantically tried to keep his mangled arm away from the dirt.

"Who'd she take, dad?" I said, but I already knew. Sydney crawled out of the shelter, white as a ghost. Haley was sprawled out by my dad. She had tried to take Faris, and Anna had Zoe. Anger seethed over me, and I released a cry of anguish that came nowhere near conveying the howling in my heart.

Sydney picked up Faris and rocked him, a soft hum slipping through her pressed lips. "They were waiting for us," she said. "We turned the lights on in the shelter and they were already there."

"The dogs?" I said only to keep myself from running into the woods after my daughter.

"Samson's dead. Bowie and Shelby are alive but hurt."

I nodded, not really internalizing the information being given. My dad was in bad shape; blood gushed from a wound in his neck as well as his arm. My mother tended to him to the best of her abilities, but it would not be enough. Devon and Jordan were still in the shelter, and I shuddered to think what that meant.

How could I have been so stupid?

Johnny and Dean bolted into the barn. "They just ran off," Johnny said, searching for his wife. "Where's Jordan?"

I tipped my head to the opening of the shelter and he hurried down. Dean bent over Haley and hauled her over his shoulder. Without a word, he lugged her to the far corner and tied her up.

"Jordan's unconscious again," my brother said when he resurfaced, holding his pregnant wife tightly. "Johnny's trying to wake her, but I don't know if he'll be able to. She got hit pretty hard in the face…she'll have some pretty bad scars."

My heart pounded, screamed, shuddered. The others gathered around those they held most dear. Johnny and Judah with their wives, my mother with my father, Dean with a thrall that had once been

180

Haley. Sydney cradled our son, and for the first time in weeks looked me in the eye. It was no longer resentment that I saw. It was desperation. Our family lay in disarray, but at least all of their closest ties were accounted for.

Jordan and my father may not make it through the night, but the only person I could find it in me to care about was my little girl.

3

"You're not coming." I had already gone to the house to grab my compound bow and returned to the barn to find my wife loading a rifle, insisting on going with me. Her entire body trembled. "Faris needs you. I'm going alone."

"No you're not, brother." Judah pried himself from Devon. "I'm going with you."

Devon began to protest, but Judah silenced her quickly. "If our child was taken, Shane would go with me in a second. I'm not letting him go in there alone."

"She's pregnant, Judah," I said so only he could hear, but he only twisted his mustache, his face stern and unwavering. There would be no stopping him.

Devon's shoulders sagged, and she kissed her husband. "Come back to us…both of you." Then she resigned herself to the shelter to be with her sister.

Dean pleaded to go, but with his wife tied to one of the barn's support beams, I knew his heart wasn't in it. I talked him into staying to protect the others. We didn't know if this was over. If Sara was right, and Faris was the one they really wanted, it may not be long before they realized they had the wrong child. I didn't want to think what that might mean for Zoe; I didn't see them bringing her back and apologizing for the mistake.

Johnny didn't even notice us, when we went down to grab some blankets. Sydney grabbed my arm as I passed and kissed me. It was intense, and I realized then that if I made it back with Zoe, I would no longer be sleeping on the couch.

"Bring her back," she said. I could still hear her voice cracking as I left the barn.

Covering as much skin as possible with the blankets, my brother and I made our way to the fence. The wall of fire on the other side continued to roar. I felt the intense heat on my cheeks and nose as we scaled the head high fence. Our feet had just touched the ground when a figure emerged from the flames and stood before us. Untouched by the blaze, Sara blocked our way.

"Do not do this, Shane McCall," she said, pleading. "Faris is the one it wants. Zoe is expendable. You cannot throw your life away like this. You must protect your son!"

"My daughter is *not* expendable," I roared, the rage surging over the woman.

"The future of mankind rests on the survival of your son," she said. "The survival of Faris rests on you. If you go after your daughter, you will not return. And all hope will be lost."

I realized then she truly did not comprehend what I was about to do. I took a breath in an attempt to calm myself, failing completely. "If ever I doubted you were not human, I doubt it no longer. If I lose my daughter, all hope will *already* be lost! God help anyone or any*thing* that stands between me and Zoe. Are you standing in my way, Sara?"

Sara's head tilted, and her eyes turned to slits, studying me, deciding if I was bluffing. I was not. She must have seen it because she gracefully stepped aside. We were about to barrel through the wall of fire when she said, "Wait!"

I went for my revolver but she made no move to stop us. Her hand merely rose in a slow sweep and the burning barrier parted like a curtain, just wide enough for us to pass.

"So she *is* real," said Judah as we dashed through the opening.

I ignored him, and entered the forest.

4

The direction was clear enough. Dozens of tracks, broken branches, trampled brush, and a trail of burning leaves pointed the way the flaming creatures had fled. Northwest. We followed quickly, the trodden ground making little to no sound beneath our feet. We were shadows in the forest; ghosts in the mist. For a long time we ran, my breath never faltering.

We caught up with the stragglers after what seemed an hour and made swift and quiet work of them with the kukri and machete. Johnny had a knack for sharpening blades, and they sliced through the thralls bloodless necks like butter, the sound of their heads hitting the ground louder than our movements. Only once did I fail to sever one completely, but Judah finished the work before the thing could utter its shrill cry.

We hacked our way through the scattered pack until it became too dangerous to continue. From there we stalked the mob from a safe distance, praying it would lead us to Zoe. A clearing soon came into view through the thick trees where a controlled fire flickered in the center. Hundreds of creatures amassed around it, huddled in clumps and cliques like schoolchildren. They sat staring into the early morning sky, captivated by the darkness above, swaying from side to side, listening to some unheard music.

One man stood apart. We knew him as Alex. He was much like the creatures that surrounded him. However, he seemed more human than the rest somehow, more in control. And he stood taller, larger than last I saw him, his features stretched and strained from the unnatural growth. Here and there, red blotches tore through his skin as if he were being eaten slowly from the inside out.

On his far side sat a small figure barely visible behind Alex's hulking shape. I knew it to be Zoe at once, and pointed her out to my brother. She sat much like Faris had, arms wrapped tightly around her knees, attempting to escape within herself. Her straw-like hair hung like a veil about her face. Such fear she must be feeling, surrounded by these monsters. I wished I could somehow make my presence known to her, to let her know her daddy's here, that she would be in my arms soon.

Sneaking in and out with Zoe undetected would be impossible. A diversion would have to be made and I would need to take Zoe during the chaos. Cautious not to speak, Judah and I made a small semblance of a plan in the darkness just outside the campfire's radius.

I moved to take my position and then thought of something else. Scanning the horde of thralls, I found my target. The naked creature that was once Anna Argo sat less than twenty yards from us in the center of the clearing, staring blankly at the black sky. I gave an involuntary snarl and pointed her out to Judah. I mouthed the words, *She's mine,* and he nodded understanding. I would have my revenge and he would keep the secret from his wife.

I gave my brother a hug, wished him luck, and crept around the tree line. I took a deep breath and then the arrows began to fly.

Judah sent the first through the head of a thrall sitting toward the rear of the clearing. It went unnoticed. The other creatures merely continued their worship of the darkness. Three more went down in the same group before the others began to stir. The effect was like a stone thrown into water. One by one, rippling in an outward arc, the thralls woke to the attack, shaking their bodies like wet dogs before leaping to their feet.

Two more went down in back, and I understood my brother's strategy. Take out those furthest away and hopefully they would believe the attack came from the wrong end of the clearing. They took the bait, rushing off to the northwest in a chorus of shrieks. He may not have done well in school, but when it came to things like this my brother was a bloody genius.

Judah continued to strike down one after another, and their numbers dwindled as they either darted off into the opposite end of the forest or fell to my brother's well-placed arrows. A few, including Anna to my satisfaction, remained crouched in the center of the fireplace like sentries. I waited no longer. The distraction had been made and it had worked better than I could ever have hoped. I nocked an arrow, and silently pulled back the string. Taking careful aim, I let the arrow fly directly into the back of Alex's skull. He dropped to his knees and crashed to the ground in a pool of dark blood. Without hesitation I rushed into the clearing and scooped up my daughter.

"*I knew you'd come,*" she exclaimed, and I covered her in my arms. Over her shoulder I observed the strewn bodies of the thralls Judah had killed and noticed that not a drop of blood had spilled from any of their wounds. I noticed also with mounting fear that my daughter's cry had gained the attention of every thrall still in range.

A large hand gripped my leg and I almost panicked. Alex attempted to gain his footing and I did the only thing I could think of. I grabbed my blade and lopped his hand off at the wrist.

I slung the bow over my shoulder and ran. One arm supporting Zoe, Alex's severed hand still holding tight to my calf, I reached behind me and yanked her gun from the waist band of my pants. "Make them count," I said to her as she took the pistol.

I glanced back only once to see Alex standing tall, yanking at the shaft sticking out of his head as if it were a splinter. "*Get them,*" he growled, his echo bouncing off the trees.

Judah's arrows continued to fly into the growing crowd of thralls, now taking out those that stood between me and my escape. Zoe fired off a few rounds over my shoulder, the gun so close to my head I thought my ears would split open.

Only one thing stood between me and the forest beyond: Anna. She screamed as I plunged forth, her eyes orange embers of fury, her mouth a gaping hole of razor blades. She made no attempt to move, but rather shifted her feet to gain a better stance. She crouched and leapt. The movement was barely visible, but I had expected it. Never slowing, I raised my blade to my right shoulder and brought it down in a powerful arc. Anna's head spiraled through the air as the kukri severed it from the rest of her emaciated body, silencing her shriek. Her remains flopped lifelessly to the ground as I rushed past.

We blew by Judah at full sprint and he fell in behind us. No more shooting, only running. The thralls gave chase, crashing through the brush. I ran like I had never run before, my heart pounding under my shirt, my lungs screaming, my sides burning. My legs became jelly, the endless miles stretching into oblivion. After every passing tree or clump of vine I would strain to see the orange glow of the fire that would welcome us back to the Argo. But only darkness lay ahead and only death behind.

My despair mounted as my fatigue peaked and I felt I could go no further. The clamor of the thralls became louder as they gained on us. But then the fiery barrier around the Argo flickered into view like it had been there all along. And then my brother cried out in pain.

He staggered to his feet only to fall again to his knees. I backtracked and pulled him up, but he nearly collapsed again when weight settled on his right leg.

"What are you doing?" he said. "For the love of God, *run!*"

Behind us, the thralls closed in, no more than a hundred yards out. To the east, the wall of fire parted, revealing the sturdy fence and the safety of the Argo beyond. We were so close. Sara stepped through the opening, beckoning us to hurry.

I peeled Zoe from my back and nudged her. "Get to the Argo, Zoe," I said, and she flew away toward Sara and the fire.

"You stupid..." Judah hissed at the pain as I threw his arm over my shoulder and we began a panicked three-legged race.

Ahead of us, Zoe darted past Sara, through the opening in the fire wall. The shrieks of the thralls rose to a deafening pitch as they drew nearer. *Too near.* Zoe climbed the wooden fence and disappeared as Judah and I reached the fifty yard mark, our pursuers trailing by about the same, closing the distance twice as fast. The thought of being overtaken and torn to shreds this close to safety drove my legs faster. I was all but dragging my brother now, and my thighs burned like the fire before us. I could feel the heat from the flames.

Sara stepped aside, allowing us ample room to stumble through the parted blaze, but she did not follow us through. We dove headlong, crashing hard into the fence, avoiding a sharpened spike by less than an inch. Twisting around, I risked a glance back, only to view the curtain of fire close.

"Move, move!" I yelled and rolled to the left. Judah cursed in agony as he used his injured ankle to propel his body in the opposite direction. But my brother's cry was drowned out by an explosion from the other side of the fire. A blast of heated air blew over me as several mangled bodies were flung through the fire and impaled on the fence between us.

Sara.

We wasted no time investigating the unexpected event that had possibly wiped out the entire horde of thralls...and the mysterious woman. Judah and I tumbled over the fence a second later.

5

My brother waved me away when I offered my hand. "See to your daughter, moron," he grinned through his obvious discomfort.

Devon came streaking from the barn, searching for Zoe, but Judah's voice brought me back. "It was supposed to be the other way."

"What was?"

"I should've been me saving *your* life...we would've been even."

My jaw tightened. "We've always been even, Judah. This isn't about keeping score."

He started to say something, but then Devon was there, clinging to his neck, so he settled for thanks.

Zoe was shaken, but she held it together well. She cried in her mother's arms for several minutes, but that was all. Once the realization that she was safe came over her, Zoe resorted to telling all who would listen how many screaming lunatics she had killed during our escape.

I was in worse shape. I had almost lost my daughter, my brother, and my own life all in the course of a couple hours. It seemed like seconds. My mother stayed with my father in the barn. Miraculously he was still alive, but he was bleeding out rapidly. His right shoulder was wrapped in a sheet that was white at one time, but now dripped a bright red. His neck, flayed open by Anna's teeth, was also bandaged, though his life's blood soaked through and freely puddled in the dirt beneath his head. Haley sat chained and gagged in the furthest corner of the barn. Dean paced in front of her, his hard stare unreadable.

"Your father wants to speak to you and your brother," my mom said.

I stood in the center of the barn, dazed. I rubbed my eyes, suddenly very tired. When I opened them, Judah had hobbled in from the yard using Devon as a crutch.

Grasping our hands, our mother led us to our father. She squeezed and went to sit with Faris and Zoe. Sydney mouthed the words *I love you*. Was it only yesterday that we huddled around the bonfire telling stories, and sharing the things from our previous lives that we missed? I missed seeing my children without a gun in their hands.

My father's breath garbled shallow, his color that of ash. But his eyes remained alert, and when they spotted us the corners of his grey lips twitched into the best smile he could manage.

Tears distorted my vision (Judah had been crying since he first walked into the barn) as we drew near and knelt beside him. He appeared comfortable and remarkably lucid for someone whose arm had recently been ripped off.

"My boys," he said, his voice tiny and clear. "I'm so proud of both of you. Despite how I raised you, you became men of honor and integrity, and you've surpassed anything I could ever have imagined. You've grown into incredible men, loving husbands, a caring father. But how you got me into this mess I will never know…"

He paused to chuckle up a few pints of blood, giving me a moment to take in his words. *Loving husband?* Some might disagree.

My father cleared his throat. "I told you repeatedly what I wanted written on my tombstone. Remember what it was?"

187

"See, I told you I was sick," Judah and I answered.

He tried to laugh, but a fit of coughing ensued. After catching what remained of his breath, he said, "Naturally, I never imagined I'd be lying here with half an arm and my thrrroat rrrripped out." His words slipped into gargled slurs, and I imagined the blood from the wound in his neck seeping into his windpipe. "So instead can you make my tombstone read, 'Ouch…that hurt'?"

He tried to laugh again and ended up coughing for several moments. Judah and I laughed with him initially, but faded to gut wrenching silence as black blood began to spew with my dad's heaves. There would be no tombstone, we all knew it. He closed his eyes. His breathing slowed until it was indistinguishable. More long minutes passed, and my brother and I searched for any sign my father was still alive. I couldn't find a pulse on the one arm he had left.

"I think he's gone, Judah." The finality of the statement stole the air from my lungs, and then the tears began to fall.

"Should we get mo—" my brother said and was cut off by a sudden gasp.

"Shhhane…Juud—" My father struggled to speak. His gazes intensified, fighting to get the words out. My brother's eyes were wide and frightened. "The light f-ffades, m-my sonsss. You think…" Again his eyes blazed through some internal struggle, and he squeezed them closed. Blood stained tears slipped from the corners. Then his lids flew open, and he continued hurriedly, his voice now eerie in its strength and steadiness. "You think this is your home, but it's not. You must…become saints…a light set apart in a world of darkness…" He grasped for air, his teeth gnashed. "You will be saints…but you are not…the navigators."

His voice diminished to less than a whisper. The fingers of his left hand closed around mine, and I felt a surge of sorrow for my brother who could not feel the clasp of our father's lifeless hand as he passed. But as I lifted my head I saw I was wrong. Judah gaped at the hand attached to my father's nearly severed right arm. The fingers wrapped tightly about Judah's, as tightly as it's opposite held mine. Overwhelming power gripped me and my heart leapt.

"Stand together," he gasped, the oxygen no longer reaching his lungs. "As brothers. The Bitter Path lies before you. Will you wa-alk it—"

His spirit left his body then. "I will walk it," I said aloud and my brother joined me.

"We are not the navigators…"

6

The revolver trembled in his hand. Judah, Johnny, and I could only watch with bated breath. There was no comfort for Dean. Though we tried, he could find no relief from his brothers who still had their wives. The creature—the thrall—that had been Haley must die. My father lay dead beside the grave of Luke Argo, waiting patiently to become his neighbor once more. Because of this, she must die. Because my child had been taken, she must die. She must die because she was no longer Haley. Above all else, she must die because the emptiness inside her had robbed us of our friend, and because the husk before us would never stop until everyone she had ever loved was dead. And so it was that Dean came to be standing amongst his brothers in the peak of night, shivering against the cold, willing himself to pull the trigger.

"She was my wife and I loved her." It was barely audible, more for himself than for the benefit of those around. "I still love her." He acknowledged us then, and I saw his gun stop shaking.

"You aren't alone," I said to my friend. I wished I could take the burden from him. That he would pass me the gun, walk away, and cover his ears. But I saw the steadiness in his hand and knew that would not happen.

"We take care of our own, right?" he said with a feeble smirk. "I think I remember that from a movie."

He closed his eyes and said something I couldn't hear, something only for him, then opened them. And with a gentle squeeze, he released his wife.

7

Three new graves. Our private cemetery grew far too quickly. My father, Haley, Anna, and Luke made four deaths in half as many years.

Only three of the graves held a body. The third we dug for Anna. The twins had not been told of her demise, but it didn't change the fact that the Anna we knew had been dead for a long time. That Anna deserved to be honored with a proper burial.

Dean asked my brother to say a few words. As he spoke, I reflected on the years I'd known Haley. The first time we met, I yelled at her for ruining a game of Trivial Pursuit. She was impulsive, irrational, and ignorant. But as the years passed, those things that drove me crazy transformed into qualities I found endearing, and we had become better friends than I would have thought possible. Those days had been so much simpler. No thralls, no one shooting their wives. Just relationships and what you made of them. Yet as Judah's kind words drew to a close, all I felt was guilt over that stupid game of trivia.

I struggled for several minutes over what to say about my father. The chapel loomed overhead, its steeple stretching for grey sky. The sun broke through the perpetual darkness, tinting gloom with a soft orange light. It was not beautiful, but appreciated nonetheless. A comforting thought came to me.

"If he were given a choice," I said, "this would be the color sky my father would've wanted to be buried beneath. The clouds are dismal, yes, but whenever the sun is persistent enough to pierce through the gloom, I'll think of my dad." My mom's near silent sobs infected me and I began to weep.

"My father was a teacher, a counselor, an example, and a friend," I said. "I told Sydney once that I would be lost if my dad died. I thought of the jokes, the encouragement, the scolding that would be lost with him, and I believed I wouldn't be able to handle life without his guidance. I know now I was wrong. Though all those things will be missed, I've learned the things he wished me to learn. He is gone from this earth, but he is not gone from our hearts and our minds."

My voice caught, and I realized I could go no further. Placing a hand on my shoulder, Judah continued for me. "With his last words, my father spoke of sainthood and brotherhood. Of standing together against the increasing darkness. Even on his deathbed—or in his death*barn* as it were—he could think only of those he loved. He doesn't have to worry any longer. He did what he was here to do, and he did it well. Today, he rests in a place far better than this. And we can be assured it is very well with his soul." My brother gazed slowly over the landscape that surrounded us, lingering on the graves of Haley and Anna. "Oh, that we all could be so fortunate."

8

My brothers and I hovered amongst the graves once the rest of our family had dispersed. Only my mother still lingered, but she remained at a distance, grieving in solitude. An image of Anna came to mind, headless in the forest. This is how it began with her, with the loss of her husband. The despair followed and then the darkness. Let it not be the same with my mother.

Johnny, hearing my thoughts about Anna perhaps, broke the silence.

"You find that pasty bitch?" he said, oblivious to his current whereabouts.

"You mean your mother-in-law?" Dean asked with a grin.

"That thing's no more my mother-in-law than I am a ho-mo-sexual."

"She used to be your mother-in-law," said Judah. "Does that mean you used to be a homo?"

"Is that why you joined the football team?" Dean said. "I know it wasn't because you were any good."

"Listen," Johnny said, casually sloughing off the jeers, "all I know is if I saw that thing again I'd shoot it with my boomstick! Boom-Yow!" He mimed firing off his shotgun. He seemed so excited about shooting Anna that I didn't have the heart to tell him I'd already done the deed.

"So what do you think Kate Beckinsale would look like as one of those things?" I asked.

"I'd do her," said Dean with a shrug.

"You're not exactly picky," Judah said.

"At least I don't pitch a tent when my dog sits on my lap," Dean came back quickly.

"He was a very nice dog."

"Personally, I love it when a girls' skin starts rotting off," Johnny said.

This was why I loved my brothers. Because we had just nearly lost our lives, and yet they still had a sense of humor.

Sydney beckoned us to the house, holding out a beer for each of us (including one for my mother who drank it in my father's honor despite her distaste). I studied mom and saw not despair, but peace. I thought of my father's final words—the most important words he could think to impart. *You think this is your home, but it's not.*

I hoped he was right. My body and mind ached, and I was beginning to doubt everything I thought I knew. The debilitating choices I'd made in the past were easing their hold over me. In its place emerged an inner assurance I had never experienced. Ironic that I should realize it at a time such as this.

My brother tapped my shoulder. He shrugged his head in the direction of my father's grave where the silhouette of a woman knelt. Sara had apparently survived the encounter with the thralls and had come to pay her respects. She rose gracefully and approached.

She remained silent for a long time, stirring an awkward tension about the group. When she did speak, it was in an unsure voice, so different than the powerful confidence she normally exuded. "I…was wrong, Shane McCall, in my attempt to stop you from saving your daughter." She wrestled with the words as if an apology had never before passed her lips. I thought it probably hadn't.

"I have watched for eons the progress and decline of the human race, the ebb and flow of your existence that has brought you to this moment and this place. I had fooled myself into believing I understood you. But I had only ever watched. Never had I even spoken to another human being before you, Shane McCall…let alone fought for one's survival."

She examined the forest on all sides, suddenly frightened. We seemed safe for the time being, but her frantic gaze brought with it a level of doubt. She settled herself quickly, bringing her focus to me once more as she rifled through a fold in her garments. Her hand appeared again in a fist, clearly having found the item in question. A few more worried glances and two quick steps brought her directly in front of me, our toes all of an inch apart.

"The object I possess," she said, gazing at her still clenched fist, her knuckles white from the pressure, "that I now bestow unto you, I have had since this…plunge into darkness began. I have been its keeper, though I know not from where it came, only who it was intended for. I accept now that it is time to pass it on." Breathing almost painfully, she stared deeply, her pale blue eyes moving steadily back and forth between my own. "But first, I must give you this."

Sara searched again through her robes and held out a rolled piece of parchment. "The only insight I have into this plague...other than my own knowledge, which is vast, yet largely irrelevant."

I took the scroll from the woman and carefully unrolled it. The paper appeared ancient, its fibers rough and prominent. I scanned over the intricately woven inscription. It contained only a few short lines, none of which made any sense, but it was the signature at the bottom that sent my heart racing.

"Faris McCall, Saint of the Boughs, Order of the Tree...my son wrote this?" I said, passing the scroll to my wife. "He's just a boy...he couldn't have written this."

"And yet his name stares us in the face," Sara said, her usual annoyance seeping back into her tone. "The meaning is clear, I hope. If not, I fear I may be speaking to a dullard...which speaks as much about myself as it does you. I normally don't associate with dullards."

Her self-righteous, insulting demeanor made my teeth grind. The vagueness of her explanations, the refusal to answer simple questions, irritated me beyond belief. But still I couldn't help but like the woman.

"Please continue," I said. "Don't let my stupidity stop you."

She nodded, a faint trace of a smile touching her lips. "It was not the boy you know that wrote this, but the man he will become."

"You mean it's from the future?" I said, more confused than ever. Sara's terse, one sentence responses wore on my patience. Maybe I didn't like her as much as I thought.

She flashed a smug smirk that reminded me of my brother. "A possible future, perhaps...though the words were as new to me when first I read them as they are to you now."

"How do we know you didn't write this yourself?"

Sara rocked impatiently on her toes. "There is much you won't understand, because your grasp on the universe is...limited. So in the interest of time, and with the consideration that the more I say, the more confused and irritable you may become, I'll make this as uncomplicated as possible. These items came to me at the very moment the *Ra'ah* appeared in the space above."

"The what-ha?" Judah said.

I had completely forgotten the others. Sydney, my mother, Dean, Judah, Johnny...they all wore matching expressions of befuddlement. "*Ra'ah*," I said. "It's what she calls the evil that fell from the sky." I motioned to the northwest. "I'll explain later."

Sara gave us a second to shift our focus back to her, and said, "The implications written on the page are plain. Faris must survive, and this…" She brought her fist level with my chest and uncurled her fingers to reveal a small glowing orb roughly the size of a marble. "…this is…honestly I am at a loss as to what this is. It burns as an ember when I am near you."

I squinted against the light, suddenly aware of heat radiating from the tiny object. Sara hadn't been kidding when she said it burned, but she betrayed no sign that it hurt her. Her eyebrows rose, and she nodded.

Hesitantly, I lifted my hand and she rolled the thing onto my shaking palm with a sigh; if it was of relief or sorrow, I could not tell. Upon touching my skin, its light went out, leaving me in total darkness. I squinted at the sky and around at the others, waiting for my eyes to once again grow accustomed to the darkness of the night. The object was no longer hot, its heat extinguished as quickly as its light when it touched my hand.

"What is it?" Sydney was the first to ask.

"A seed…I think," I said, not completely sure I was correct.

"A seed it is," Sara confirmed with quiet awe. "Though it is not of any tree or plant I am familiar with." Then for added mystery, she said, "And I am familiar with many things."

"Let us see it," Dean said, and I turned, holding out my hand.

"What the hell are we supposed to do with a seed?" Johnny asked in the tone he normally used when faced with something he couldn't shoot or slice.

I already had an idea what to do with it, and when the seed began to tremble in my hand I became sure. "We plant it," I said, moving slowly in the direction of my father's grave.

As I drew nearer to my father's final resting place, the seed's vibration increased. When I reached the grave, it lurched from my hand, landed in the center of the mound, and began to burrow. I fell to my knees, not out of panic but from sheer curiosity. I sensed the seed was now exactly where it wanted to be, and was fascinated by the fact that a seed could actually *want* to be somewhere.

Then it was gone.

I rose to my feet, unable to conceal the smile spreading across my face. I felt renewed somehow, refreshed like I had just woken from a good night's sleep and jumped into a pool of cold water. I studied my hands in astonishment, barely recognizing them. My brother, Johnny, and Dean gawked at me with the same emotion on their faces. They felt it, too. And Sydney, my mother…they basked in a glow that made them seem younger, revitalized.

"What does it feel like," Sara asked, her voice sounding distant in the midst of the elation I felt.

"I…" I began, stumbling for the words. "What is it?"
The strange woman gazed at me in wonder. "You don't know?" She tilted her head, pondering this fact. "It's redemption."

9

We walked together about halfway to the house before Sara stopped us. "I cannot stay here with you," she said in a forlorn voice. "There are things I must do, but I shall return when I am needed." She aimed her focus at my brother's swollen ankle. "I can restore you before I go, brother of Shane McCall."
"Restore me?" Judah asked, his full weight teetering on his left leg.
"*Heal* you. I can mend your leg, make it well, fix, repair, improve…I can go on."
He considered the offer and then shrugged. "Okay, sure."
Sara closed her eyes and smiled. She opened her mouth to speak, but the incantations I expected to come out never did. Instead she said, "You are healed," and opened her eyes.

The ritual spanned all of five seconds and more than one of us actually laughed. My brother wasn't one of them. He placed the toes of his broken leg onto the ground and increased the pressure until his entire weight leaned on it. He looked up, astonished. "I'm healed! Hallelujah!"

A mixture of shock and joy spread through the group. Amidst the jumble of congratulations and awed exclamations, I spied Sara turning to leave unnoticed, and a disturbing thought occurred to me.

"Sara!"

The beautiful woman turned as if she had expected my call. "If you could heal my brother, why didn't you heal my father?" The excitement faded at once and all eyes bore into the strange woman.

She nodded gravely, picking her words carefully. "My powers are great, Shane McCall. It was not beyond my ability to save your father. It would have, in fact, been easy for me to do so." She raised a hand as we started forward in protest. "What was difficult was to allow him to die. To let him fulfill his purpose without interference. He did not suffer, he felt none of the excruciating pain that attempted to ravage him. I interfered that much, so that you could hear the wisdom he passed on to you."

I asked the only question I had left in me. "But why?"

"Why must someone die while others live on? I do not have all the answers. I do, however, know that you have slumbered through your entire life, Shane McCall, crippled by your fear of responsibility. The light rapping had turned to pounding, but still you did not open the door to your destiny. It was not until your father passed that you finally accepted your calling, when the wind of fate blew the door open and you were forced to stare yourself in the eye. You think you have been redeemed, Shane McCall? Then heed your father's final words. You are the saints this world so desperately needs. You are the light in the darkness."

She swept her robes into a polite bow and was gone.

Patrick Fitzpatrick

1

The sand squished between my toes when the cold water rushed over them, the white froth swirling about my ankles, the gritty buildup around my heels eroding as the wave washed back out to sea. Goosebumps covered my skin, the wind cool and refreshing after the hot summer we just had. In another few weeks, the air would be too cool for the beach. The surfers would brave it in their wetsuits, but those in shorts and bare chests—or girls wearing much less—would find the ocean less enjoyable.

Someone called my name from the ocean, and I scanned the horizon to find the source. I didn't remember coming here with anyone, though for some reason I couldn't remember much of anything. I was just here, at the beach, alone...

My name came again, this time louder, closer. But there was no one there. I searched the length of the shoreline to my right, the sloping dunes behind, and around the opposite stretch of beach. Empty.

As I came full circle, my feet sinking again into their soggy holes, I was startled to find two small boys hurdling from the water directly in front of me. I recognized one immediately, his abnormally large head bobbing awkwardly atop his skinny neck and body. The curly light brown hair, the He-Man swim trunks. *Judah.*

The other boy, the one calling my name, took longer to place. He was older, less clumsy than my little brother; his hair straight and blonde, eyes adventurous and laughing. "Shane," he said again, and a splat of wet sand hit me in the stomach. "My parents said we have ten more minutes. One more game of last man standing?"

Then my legs were taking me into the ocean. The two boys turned and leaped over a small wave, my brother not quite making it, and suddenly I knew who the second boy was.

Sean. But he's dead.

I shook my head, knowing that wasn't right because here he came, sloshing back, telling me to hurry up. He tugged at my arm, and as it pulled into view I saw it wasn't my arm at all. It was that of an eight year old boy. That couldn't be right either. I was a grown adult with two kids of my own. Still the body seemed to fit me, and I seemed to know it. The legs and arms, fingers and toes, had familiar features, responded to my commands like they always had. Like they still do.

We waded to where the shore pound broke, no higher than Judah's shoulders.

"Here we go," Sean screamed as the first wave swept over us. It was small, maybe waist high, and even Judah had no problem keeping his balance. The next rose slightly larger, and the third sent my brother floundering toward the shore. Now it was just me and Sean. I dug in as the fourth wave crashed down, the set gathering strength, but not enough to declare a winner. Two more came and went, until finally one came in with sufficient force to knock Sean off his feet.

He came up laughing, my brother right on his heels. Facing the beach, I noticed a pair of adults waving in our direction. Sean and Judah barreled past me, but I was distracted by the new arrivals. I looked around and could see no one else.

"I think your parents are calling us in, Sean," I said over my shoulder. I turned in time to see a huge wave curl over the two boys. They faced me, hearing my voice, their backs to the hulking wall of water. "Watch out," I shouted, pumping my thighs through the ocean, sweeping at the water with my hands to gain speed, but it was too late. The wave seemed to pause, to emphasize its raw power, and then it was smashing down.

I dove under the whitewash, losing ground as it swept me in the wrong direction. I broke the surface, and found I was alone. I dove again, feeling around, afraid to open my eyes in the stinging salt water, and found no one. I plodded further out, inhaled, and plunged beneath the surface. I clenched my teeth and opened my eyes. The salt stung, distracting me for only a second, and then I saw something floating a few feet away. Sean swayed with the motion of the water, unconscious, unbreathing. I reached out, but a booming voice thundered in my head.

"Not him," it said, and I listened. I pushed Sean toward the surface with all my strength and swam deeper. I was running out of air, growing desperate, about to go back up when something brushed my leg. I sloshed around and found myself staring into my brother's unseeing eyes. I grabbed him, pushed off the ocean floor, and kicked as hard as my child's legs would allow. I shoved Judah's head into the cool afternoon air, and suddenly a deafening *GONG* clattered through my skull. Another followed, and then silence.

Gasping, I wrenched Judah out of the water, desperately searching for help. *GONG, GONG,* the sound came again, louder. It wasn't in my head either; it was in the sky, the sand, the sea. I dismissed it, bent over my brother, and recoiled. The boy in the sand was the same age and size as Judah, but it was him no longer. It was my son, Faris, and I was no longer eight years old.

The echoing thunder blasted through me again, and I was shaking. The second blast opened my eyes. And my wife's face hovered over me.

2

The chapel bell rang twice more and I bolted down the stairs, strapping my guns to my waist, and burst out the front door before the reverberation faded over the hills. I shivered as the first flakes of snow touched my bare shoulders, and wheeled around the corner, sprinting northwest, *two tolls, two tolls,* my only thought. I slept in my jeans and boots in case of just such an emergency, though slumbering through two passes of the bell defeated the purpose.

I was the last to arrive. Judah, Johnny, and Dean already stared off into the woods when I skidded up beside them.

"Nice of you to join us," my brother said, and I wrapped him in a bear hug so tight he had to slap me before I would release him. "What's that about?"

"I just love you," I said, raking over the tree line.

"Fag," he said. "You see anything?"

The others shook their heads. "Who's up there?" I asked.

"Mom, I think."

"Probably a false alarm, she can't see three feet in front of her. Who let her take lookout anyway?"

"You did," they all said at once.

"Oh, right." I couldn't make out anything through the haze and trees. I searched for the moon, but it cloaked itself behind invisible black clouds. It felt early.

"There," Johnny said, pointing to the right near a clump of white oaks. A figure squeezed between the pale trees. And it seemed to be dragging something…its movements too calculated to be a thrall.

"Holy…" Judah said, as the shape stumbled down the trench and halted at the fence. "Is that…?"

I recognized him a moment later. "It's Patrick Fitzpatrick."

3

We approached warily, knowing all too well that familiar faces didn't always mean good intentions. But when the chains on his wrist came into view, I left caution to the wind and ran to the man. His face was cast in shadow, long hair hanging in tangled knots over his cheeks and forehead. I reached the fence, and followed the chains to the snow covered ground.

"Oh…" I managed to say before my stomach twisted and I had to avert my eyes.

Johnny hurdled the fence before I could warn him. "Mother of a retarded whore!" He retreated back over the fence a second later.

"Patrick?" Judah said. "Can you hear me?"

His head creaked up. "Yeah, a deaf man could hear you," he said. "Can you get these off of me?"

"Are they…?"

He nodded. I stuttered, then scaled the fence. Stepping carefully around the frozen lumps at the end of the chains, I drew my gun. "Lift your arms."

He obeyed to the best of his ability, but he could barely get them above his waist.

"Now hold still." I pulled one of the chains tight from his wrist and shot it in two. I did the same with the other side, and then helped

200

Patrick Fitzpatrick crawl under the fence.

In the light, Patrick Fitzpatrick proved a bloody disaster. Long, deep gouges ran the length of his arms, neck, and face. He was missing four fingers and even more toes. But the real shock came when Devon removed his shirt to inspect the wounds to his torso. His back resembled his extremities, multiple slashes crisscrossing in gruesome patterns. His chest was something different altogether.

"Remember, I'm just the messenger," he said, and then he passed out.

From clavicle to naval, carved deep into his flesh was a message. An impossible ultimatum. It read:

THE BOY =
ARGO LIVES ☐
ELSE =
ARGO DIES ☐

4

"My step-girls," Patrick Fitzpatrick said through heart-wrenching sobs. While he lay unconscious, Judah and I had hauled the mutilated bodies into the cemetery and dug the necessary holes. He had awakened by the time we finished, and sat hunched over a bowl of light broth.

"What happened?" Jordan said.

He told us his story. I almost wish he hadn't.

His ex-wife was nowhere to be found when he got to her house in Knoxville. Most of the streets were deserted, hardly any cars in the driveway. A few people roamed the neighborhood, ignoring him as he passed. He found the girls in a small hidden compartment in one of the bedroom's walk-in closets. It took almost a half hour of calling their names to get them to come out.

They were starving and scared. They hadn't come out of the closet, except to eat what little food was in the kitchen, for nearly a week.

"Other people came lookin' for 'em, but after the first screams resulted in four dead people in their livin' room, they didn't come out no more." Patrick Fitzpatrick hung his head in his hands. "Don't know why they come out for me. Wish they didn't."

True to his word, he headed back to the Argo to return Luke's truck. It broke down about five miles northwest.

"That can't be a coincidence," Johnny said. "That close to the pit?"

Patrick Fitzpatrick's head wagged slowly. "It wasn't no coincidence. Them things piled on me like stink on shit the minute I got outta the truck. Didn't kill me though. Cut me up, took some fingers and toes, then made me watch as he stripped the skin from my little girls."

"Alex?" I said.

He shrugged. "Never said his name. That was recent though. He kept 'em alive for over a year in that pit. I never saw 'em though, just heard their screams. He kept me chained up, wouldn't kill me…said I was Plan B, but he kept changin' the letter of the plan on down the alphabet. Think I ended up on Plan E or F."

"In the end, he butchered the girls and chained 'em to my wrists." I pictured him on the long journey through the woods, dragging the carcasses of the daughters he meant to save. Wanting to end it all. Not doing it because of the debt he thought he owed us.

We should have known better than to take our eyes off him.

The next morning we found him hanging from the barn rafters, the message even more petrifying as it swayed at the end of the rope.

Silence

1

Patrick Fitzpatrick was buried in the cemetery beside his girls. The threat was real, but the consequences never came. I never really got over Patrick hanging himself or the dead girls, but most of the others chose to erase that single night from their minds. Especially, Judah and Devon.

That was five months ago. They passed like a dream in which new life was given to our family. The baby Levi, my nephew, was born into the lull between two storms. Overwhelmed by their joy, my brother and Devon played the happy parents perfectly, as one would expect and none could blame. The excitement was intoxicating: Jordan spoke frequently of having a child of her own, and even Sydney whispered hints of wanting a third. My mother, using the new addition to distract from the loss of her husband, was as enthralled with Levi as the terrible creatures were to the darkness they served.

Life also bloomed from my father's grave in the form of a young tree. There was no mistaking the origins of the sapling, first sprouting and then thriving within weeks of the tiny seed's planting. Few leaves adorned its milky branches at first, but they were unlike any I had seen in all the years I spent exploring the forests surrounding the Argo. Pale green, shaped like thumb-sized tear drops, they seemed to illuminate the darkness with an inner light, although no light was actually emitted. They didn't merely glow, that would not do them justice, and the tree could be seen from a long distance in the blackest of nights. They did not radiate light; they *were* light. By all accounts, this tree was the most magnificent thing I or my companions had ever seen. It flourished during that fleeting time of peace, much like our family flourished, its branches stretching ever outward and upward at an unprecedented rate. Unaccustomed joy filled us as we crouched under the tree's low boughs, and we frequently would find one another lounging beneath its shade and shelter. I often imagined its roots enfolding around my father's body in a protective embrace as I sat with my back against its trunk, grown to the thickness of my bicep in mere months. I found this vision comforted me greatly.

And what of the creatures, the thralls? Like Patrick Fitzpatrick, they seemed to disappear into the corners of their minds.

Only Dean and I seemed to remember their existence, their threat. Not wishing to grow complacent, he and I would venture into the forest on "reconnaissance" operations. I often brought Zoe and Faris on these outings with the hopes they could acquire the knowledge needed to survive in the plausible case they were forced to grow up without parents. Dean taught them to set traps and to make secure campsites, both of which he learned during his time in the military. He never talked much about what he did or where he'd been deployed, but his knowledge of ensnaring enemies, explosive devises, and creating nearly invisible shelters (these usually in trees or holes in the ground) proved incredibly useful. A few weeks of training and my children were able to do these things better than their father.

Generally lacking in the useful skills category, I was able to teach Faris and Zoe to track wild game and move through the brush in near silence. Both skills I learned in the heat of the moment, usually by the seat of my pants, and I wanted my children to be confident in their abilities if the time came when they'd have to use them. As in the case with Dean's lessons, Zoe and Faris absorbed every instruction with zeal, far surpassing my level of aptitude in a matter of weeks.

I became confident they would at least survive without me. Rapidly approaching adolescence, Zoe had already assumed the role of secondary guardian over Faris—much to my son's chagrin in most cases. However, she was less bossy than concerned, which made me wonder if the seven year old could foresee what to expect in the coming days better than her father. Sara made clear the importance of Faris's survival, and perhaps this played a subconscious role in Zoe's increasing protectiveness of her brother. But as I observed them in the forest and around the property in those silent months, I noticed more than just a defensive quality in their relationship. They developed a bond—perhaps upon Zoe's return to the Argo following her kidnapping—that grew much stronger than the simple little brother/over-protective sister relationship common amongst siblings. This bond was suddenly just…there. They were inseparable, always in agreement, and *never fought.* It was a stretch for me to make it a few hours without arguing with Judah, let alone *never* fighting; and here Zoe and Faris, two children, could do it for nearly a year.

Over time, their signing to each other even stopped. I asked Zoe about this once. She said she didn't need to sign because Faris always knew what she was thinking.

"It started after Grandpa died," she said like it was the most normal thing in the world. "He just knows what I'm thinking and he can tell me things without speaking. I can't do it, I tried. Faris says to stop trying to think at him because it makes me look stupid. All I have to do is think it and he hears it."

I was aghast. It wasn't until Zoe tugged on my arm that I realized my mouth hung wide open.

"Sorry, honey, I was thinking about what you said, about Faris's voice." I could never dream of my son being any more perfect than he already was. But I had never heard him speak; his small voice remained absent for a reason only he knew, and I found myself entranced by the idea of finally hearing it. I hesitated…my eyes teared up, then whispered, "What's it…sound like?"

"It's cute, daddy," Zoe giggled. "Like I always thought it would be. It's a little weird not really hearing it, but still hearing it, you know?"

I beamed. "Do you think he'd be able to talk to me?"

She just shrugged and walked away. Darling child.

2

Sara says it's the tree that lets me do it.

I hugged Faris so fiercely he wouldn't have been able to speak if not for his special talent. Zoe was right: his voice sounded exactly as I imagined it would.

Holding him at arm's length, unable to release his shoulders, I asked, "When did you talk to Sara?" Concern came over me, and he could see it.

You don't have to say it out loud, daddy. I can hear your thoughts.

You can hear me? I concentrated intensely. *This is so weird.*

I can hear you. You don't have to try so hard. It's nice to talk to you, daddy.

I almost broke down right then. My legs began to wobble. My little boy was *speaking* to me, his tiny voice as perfect and innocent as his face.

My boy..., I thought, struggling to keep the conversation going. Ironic that my ability to come up with something to say would cease at the moment my son finally found the power to reply. Finally, the question I'd always wanted to ask came pouring out of me. "Why don't you speak, Faris?"

He tapped his index finger to his temple, thinking. I remembered Judah doing the same thing as a child. *The world is too loud as it is, daddy.*

My jaw dropped. Everything he said amazed me.

I love you, daddy. Let me do the talking, okay? I nodded and he continued. *Sara speaks to me sometimes, but she never comes to see me. She says it's the tree in the cemetery that's letting me do this. But she says I always had it in the first place, that the tree is just...*akivating *it.* The mispronunciation reminded me of how young he was. Hearing him string sentences together made him seem so...old. *I don't really understand it. Sara says I'm special and when the time comes, I will go with her to a safe place.*

"Whoa, whoa, whoa," I said aloud. "Over my dead body you'll be going with her."

I think that is the point.

When he did not go on I took a minute to consider his words. *She's not going to kill me...is she?*

He laughed and this time I did break down. The sound of his chiming laughter in my head was too much.

Daddy? Faris placed a hand on my head and waited for my sobs to subside. *I love you, daddy. And Sara would never kill you to take me.*

"Then they're coming again," I said aloud and stood.

He nodded. *Soon. Their master is building a new army. It took a long time after Sara destroyed the others. She's been running since she did that. But she's been running since the first time she helped us.*

"Running from what?"

With your mind.

Sorry. Who's she on the run from?

She flees from others like her...but really there's no one else like her.

206

She says they're not supposed to interfere with the way things should go. When she helped us, she made herself an outlaw and the others are after her. But Sara says not to worry about that. She will come when she can to take me to a safe place. Somewhere the thralls can't get me and the others don't know about.

Because we will not survive this time. The statement had a certain truth to it. Cold fingers made their way up my spine. *Have you spoken to your mother?*

His face went sad. *I can't. I try every day, but nothing gets through. I couldn't hear her either. I told Zoe not to tell her about what I can do. I don't want to make her sad. So far, the only people I can hear are you and Zoe. Zoe was first and I told her not to tell you for the same reason as mommy. I'm surprised she kept the secret* this *long. I tried it on everyone and until now, Zoe was the only one I could get through to. Maybe the ability will get stronger over time?*

"Maybe," I said. "But I think we should tell your mom."

He nodded, his gaze shifting over my shoulder.

"Something else you want to tell me, son?"

Only..., he let the word hang for a long time. *It's...I kinda lied just now...when I said you and Zoe are the only ones I hear.*

Who else then? I didn't like where this was going. If it was something good, he would have already told me. A minute passed and he didn't answer. *It's okay, Faris. Just tell me. Who else?*

It's not a who, *exactly.* He strung out the last word, taking it apart in syllables.

You don't mean...you can hear them?

His teeth clenched between his thin lips.

What do they say? I asked, truly curious, for all I had ever heard from them were high-pitched shrieks.

Well they *don't say anything. They just scream...all the time. They're hurting, but the pain will never stop. I think the sounds they make are their hearts crying or something...because of what they lost...its unbearable. There's a lot of them now, and it's getting hard to tune them out.* He hesitated again; this time his face was frightened. *The master, the one that was here...Alex. He speaks. He calls to the thralls, organizes them. It took him a long time to gather them, but they always answer his call. He almost has enough now.*

"We're in trouble, I think." I knelt before my son and hugged him again. "We need to prepare."

That's not the worst thing…

I held him out from me as I had before. *How can it be worse?*

His fear was palpable, his pale blue eyes round and bulging. *Because…he knows I can hear him.*

A lump took shape in my throat and I tried to swallow it down. "How can you know?"

I know because he calls for me even more than he calls for the thralls.

3

"But Levi…Zoe and Faris," Judah cried over the panicked commotion that broke out across the compound after I announced the return of the thralls. Several attempts were made by Dean and I to relay the dire nature of the situation before my family finally awoke from the la-la-land they'd been living in. I actually had to slap my brother across the face before he internalized the message. "How can we protect them from another attack?"

I explained that Sara was coming to take the children somewhere safe, though my words felt weak. The woman had yet to show herself, the vague words…*thoughts*…of my young son the only glimmer of hope I had to go on. This revelation brought on a roar of dissent, but what had I really expected? That we should willingly give our children to a woman we knew next to nothing about?

The message was clear: give over Faris, and we all live; choose anything different and we all die. I had dreaded the decision the group would make after Patrick arrived with Alex's demands. Hadn't I even allowed them to slip off into their happy little world just to avoid that discussion?

Now there was a third choice. One that surely meant certain death for us, but offered hope for our children.

Sydney adamantly refused at first to allow the strange woman anywhere near Faris and Zoe, though I saw the painful resignation in her eyes even as her mouth spoke to the contrary.

"Faris and Zoe will go with Sara when…*if*…she returns, Judah," I said calmly as the agony of leadership burned like a hot coal in my stomach. I was forced to do it again, make the decisions no one else would, and I hated myself for it. My brother was a wreck on the outside, but I saw the rage welling up through the tears. Devon was a stone, and I knew she would not be moved.

"My children will go," I said, this time speaking directly to Devon, "and perhaps they'll live." My throat caught as I attempted to finish the words. "I hold out no hope for our survival, but I do for theirs...*if* they leave."

Once again my words rang empty.

"I want to stay and fight, Daddy," Zoe demanded, stomping her small feet on the ground and crossing her arms.

I broke down then and hugged her tightly, refusing to let go even as she cried to be allowed to stay. She would fight bravely and brilliantly, of this I had no doubt. But she would also die miserably; of this I was absolutely sure. In the end, it was Faris that calmed her with words only she could hear.

In the end, it was also Faris that convinced my brother to let go of his only child. Slowly approaching his uncle, my son put his arms around his leg. My brother's course was decided with that hug.

4

Winter brought foul flurries of snow and ice that covered the landscape, making life nearly unbearable. I dreamt of Florida winters that at times felt much like Florida summers, where we would pass the time outdoors in nothing but shorts and a tee shirt. And although many winters had come and gone since we moved to the Argo, Christmas all but forgotten, this winter seemed the most hostile. We stood near the chapel, gravitating to the tree, huddled for warmth in several inches of snow, too numb to take up the effort of making a fire.

She came like the wind, a thief in the night, and that was how we received her. A threatening menace had never been how Sara was viewed through our eyes, but in that moment she was terrible. We laid our hopes for our children's survival at her feet, yet we could not dismiss the thought that she was *stealing* them for her own unknown purposes. The wind blew thick swirls of white through which only the black backdrop of the night could pierce. Sara, a ghost in the darkness, stepped through the wisping veil and stood before us ere we ever saw her approach.

Her manner of appearance did nothing to alleviate the tension that wound through us like a tug-of-war rope, pulling us in two directions: our selfish desire for our children to stay with us, and our hopes that they might survive. We agreed, for the most part, albeit reluctantly, to give Faris, Zoe, and Levi over to Sara's care, but I could see minds changing as the woman, witch, or whatever she was, came nearer. For years it seemed we stood in silence and then she spoke.

"You have made your decision, then, though I see by your scowls that all do not agree." Her gaze fell on each of us in turn, lingering upon my son for many moments before returning to me. "I will protect him with my life, I assure you, and under my guidance, he will do great things. Shall I take him now, then?"

I squinted through the snow, not overly thrilled with her use of the word *guidance*, nor the "great" things my son would do under it. I was also suddenly aware that we had not fully understood her intentions. "You'll take them all, Sara. We wish for all of our children to survive, not just the one you favor."

I heard my brother inhale beside me with a hiss, but I didn't turn my eyes from the woman before me.

She took a moment to consider my words. "I did not intend to take them all."

She said nothing further. The tension mounted, this I could sense without seeing the grimaces, the anger on my brother's face. And as the silence stretched on, it finally broke.

"You condemn my son to death because you didn't *intend* to take him with you? And what about Zoe? You think Faris would leave her here to die?" My brother stepped forward, hand on the hilt of his gun, eyes blazing in a way I had only witnessed in battle. "You've been around a long time, I'm sure, but you know nothing of the humanity you claim to have watched for centuries. We are blood, woman. And we do not give over our blood so lightly."

Johnny and Dean moved to my brother's side, prepared to fight. The children were just as much theirs as they were mine and Judah's. My brother's words ignited them.

"Stay your hands, brave men," said Sara, perhaps sensing her growing peril, though laughter brimmed her words. "You speak true, Judah McCall, I am only now learning what it means to be human. If I had entered your world as a participant ages ago instead of merely chronicling it, things may be different. But as they are, I know only an inkling of the inner struggle you face." She paused for a long time, considering her alternatives. "I will take the other two as well. They may be of use to me. The power of blood shows itself to be a strong motivator, and this too may be advantageous."

Glancing at my brothers, I saw they were in agreement, though not entirely pleased. She spoke of my daughter and Levi as tools for some elusive scheme, and it was not sitting well with any of us. I turned and nodded my consent to the beautiful yet powerful woman that would take our children from us.

"Come now little ones," she said softly, a failed attempt at emotion.

"First," I said, my hand raised. "First, tell us the rest of what you know."

She took another of her long, considering pauses and said, "Very well. But I do not hold all the answers." Another pondering expression. "The thing came through a gate..." she blurted, as if tricking herself to say it, "...though it was not mine. It couldn't have been mine."

We stared, stricken by this ambiguous revelation. The woman gauged our reactions, possibly contemplating the consequences of her next words.

"Umm," my mother's timid voice cut through the silence. "What do you mean, a gate? Are you saying you may have brought it here?"

A collective gasp. The murmurs began, rising to the point I could no longer tell who was speaking to whom.

"Quiet!" I shouted, my head beginning to ache. It wasn't enough we were losing our children, but here we were acting like children. "Explain yourself, Sara."

"Beings such as I may open doorways. We use them to travel, and for...other purposes. It was through one of these that the *Ra'ah* has come." She sighed, the implications laid bare. "I say *we* because there were once many more with this ability...this gift. But I alone remain. I did not open that gate, Shane McCall. I did not bring that thing here. I couldn't have."

Her conviction swayed toward the end. Sara was the sole remnant of her race of whatever-they-were, the only one who could have opened that door. There was only one obvious conclusion, and she knew it.

"I do, however, know what it is," Sara continued. "It is evil in its purest form. An infecting darkness. And darkness tends to spread as it has throughout the world we inhabit. This darkness has taken a vessel, the man you know as Alex. He had been taken ere you ever met him, though I believe you caught his glimpse on that day in the mist. Its influence stretches far, entering all manner of beings, but it is humanity it craves, because humans possess souls. It has never been this powerful before. It devours the will of a person, drinking its life, its purpose, and when that is no more it devours the soul. What is left is a mindless, bloodless corpse, walking the earth with no guidance but what the master gives it."

"So how far has this spread?" Dean interjected, lifted from his stupor enough to form a coherent thought. No doubt that thought was of Haley. "And why have some of us been affected while others have not?"

"Good questions, both," said Sara, "though I only know the answer to one. There is nowhere within the sphere of our existence that the *Ra'ah* has not been able to reach. The world as we know it is over. But there are pockets of individuals, like yourselves, that have resisted its influence. I know not how this is possible, though I have my theories. I dare not voice them, however."

"You've seen these others?" Jordan asked, hopeful in this revelation.

"I have. And I have assisted some of them, though none as much as you. But do not place your hopes on such things, dear. They cannot help you, as they must help themselves."

Jordan hung her head, all hope drained from her pretty face. Hers was not the only gesture of defeat. My mother clutched Faris and Zoe to her as if the thralls surrounded them; Devon and Sydney uttered involuntary gasps through their teeth, barely audible above the swirl of the wind. I shivered as I thought of the inevitable battle fast approaching. And we would receive no more help. Once Sara left us alone without our children, she would not return to save us as she had before.

I turned my back to the witch. I no longer thought of her as an ally, but rather one outside the laws of nature with her own goals and her own ambitions. Ambitions that included the *guidance* of my son and the *use* of my daughter and nephew. Not to mention that she may or may not have brought this whole thing upon us in the first place. I inhaled deeply, realizing it no longer mattered if she had. If she didn't take them now, my children would not survive. That was all that mattered.

Kneeling, I drew Zoe and Faris close to me, tears already stinging my eyes. Sydney dropped to her knees beside us and wrapped her arms around them.

"Look out for each other above all else," I whispered. "This woman, whatever she is, has offered you safety, and you must accept it. But that is all you must accept. You are *my* children, and you have strong minds and strong wills. Listen to your hearts, and they will tell you right from wrong. And you must heed one another's cautions…what one of you may not see, the other might."

"Daddy, I don't want to go," Zoe whispered, as if she could stay here to die. "I can fight beside you."

I had not the words. Faris put his hand into hers and I felt something pass between them. She lowered her head and nodded through heaving sobs.

"Know that we love you above all things," Sydney whispered into their ears as she hugged them tightly. "We do this because we can't save you ourselves, and we'll regret it for the rest of our short lives." Her words cut off as she too began to weep. She took the shamrock necklace she wore from around her neck—one of my favorites—and clasped it over Zoe's, fresh tears pouring from both of their eyes.

We stayed like that for an eternity, neither of us willing to let our children go first.

"It is time." Sara had her back to us, making intricate gestures in the air with her pale hands, low sounds issuing from her lips in a language I did not understand. She clapped her hands together quite suddenly and as she did this a sharp crack sounded from the air in front of her, trilling off into the hills.

"Behold, a *gate*."

A slit of bright light appeared perpendicular to the snow covered ground and stretched to the heavens beyond our vision. Her hands began to part and the slit opened wider until her arms reached their full span.

Stunned, we watched as she turned, the pillar of light nearly swallowing her, and beckoned the children forward with a sweep of her hand. With trembling arms, my brother lifted Levi from the arms of his grieving wife and gave his only son over to my daughter. The sorrow and anger on Judah's face burned so powerfully that I had to turn away.

Faris and Zoe, who now carried her infant cousin, made no move to step toward the light, their feet frozen to the ground. Sara smiled not unkindly and beckoned once again, this time placing first a leg, then an arm, and then half of her body within the doorway of light. Seeing her unharmed, Faris and Zoe took a small step forward, their frightened faces peering up at their mother and father. Tears streaming down my cheeks, freezing around the collar of my ragged jacket, I tried to smile, and nodded. "I love you, Zoe. I love you, Faris," I said to them, but neither turned from the gleaming pillar.

I watched as my children approached the doorway that would take them to a place only Sara knew and a sudden impulse took me. "Wait," I called, and I rushed to them, undoing the buckle of my gun-belt as I went. "Take these, son."

He turned at my voice, and so did Zoe and Sara. "They will have weapons where they are going," the witch said, almost amused.

"But he will not have *these* weapons," I snarled. "They were meant for you, Faris, I see that now. I would not have you leave without them."

He beamed at me and hugged my waist. Then he took the guns in his hand and followed his sister through the door, but not before sending his words through my mind; the last thing my son said to me before disappearing from my life forever. *We'll see you again…beneath the boughs.*

5

That night was a long one. My brother, Devon, and the others retired to the solitude of their rooms as soon as the gate disappeared. But Sydney and I lingered in the snow staring at the place we had last seen our children, feeling the hole in our hearts expand wider than the door that swallowed them. I sank to the cold ground. Sydney's arms wrapped me tightly and we wept together.

After the hope that the gate would open again and Zoe and Faris would come running into our arms dwindled to shame and despair, we finally wrenched ourselves from the yard and returned to the house.

"I regret it already, Syd," I said.

"I do, too, Shane," she said. "But I think when they come, our shame and regret will not be as strong." I saw in her eyes the reason I had loved her my whole life. They sparkled green with the remnants of the tears she had shed, but it was the fire behind them that sparked me. She hadn't lost hope. "When the dying begins, we'll rejoice together that our children aren't here."

I kissed her and she returned it with her whole being. We made love for the last time that night, and for an instant the crumbling world around us melted away.

If only I could have died then.

Together We Fall

1

*GONG, GONG, GONG...*The repeated clang of the church bell woke me from an unexpectedly peaceful sleep. It continued to toll with no break to indicate a clear direction of attack. I sprang from the bed, searching the side table for my guns. But they were in another time and place, and the harsh reality of what was happening hit me with the force of a cyclone. Sydney had been jolted from her slumber as well and now stood naked on the opposite side of the bed, her face drawn and frightened.

"They're here," I said, my voice barely a whisper though it sounded like a thundering roar to my own ears. I crossed the room and held her tightly for several seconds, although I knew I should already be armed and in the yard. Preparations, like last time, had already been made as best they could for the upcoming fight, and our ability to stave off as many thralls as possible depended largely on our quick response time. Still I clung to my wife, knowing I would never see her this way again. Finally, Sydney told me to go and kissed me passionately one last time. I felt movement in my groin and she must have felt it too because she giggled, and then pushed me away to get dressed.

I was clothed and standing in the misty chapel yard with my brothers and family (what was left of them) a minute later, the tree sprawling over us, a brilliant light in the darkness reminding me of my father's last words. All were armed with their weapons of choice. I had thrown my bow and quiver over my shoulder, shoved a Glock .45 in my jeans, and cradled my shotgun in both hands.

The screeches bellowing from the forest beyond the Argo's northwest border told me all I needed to know. No thralls had yet been spotted, the shrieks still a few miles off. We still had time. Torches were

216

already lit here and there to provide some light, knowing the assault wouldn't come in broad daylight. Dean assured us the gasoline-soaked crates we had filled with Luke's dynamite were in position around the border and strategically placed about the yard. Judah nodded toward a quiver of arrows—the tips wrapped in gas-soaked rags—as confirmation he was ready to light and fire them into said crates when the time came.

"I'm sorry it's come to this," I said. "I can't begin to guess tonight's outcome, but whatever comes, know that I will fight for each of you and I will die for each of you."

"As will we all, brother," Judah said, not able to keep his grin contained.

I shared the feeling. I was scared to death, but at the same time eager to bring down as many of those things as possible. I only hoped to have one more chance at Alex.

The others nodded or voiced their approval.

"We've lost loved ones," I said. "We've lost our *children*. But we have not lost our resolve, our love for each other, or our souls. Stand with me my brothers, my sisters, as I stand with you, and together we'll show the world what strength truly is. Stories like ours have a way of surviving, and the deeds we do tonight will be remembered. The name of McCall will live on through our children, Judah. Let our actions tonight bring honor and not shame."

The pale branches spread over our heads, a protective canopy diminishing the darkness. "We will be together again in glory after this is over and there will be no more pain, no more tears. I will see you again beneath the boughs."

2

Darkness spreads like wildfire, but more quickly. Turn off the lights, blow out a candle and the dark closes in, its fingers grasping for your neck. But the tiniest pin point of light will send it scurrying off in fear. The smallest, dimmest ray will obliterate the night as it does each dawn. Darkness can only survive in the complete absence of light, but I have come to appreciate that light is never completely absent.

We waited in close groups as the wailing thralls drew nearer. The wind picked up, whisking away the mist that hovered waist high above the ground, along with the light of our torches, and the darkness swept in. But again, light is never absent. The tree's soft brilliance intensified, casting no shadows though the light shone at our backs, and when the shapes became visible through the woods we feared them not. I resigned myself to death, but I would no longer dread its coming.

3

Thralls, so many thralls. They poured from the trees near the barn, teeth gnashing, their only goal to kill and destroy. Judah knocked his first arrow and I lit the rag on the tip with my Zippo, then lit the cigarette hanging from my tightened lips. That lighter, a gift from the past given to me by my wife depicting a sunken anchor, rarely failed to light and it didn't tonight. I drew on my cigarette.

Judah let loose the flaming arrow with the precise accuracy he had practiced for years to achieve. It stuck in the crate as the thralls passed, sizzled, and then set the wooden box ablaze. The crate exploded, sending limbs and gore flying to the four corners of the earth.

Gunshots filled the air as I lit the second arrow. My brother shoved the arrow into the dirt, feathers first, to use as a torch to light his remaining quiver.

I fired off round after round of buck shot into the mob of thralls. They came in such mass it was impossible to tell whose shots went wide and whose aim was true. I estimated them to be in the hundreds. The dogs attacked the horde head on, Shelby and Bowie sinking their teeth into the necks of thrall after thrall with killer instinct.

Another crate exploded to the left of the first, tearing several more thralls to pieces. Sydney and my mother emptied their magazines quickly; if they landed half of their shots, I would be pleased, but there was no way to tell. I figured if they pointed toward the mob and pulled the trigger they were likely to hit *something,* the creatures flocked so closely together.

Crate after crate erupted under Judah's destructive bow. A mutilated head hit me and I saw a forearm flop over my wife's shoulder. I struggled to bottle the urge to hurl, but Sydney hardly

218

noticed. She just continued to point and pull her blessed triggers.

Mounds of bodies littered the ground along the Argos border in a matter of minutes. The first wave gained no more than ten yards from the tree line, still giving us a comfortable amount of leeway.

Several more thralls darted from the dark of the forest, but no more followed. I believe every one of us sent at least one bullet through those last unfortunate creatures.

4

"Reload, people," I yelled across the property. The first wave had been defeated, but there would be more, many more.
"Oh really, Shane?" Dean shouted. "Because I was thinking about just throwing my gun at the next one that runs toward me."
"I really hope you survive this, Dean, so I can shoot you myself."
"Please, I'll survive longer than you, no doubt about it."
I laughed and lit a new cigarette. The dogs came hobbling back, all wounded but still on all fours.
"Light me one, Shane," my mother's voice startled me.
"Uh…sure," I said and handed her the one I just lit. I didn't have time to light a second.

5

Judah saw them first and released an arrow into their midst, but they formed such a tight group that the shaft was intercepted by a passing body. The thrall caught fire and spread the flames to the three running next to him. I shot the one in the middle, center mass, and sent the thing hurdling into the dynamite. The explosion was powerful, spewing flaming body parts across the sky like shooting stars.
It did nothing to slow them. Dozens upon dozens crossed the borders of the main property, scaling the fence like it wasn't even there, the shrieking overpowering the roar of our weapons. And the high-pitched sounds weren't only coming from the area to the northwest. I turned to the west, then north to see a multitude on our flanks.

Loads of grenades dangled from the trees surrounding the borders to each end. A series of tripwires would pull the pins and drop them to the ground in the event the assault crossed that way.

I kept my focus forward as the grenades fell one by one. *Kaboom! Kaboom!* The shrapnel ripped through the passing thralls. All were not stopped, but the grenades thinned the herd significantly.

"Spread out," I shouted, moving to the second (and last) phase of our plans; the phase where everyone pretty much fended for themselves and hoped for the best.

The dogs stayed closer this time, routing the thralls like sheep, snarling viciously, too agile for the thralls to sink their teeth into.

Johnny, Dean, and Jordan moved southwest to protect our backs, while Judah and Devon took the northeast. This put Sydney, my mother, and I in the center of the main attack.

"Light that fuse, Mom," I called over the blast of my shotgun, tossing her my Zippo.

She fumbled it, quickly recovered, and lit the long trail of filament that traveled northwest, split into four separate fuses that led to large crates of dynamite placed in the barn and three other locations in the woods. The spark moved along the fuse at a crawl and I began to regret not lighting it sooner. It reached the junction several seconds later where four separate sparks would go their own ways, hopefully at a quicker pace.

We continued to shoot into the fray, taking out as many as we could, praying the sparks would reach their destination before we were overrun. The thralls were much closer now, those in the lead a mere ten yards away and closing fast. Some actually stopped to investigate the fuses as the flames crept past, their intelligence far too low to think to extinguish them. By the time the dynamite finally blew, we were firing at nearly point blank range, our faces and clothes covered from the blowback.

The explosions were deafening, sounding off one after the other, beginning with the barn. Splinters of wood from the building and trees along the border showered upon us and the thralls, driving us to duck and take cover under our own arms. Those thralls nearest the blasts disintegrated instantly, while those further off were blown in all directions in thousands of pieces. The ones closer to us found themselves impaled by planks and branches that severed arms, legs, and heads. Our group was too far away for the force to affect us, but a stray chunk of the barn arrowed itself into my mother's thigh.

She screamed and fell, and for an instant I thought one of them had gotten through. I spun to help her, and that was when our luck began to turn against us.

6

Johnny was the first to go. As I yanked the plank from my mother's thigh, I saw the horde close in on our group to the south. Dean knocked them down quickly but there were too many. Johnny drew his kukri and began slicing like a butcher, Shelby right on his heels. One grabbed hold of Jordan's arm and Johnny hacked the hand off at the wrist. He shoved Jordan from the tangle and to the ground where she would be safe for at least a few seconds. That action cost Johnny his life.

Five thralls overwhelmed him, Shelby leaping to his aid, but to no avail. Gnawing and ripping, they dug into Johnny's flesh as if it were butter, tearing chunks of meat from his shoulders and ribs, spitting them out and going back for more. His screams came as horrifying gurgles as he choked on his own blood.

I saw this in the lull the exploding crates had created, and found Dean, who had been left abandoned for the time being for the prospect of an easy meal. He shifted his head to Johnny and I nodded. He raised his pistol, aimed, and shot our brother between the eyes. Shelby, who refused to leave her master, met a far more agonizing fate, for no bullet eased her suffering.

There was time to be grateful my children were not there at that moment; that any fate they might find would be better than dying like Johnny had. And then they were on us. Dean and Jordan rushed to our side, abandoning the lost cause that was our left flank. *Tat-tat-tat!* The thrall that lunged toward Sydney took a sharp turn in mid-air as Jordan's AR-15 blasted it from existence. Sydney sighed with relief, then fired three shots over Jordan's shoulder, filling the skull of a sneaky thrall with holes, returning the favor.

A few more attacked from the center, but Dean and I took them down easily. Johnny's body was being devoured to our left, a final sacrifice that kept our assailants at bay and satisfied for the time being.

Dragging my mom to her feet, we backed toward Judah's end of the yard, but my mother stopped me in mid-stride, pushing me away.

"You have grenades on you?" she asked, her voice pained, but her eyes determined. When I didn't answer she said, "Give me two grenades, boy."

I shook my head, knowing her intentions and knowing at the same time there was no time to argue with her. Dean, Jordan, and Sydney kept moving to the right flank.

"Give them to me, Shane."

Defeated, I placed the only grenades I had into her open palms. "There's still time," I begged, but it was useless.

"And this will give you more of it." She hugged me, and said, "I love you, Shane, beyond all else. Beneath the boughs, was it?"

I nodded grimly, wanting to tell her how much I loved her, but she was already hobbling off to the northwest where a fresh wave of thralls had just emerged. I inhaled deeply, the air already tasting like rotting corpses, and turned my eyes from my mother, a woman who had lived her life for her children and would now die for them.

Could I do the same?

There was an explosion, and as I ran to join what remained of my family, my shotgun vomiting shells in every direction, I wasn't so sure of the answer.

7

The next few minutes were a blur. In droves they came, taking us down one by one. I reached the group in time to see Jordan being dragged away by her hair, kicking and screaming, still fighting with all her might as the jagged teeth and fingernails sliced through her body. Jordan's head was pulled from her shoulders with a sharp snap, and carried off into the night, a trophy for the dead.

We pumped out hundreds of rounds in those last minutes, covering one another as others reloaded, but there was no end to the onslaught. I was bitten or clawed more than once, as were we all, until we simply could not defend ourselves any longer.

Dean and Devon went out together, and I could do nothing to stop it. Surrounded by the horde, they were cut off from the group. We were having problems of our own by then, but I heard Devon's voice over the din, screaming, *"Do it. Do it!"*

"No," screamed my brother, attempting to charge into the fray, but I grabbed his arm.

"Remember the Argo," Dean shouted, and another explosion ripped through the mass of bodies. Judah, Sydney, and I were thrown several yards before skidding to a stop in three bloody heaps. I shook the rattles from my head and saw Judah stumbling and wailing around the place his wife had last been standing. There was nothing remotely identifiable in that mess.

"Judah, get back here," I called, helping Sydney to her feet. I pulled her toward me and was yanked backward. Sydney cried out in pain, as a thrall dug his teeth into her left bicep. I pulled again out of sheer reflex and she moved to me easily this time. Her eyes expanded as they met my own. She no longer screamed. A spurt of blood caught my attention and I followed it down to find her left arm had been ripped off just below the shoulder.

She pivoted slowly to find the creature hunched over, feasting on her appendage, the blood oozing down his leathery maw. She half-stepped, half-staggered toward the thrall. "Sydney?" I said in what little voice I could muster, but she made no response.

She lifted her leg and brought her foot down into the thing's temple, heel first. It dropped the arm and rolled. Searching for a weapon, and finding none, she picked up her severed arm and continued her advance. Holding hands with herself, she swung with all her might, bludgeoning the creature that had wounded her so. The thing's head was nothing but a mass of grey mush when she finally relented.

"What the—" Judah said from behind me.

I was numb. My mouth hung open in disbelief, and then my wife collapsed. I rushed to her, fully aware of the circle of pale shadows surrounding us. But they kept their distance. Her head in my lap, I patted her face to revive her. Her eyes opened, circled, then focused on me. Judah had dropped to his haunches nearby, checking the enemies that surrounded us.

"Syd? Baby?" I said. "Stay with me, it's almost over."

She smiled. Beautiful as ever, her lion's mane of red hair tumbled about her face and shoulders. Her lips parted, but she could do no more.

"I know, Syd. Don't try to say anything." I gazed into her fading green eyes, and grinned. "You're pretty bad ass, you know?" She laughed, splattering blood into my face. I wiped it away and put my hand on her cheek. "Go to sleep, my wife, and know that I love you."

She gave a frail nod and closed her eyes. I felt her inhale and exhale a few more times and then she was still. I too closed my eyes, taking my own long breaths, and noticed the screeching had stopped. It had been replaced by laughter.

8

The laughter continued for a long time, but I did not open my eyes. I knew what made that hateful sound. I felt my brother sidle closer and I finally opened them.

"Ah, the Brothers McCall," said Alex, again laughing his evil laugh. "A good fight, but very unnecessary."

I surged to my feet and Judah followed. I still had my bow slung across my chest, but the arrows had fallen from the quiver, most likely during the explosion. The only other weapon I had was the knife on my hip. I could only hope Judah would be able to defend himself.

"I want the boy," the spirit growled, this time void of laughter. He towered above the other creatures. Dark blotches partially covered his face and bared chest as if it decayed as he walked. He was an animated corpse, albeit an enormous one. In his eyes, however, raged an inferno of orange flame.

"Well," I said, "you can't have him."

Alex snarled. Flicking his head to the thralls beside him he said, "Search every inch of this place. Then burn it to the ground."

I shook my head and laughed. The thralls scurried off to do their master's bidding in silence, leaving us alone with the *Ra'ah*.

"He will be found, foolish man. And when he is, I will take him for my own. This body is…lacking."

The last thing I wanted was to have a conversation. He was goading me, trying to get me to give away something. But I had nothing to give, and I had never been more grateful for Sara. Alex would kill us, no doubt about that, but he would never find my son.

"Have you nothing to say, Shane McCall? Or you Judah of the same name?" The hand I hadn't lopped off clenched into a tight ball, the muscles in his jaw tensed. I could see his patience was wearing thin. He paused, giving us time to speak, to beg, or whatever he expected us to do. When he got nothing, he growled, "Very well."

He lurched forward. In one swift motion he held my brother by the neck in his one huge hand. Judah's feet dangled, kicking and flailing, his face already turning purple. "Tell me what I need to know or your brother will die a painful death."

I sprang forward, yanked my blade from its sheath, and jammed it into the side of Alex's throat. It didn't go in as easily as I expected. Unlike the thralls, Alex's body was hard, almost solid. The blade went in no more than two inches and snapped at the hilt. His other handless arm lashed out, snaring me about the neck in a vice-like headlock. The pressure was unbearable. I felt myself being lifted.

"Ah shit, Judah," I eked through the pain in my temples, straining to shift my eyes far enough for his face to enter my limited field of vision. "I love you brother."

I heard low growls below me. Bowie had appeared out of nowhere, thrashing at Alex's calves and upper thighs, but a swift kick sent him sailing into the distance. Then I was soaring through the air.

My head slammed against something hard, and my consciousness began to slip away. The last thing I heard before the lights went out was my brother screaming my name.

The Boughs

1

And so we come to the end of my accounting of recent events. I am still among the living; an obvious statement considering I am writing these words. But that will soon change. I have no illusions to the contrary. My journal, in which the entirety of this tale has been written, is securely locked in the fireproof safe in what was once the den of the Big House should anyone care to read it. I write now on the walls of the chapel with an old ink quill I found in a discarded desk drawer. I would have written anyway—in my own blood if necessary—had there been no other option.

2

I woke to the smell of smoldering cinders and my brother staring at me through wide, smirking eyes. My head cleared slowly, and I rubbed the top of my skull where an enormous lump had formed. There was no telling how long I had been unconscious, but it was a matter of hours rather than minutes because the sun was popping its head over the horizon and the snow on the ground was already turning to slush. I took in my surroundings quickly, confused in the fact that I hadn't become a late-night snack for hungry thralls.

The Big House was a mountain of smoking rubble as was every other thing that could burn on the Argo, with the exception of the chapel, which stood unharmed.

My head had hit the trunk of the tree in the chapel cemetery; I had awoken on the grave of my father. Not the worst place I could be—it had saved my life, a conclusion I would come to very soon.

I stood, wobbly at first, and trudged to where my brother's head simpered, impaled on a stick in the outer yard of the cemetery. I was out of tears, but I felt the sorrow building as I beheld the remains of my brother. The words "BRING THE BOY" were carved into his forehead, but that was not what caught my attention. A crooked grin I knew well stretched across my brother's face, and I laughed. I had seen that smirk many times. It was indomitable, arrogant, relentless. I freaking hated that smug grin. Never had I felt such a powerful combination of pride and grief.

I buried Judah beside my father. Beneath the boughs. I regret that I could not find the remains of the others to do the same.

For a long time I sat under the tree, running through the events of the previous night, or just staring into the forest. Movement rustled the bushes across the lawn and I stood. Too small for it to be a thrall, my heart leapt in my chest.

"Bowie," I called, and my raw throat seared in protest. I called again anyway.

The black canine lifted its ears and cocked its head in my direction as if my voice were the last thing it expected to hear. Limping impatiently, Bowie made his way to where I sat. Elated that *something* had survived, I spent an age stroking his fur, accepting his licking tongue on my face with a sense of fierce gratitude.

His front leg was clearly hurt but I could find no break in the bone. It would heal, but even then I doubted it would ever have the chance.

Several questions remained unanswered. Why was I alive? Why was the chapel still standing? Where were the creatures that only hours before were so hell-bent on wiping out our existence?

I peered into the canopy of leaves above, and the answer to all my questions came to me; its truth beyond doubt.

The tree.

3

The details of my situation came clear to me then. The chapel, towering within mere feet of the glowing tree, still stood untouched by evil hands. All signs of last night's struggle were absent from the tree's vicinity, as if the thralls had avoided it entirely. Even my brother's head had been placed far outside the radius of the churchyard.

I was alive because I was thrown beneath the protective shade of the boughs; a mistake Alex was surely ruing.

So what now?

The carved words upon my dead brother's forehead flashed across my vision and the only answer to that question stared back at me from his bloodshot eyes.

I kill it.

But how? My blade had barely pierced its skin; had, in fact, broken in half during the attempt. I had a bow with no arrows, and surely a few wooden shafts—

Wooden shafts.

The tree rose before me, bright and vital in the purest sense. The *Ra'ah* could not bear to enter its presence. But would it do more than protect? Was it possible that this tree could assist me in vanquishing my foe?

I reached up, gently caressing the pale green leaves, an action I realized had never been done. We spent many hours under the tree, leaning against its trunk, soaking in its shade, but never had it even occurred to us to *touch* its branches. Serenity coursed though me as my fingertips made contact with the tear-drop shaped leaf. A shiver ran up my spine, standing the hair on my arms and neck on end.

"Will you aid me?" I asked. It seemed only right to request a gift so potentially powerful rather than just taking it.

An answer did not come in the form of words or sign, but I knew the reply just as I knew the tree had saved me from agonizing torture at the hands of the *Ra'ah*. Again, I reached up, taking hold of a single thin limb roughly the length of an arrow. I began to pull, but the branch *released* itself from its larger bough as if it had been waiting to be chosen.

The limb was straight and true. Sharp at one end and devoid of leaves, it even had a small notch at the opposite end that would easily fit over my bowstring. I had envisioned the carving and sharpening that would need to be done, but I saw now that alterations would be unnecessary. It had no guiding feathers, of course, but I believed the shaft to be perfectly made for the task at hand.

My arm ascended into the leaves to pick a second, but I

suddenly thought better of it.

Thump. I circled around the trunk to see what had fallen. A shorter, thicker piece of wood lay upon a tuft of grass, and I picked it up. About a foot long, it was straight like the arrow, but much sharper. Halfway up the limb, it angled inward, coming to an acute point, much like a stake used to slay a vampire.

I could scarcely imagine how I'd get close enough to use a wooden knife, but it brought me comfort nonetheless.

4

My family was slaughtered two days ago. A feeling of loneliness so deep has gripped me that I long to join them. Alone, with only Bowie to keep me company (and such a blessing he has been; I believe I may have already gone insane had it not been for him), the faces of the dead plague my waking eyes. I dare not describe the things I see when they are closed.

I remain in this chapel only to finish my tale, but words have eluded me of late. My brother, Judah, would never have had this problem. Words had a way of spewing from him like a fount of ever flowing water. Diarrhea of the mouth, my father called it. How speaking of them in the past tense turns my empty stomach.

Perhaps I cannot finish because, when I do, the only task I have left must at last be done. In the face of everything I have seen, still I doubt, still I waver. How can one such as I be chosen for such a purpose, when so many souls are at stake? If only this burden would be lifted. The bitter path before me is paved with the dead, and as I tread upon them I tremble, for I see my wife, mother and father, my sisters and brothers. I see things I have done, choices I've made, and from the depths of my soul I scream for deliverance.

But I have hope, as fragile and fleeting as it is, rousing the hearts of men, lifting them above the squall, only to withdraw and send them plunging through the hail and rain and sleet and snow. Hope is a promise unfulfilled, a salvation I long for, but cannot obtain on my own.

The hearts of men are ships at sea. The calm brings fleeting comfort and peace, but it is through the storm that conviction is proven: whether to be tossed asunder by the wind; to be cast into the deep by the torrent; or to have the courage to stay the course.

So I cling to the tree, the boughs, the light in the darkness. An anchor in the storm, a rock that does not falter, a foundation upon which the hopes of mankind are tethered.

It is there, beneath the boughs, that I will see Faris and Zoe again. It is here, from this chapel, that I step upon the bitter path, and as the darkness is proclaimed through the wails of the Enthralled, so let the tree's light be revealed through the cry of my heart.

Shane McCall

Winter, 2017

The End

If you enjoyed this book, please take a moment to review it on Amazon for other readers to discover it.

Become a fan

 @dryangishauthor   @dryangish

Ryan is available for author visits & conferences. Email awriterforlifecoach@gmail.com for dates.

ABOUT THE AUTHOR

D. Ryan Gish is an avid reader of imaginative fiction, and prefers stories that invent new worlds or modify the one in which we live in some strange new way. His writing tends to drift toward these areas as well. Ryan's debut novel, *Enthralled*, was inspired by his close group of friends, although the characters are complete works of fiction. He currently lives in Florida with his three children.